THE VEILS OF VALORIA

BOOK ONE

KIRSTY F. McKAY

Published in paperback in 2019 by Sixth Element Publishing
on behalf of Kirsty F. McKay

Sixth Element Publishing
Arthur Robinson House
13-14 The Green
Billingham TS23 1EU
www.6epublishing.net

Printed in Great Britain.

THE VEILS

OF

VALORIA

BOOK ONE

In loving memory of my grandparents, Vera & Duncan Thomson.
A dream realised and a promise fulfilled.

*"Darkness throws its blanket of black and
evil bleeds the goodness from the land
Crimson innocence ebbs away as forests burn and flames are fanned.
A venerable spirit plummets from its lofty height,
the rivers foam in sickly red.
Nightmares shuffle free from their restraints,
as chains and shackles are easily shed.
As insidious forces rise and crush a realm asunder,
an ageless prophecy is born.
The veil that once held back the burning light,
is gossamer thinned and torn."*

CHAPTER ONE

Guisborough, North East England

The storm howled with frustration as Finn escaped from its wildness and cruelty into the only sanctuary he could find. Hidden within the darkness, ignoring the foul stench that made him almost retch, he squeezed his eyes shut and instead whispered a thank you. Despite his current discomfort, an overwhelming surge of relief flooded through him, knowing that the force raging outside was enough to mask the sound of his teeth chattering in the confined space, and the tremulous pounding of his heart.

Paying no heed to the cold that bit its way deeper through sodden clothes, Finn attempted to adjust his position and relieve the grinding ache of his limbs, crushed in his haste to seek protection from the tempest. His wound screamed out in protest, and he clamped a hand firmly over his mouth and waited for the pain to subside.

A sudden warmth seeped down his leg, confirming the injury much more than just a mere graze. Unwilling to yield to its torture, Finn gritted his teeth and instead suffered his torment in silence, not daring to risk revealing his location. The storm's arrival thankfully had brought him back to his senses, and saved him from making a terrible mistake. No longer would he give in to the fear that had threatened to take hold these past few days. If that meant he had to hide away in this wretched tin can, then so be it.

Something scuttled from the furthest corner and briefly brushed against his ankle. Swiftly pulling his leg back, Finn smothered another cry of agony, and prayed that the scent of blood held no attraction. His attempts to search for whatever it was that had stirred, proved futile in the darkness. Head swimming with the intensity of his senses magnified, Finn waited for his companion to return, a sigh escaping when he felt nothing further.

Running a hand through his hair, he swept back the tendrils that had fallen, and dripped water onto his face. His eyes were stinging, a consequence of the contaminated atmosphere of this world or the noxious smelling contents of this strange sanctuary, Finn could not be sure. From his observations, both were a distinct possibility given that the dwellers of this world paid little regard to their natural environment.

Rubbing the irritation free from his sight, his hand grazed against his skin and prompted a pang of longing in response. How he missed the comforts of his home, his usual well-cared-for and groomed appearance a far cry from what he must look like now.

Losing count of the number of times he had wondered that day, Finn considered once more why he had been the one sent to find her. What had possessed him to agree? Perhaps it was utter madness that had goaded his decision.

Yet, as he sat alone in the darkness of this strange tin box, he realised that he could not escape the real reason behind such folly. It was neither bravery, nor stupidity, that had driven him through the portal. But a feeling that he could not understand or explain.

Powerless to resist the need to respond to her call from across time and space, Finn had willingly agreed to the Council's request, and had stepped through the portal without any hesitation, or consideration as to what he may find waiting for him on the other side.

Listening to the damage created outside, he felt pity for the village inhabitants, doubting whether they would have seen the like of such a power before. It had been fortunate for them, that in the split seconds before the storm's arrival, he had sensed the sudden and unnatural shift in the air around him, and had run, guided by an unknown instinct to head away from the centre of the village, and in doing so protecting the occupants from its eye.

The storm had immediately given chase, it had seemed with one purpose, to thwart him. After a few moments of taking refuge however, Finn realised the storm had in fact been a blessing in disguise.

Hidden away in this temporary sanctuary, the gift of time had been offered. An hour or two at least for him to gather his strength, and create as much distance as possible between him and them. The creatures that lurked within the shadowlands, and thrived on the pain of others. They were driven by an inexorable thirst to consume. Devoid of any emotion, and with no physical form, these abominations were known only as the Fallen, the source of all nightmares.

Their power should have been unable to reach beyond the dream realm, or so he had first thought. Somehow the Fallen had been able to shed their shackles, and within days of Finn's arrival snapped like wolves at his heels.

Kane, Finn cursed, the anger rising from the pit of his stomach. The Master's latest Commanding Officer had found not only the means to bring these creatures through a portal, but also to give them substance, and enable them to travel in this world.

Last night had been close, too close, Finn reflected, his blood running cold at the thought. Thankfully luck had been on his side, and albeit only narrowly he had evaded their capture.

Finn imagined that mistake would have cost Kane dearly in the eyes of the Master, and he felt a momentary flicker of satisfaction.

Tonight, his fortune had changed, and Kane's determination not to fail a second time had Finn backed into a corner. With all hope gone and nowhere to run, Finn had finally resigned himself to whatever fate held in store.

Sensing his surrender, and that he had almost risked it all, the storm had exploded around him, leaving little doubt in Finn's mind of the message delivered by the Council. Its intensity and pursuit of him had made that all too clear. Their anger was palpable with every piece of debris that clipped the back of his heels, and finally crashed him to the ground. Finn had only briefly registered the searing pain in his leg as his survival instincts seized control and spurred him on.

The storm seethed around him, and in its air carried along a rush of depraved excitement. Kane had closed in on him with such an eagerness to have ignited the Fallen's appetite. Their hunger was insatiable.

Unable to see his way through the deluge, Finn had scrambled to his feet and searched for somewhere to hide. With his heart hammering and fighting for breath, he jumped into the strange metal container, and immediately smothered the urge to vomit. No option but to wait to be discovered, unless lady luck had finally switched sides and smiled favourably on him once more.

The minutes that passed by felt like hours. Finn reached forward with his senses as far as he considered safe and scanned the surrounding area, careful to avoid alerting Kane to his presence. Confusion and frustration hung in the air, the only emotions he could detect. The creatures had lost his trail and moved on into the distance. The storm, he realised, had fulfilled more than one purpose. *Was that the Council's intention all along?*

As much as it pained him, Finn had to admire their ingenuity. It was a damned impressive effort, although a surge of annoyance still tugged in his abdomen, at the not so subtle reminder that they watched him closely and monitored his thoughts. In particular, Mercadia, an Elder of the Council, charged with the task of keeping a close eye on his progress. Her magic was born from a bloodline that enabled her to extend her abilities far beyond the boundaries of their world.

Incapable of blocking her frequent intrusions, Finn remained an open book for Mercadia to study, and he was powerless to hide his thoughts or fears. He could still feel the trace of her touch before the storm's eruption, and the hint of temper and disappointment moments before she had unleashed her power. Her sudden silence from his mind could be explained, given that it would have taken a phenomenal amount of energy to conjure such a storm, and send it through the portal. Knowing Mercadia as well as he did, she would not resist leaving him alone for too long.

Finn wished he possessed the same ability as his brother Aaron, his envy and regret stinging deep. If only he had paid that little bit more attention to their father's lessons, and shared the same devotion to the practice as his brother had, Finn may not be in this position now. Aaron at a young age had not only mastered the Shroud, but had spent many years perfecting it, and moving well beyond their father's teachings. Although Finn would never bear the same amount of power, he wished that he had at least taken the time to learn and understand the Shroud's secrets.

A master in the craft, Aaron's skills had ensured that he remained a closed book as far as the Council or any others were concerned. Even Mercadia, with all her skills and thousands of years of knowledge, had failed to break the Shroud. Aaron's mind could not be infiltrated, creating a perfect mole. One the Council had then wasted no time in enlisting, and successfully planting into the Master's faction.

Two seasons had passed before Finn learned of his brother's fate, the guilt now accompanying that familiar bite of regret. Had he not ignored Aaron's invitations to spend time with him and pass on their father's knowledge, Finn might well have discovered the Council's intentions, and dissuaded his brother from going along with their crazy idea. Finn could only pray that his brother still lived, and yet he feared what would remain of the man he once knew. The darkness of the Master was known to change and infect the nature of those around him. None had been able to resist his lure. If Aaron was to keep up his pretence, would he be asked to do the unimaginable, and compromise the good within him? It was a risk that the Council seemed happy to take.

Mercadia, sensing Finn's guilt from the moment he had sought counsel on his brother's whereabouts, had fully exploited his skills to the Council's advantage, coercing Finn into their services too. No other Tracker had ever come close to his ability or success. The capture of the Silver Stag the Council's proof. Finn had vowed this would be his last quest, until Mercadia explained the prophecy, requesting he be the one to locate the girl and bring her back to their world. Finn had immediately agreed.

With little else to do now, but wait for the storm to subside, Finn took the opportunity to rest. Closing his eyes, he succumbed to the demands of his exhausted body and drifted into sleep. His consciousness released, he travelled deeper towards the realm of dreams, and to her once more.

A smile formed on his lips the moment he stepped through the doorway. The emerald eyes that had haunted Finn each night since the arrival of the Silver Stag, stared back into his own. Her fingers brushed a lock of her long chestnut hair behind her ear. When she smiled, his abdomen stirred with need.

Unable to deny himself of her touch a moment longer, Finn rushed towards her, his extended hand eager to grasp hers and pull her close. A sudden spark of light almost blinded him, as their fingers collided and locked together, the energy created, making him unusually giddy.

She dropped her arm instantly, her breath released in short sharp gasps. Overcome by his desire to reassure her, Finn reached forward once more, sensing her conflict as she immediately retreated from his touch. In any other situation he had faced, he had always known what to say, but this time the words suddenly eluded him. With all ability of speech gone, Finn's eyes instead implored her to trust him. His emotions exposed and laid bare for her to see.

Her gaze searched his face, and she bit down on her bottom lip.

Finn's heart wrenched as tears escaped from her eyes, and she turned away from him to whisper, "I'm sorry, I can't do this."

Finn lunged forward but was too late, his hand grasped air as she vanished into the light. Bereft, he jolted awake.

The storm's hush suggested that sufficient time had passed for it to lose all momentum and grip on this world. Only the faintest of rustles and an occasional roll of metal across the ground could be heard. Finn winced as he adjusted his position once more in the constricted space.

Completing a perimeter scan, he confirmed with relief no trace of Kane or his minions. Long gone by now, and no doubt reporting back to their Master on yet another failure. Satisfied that the immediate threat had passed, Finn released a healing orb and heaved a sigh as the pain from his knee dispersed and his wound closed. He waited patiently as the sphere continued travelling deeper through his core, in search of other injuries, the warmth from the healing energy treating and comforting the rest of his tired, and bruised body.

Allowing the extra time for the orb to complete its task, Finn's thoughts returned to his nemesis, unable to comprehend precisely what favour Kane carried with the Master. From the stories he had heard whispered late on an evening, in the quiet corner of Candlebridge Tavern, the Master considered forgiveness a weakness. Mistakes, however small they were, resulted in punishment by extreme torture, or if you happened to be fortunate, death.

For Kane to therefore retain his position of power for so long made him no fool, and he undoubtedly demonstrated a much higher level of intelligence than his predecessors. Finn grimaced with the realisation that he must stop underestimating Kane if he were to stand any chance at all of succeeding in his quest.

Reflecting on the potential of what Kane might do next, Finn considered that this might be an opportune time to move. Slowly he lifted the lid and climbed free. Raising his head towards the night sky, Finn pulled the crisp, fresh air deep into his lungs, exhilarated by the newfound energy coursing through his veins. The smell of the sanctuary faded in potency with each breath inhaled, although a faint pungent aroma could still be detected clinging to his clothes.

An assessment of his physical body confirmed that the orb had successfully treated all of his injuries. Finn's muscles no longer resisted any effort to move, as he stretched in each direction with ease. Lunging forward into a fighting stance, he kicked alternate legs into the air, his strength, balance and coordination returned. Satisfied with his recovery, he navigated his way through the scattered wreckage without any hindrance and turned onto the main road that led towards the village.

A chill hung in the night air, but at least for the present moment, all remained calm. Finn shoved his hands into his pockets and increased his pace, hoping to encourage some heat.

"Where are you going, Finn?"

Irritation soared as Mercadia invaded his thoughts, and re-established her link to his mind. He pressed his lips firmly together and concentrated on the road ahead.

"I'm warning you."

Finn knew his silence had irked her by the slight rise detected in her tone. His observation of this only further added to her annoyance.

"Do you need me to send another message?" she said through gritted teeth.

A smile broke free at how he managed so successfully to climb underneath her skin, like an annoying itch that she couldn't quite reach to scratch.

"Answer me."

The sharpness of her tone signalled that she was tipping close to the edge.

Finn ran a hand through his hair and sighed loudly. "Are you going to watch my every move?"

Mercadia's voice was somewhat calmer, now that she had elicited a response from him. "That depends on you."

He paused and reached his senses ahead, in search of shelter for the night.

Mercadia seemed to consider for a moment too. "Down there," she instructed.

Finn rolled his eyes. "I know that."

He jogged to the entrance at the side of the main road, and pushed back the overgrowth that had obscured the signpost marked Somerbrook Bed and Breakfast. In the distance a faint glow of light. A scan of the area confirmed a safe haven for the night. "This is my decision, not yours," he muttered.

"Sure," she said.

Finn sensed her smirk and his annoyance rose. She also, it would seem, had a way of crawling beneath his skin.

Eager to be free from the cold, Finn hurried towards the light and grimaced as he drew closer. Somerbrook Bed and Breakfast was also a victim of the storm's wrath. He scowled at the debris scattered in all directions across the lawn, and pots smashed by the doorway, their contents hurled across the steps. Stumbling over broken pieces of wood, Finn seethed. "See what you've done?"

His words were met with no response, although he detected the slightest flush of shame.

Finn advanced to the whitewashed building and sensed movement from inside. Relieved to find that someone was still awake, he knocked gently on the door and waited patiently for a response. A few minutes later, an older gentleman greeted him.

"I'm sorry to bother you, I know it's late, but I was hoping you may have a room for the night," Finn said.

The man didn't look at all convinced, as he considered Finn's appearance.

"I don't blame you for being cautious, and I realise I look a state. Please believe me when I say that this has been the worst night of my life."

His appraisal of Finn continued, although there appeared to be a slight shift in Finn's favour. "Caught in that storm, were you?"

Finn nodded. "There wasn't time for me to find somewhere safe. I had to jump into the nearest shelter. I guess it could have been much worse."

The older man studied him for a few moments more. Finally, he seemed to make up his mind, and opened the door further, inviting Finn inside.

"Took us all by surprise that one did, never seen the like of it. Everything was crashing around outside. Nearly lost me bloody roof as well as the fence. Thought the windows were going to shatter on us, they shook so hard." He eyed Finn up and down. "Still, it looks like we were more fortunate than you, lad."

"Is everyone here alright?" Finn asked with genuine concern.

"We're all fine. Have just settled the Mrs down with a cup of tea. She spent the last hour hiding under the stair cupboard. Inherited that from the Dragon," he tittered.

"Dragon?" A slight surge of panic rose. The Council had made no mention of any dragons coming through the portal.

"Aye, and that's a polite name for her."

A female voice shouted, "I heard that, Patrick!"

Finn couldn't make out where the sound came from but sensed that she was close.

"Sorry, dear!" Patrick pulled a face and brought his hand to cover his mouth. "Got the bloody hearing of a bat that one."

Chuckling, Finn followed him into an area marked Reception.

"You wait there... Mr?"

"Just call me Finn."

"Well, take a seat, Finn, while I grab the register and your room key."

Sinking back into the worn fabric sofa, he waited as instructed, reflecting on the events of the night. Finn had escaped the Fallen's grasp once more, but that had only been made possible with the Council's help. He wondered how Kane would justify that mistake to the Master a second time.

Perhaps Kane could use the Council's sudden interference as his defence, and safeguard himself from being feasted on by the Weavers. Finn shuddered at the thought, recalling Merrick's words of warning that night in the tavern as he slammed his tankard on the table, his breath soaked in ale and his clothes covered with grime. Merrick had leaned in close to whisper to him, "*Choose death, and if he offers no choice, take death before he takes death from you.*" When Finn had asked for further explanation, the older man paled before recounting the events of the night he escaped from Moren's citadel.

"*I was one of ten to have survived the siege and remain behind. The Master's soldiers had rounded us up like cattle and took us to the dungeons where we were given a choice, to live and serve the Master or suffer a worse fate than the ones who had died fighting him. I foolishly agreed to serve as did the others with the exception of Margarite. Her son was slain by the*

Master's hand and she could not bring herself to do his bidding no matter how much we begged her. I will never forget the Master's smile as he gave the order, but not to execute Margarite, no, what he had in store, a far worse fate then death.

The Master's soldiers instead laid Margarite on the ground and shackled both arms and legs. The rest of us to remain and watch while he opened a portal. I had never to that day believed in demons until I came face to face with that yellow eyed creature. It revelled in our fear, I remember being grateful to poor Tobias for losing control of his bladder, it dampened some of the smell from the demon's putrid skin.

The Master whispered in its ear, the demon picking from its back two parasites and dropping them to the ground. They crawled to Margarite, one on each side. She struggled against her shackles and screamed for mercy. The Master laughed, as they burrowed through her skull, to expose her brain. White viscous tentacles weaved in and out of its mass. Margarite ceased to move. Her eyes closed, her face riddled with pain, and then she screamed. She did not stop screaming. The Master warned the same fate would befall us if we dared to betray him.

Every day all that could be heard from the dungeon below was Margarite's blood curdling screams. Tobias soon joined her after serving food to the Master's disliking. I could bare it no longer. I begged the others to escape with me but they were too afraid and so I crawled my way alone through the tunnels to the Citadel's outskirts. I smeared myself with the blood and intestines of the dead and hid beneath their bodies waiting for nightfall. I made it to Moren's borders and passed through into Valoria before the Elders raised the Selensia."

Finn had never forgotten Merrick's tale and had no desire to come face to face with the demon he spoke of, or the parasitic creatures known as the Weavers. He wondered if faced with the choice what Kane's preference would be. Either prospect for his nemesis held a certain appeal to Finn, and it would certainly buy the Council more time. Especially if the Master were to be forced to hunt for another Commanding Officer. Not many, he imagined, would have the sheer stupidity to sign themselves up for that role, unless they had an unfortunate penchant for pain and torture.

However much the prospect of Kane's demise excited him, Finn knew it would be more wishful thinking on his part. The chances of Kane being spared, even following the recent failed attempt to capture him, increased by the sheer fact that the Master was indeed running out of time. Kane, with his apparent level of intelligence, would use this to his advantage, and situations reversed, Finn would, of course, do the same.

Patrick returned, clutching a small book and key in his hands. He drew out a pen from his shirt pocket and offered the book. Finn accepted and scribbled his name, next to the X on the page highlighted. "Thank you."

Patrick smiled warmly. "We have two other guests here, so be sure that you don't wake them. Your room is on the second floor. There's an en suite bathroom, plenty of clean towels and toiletries for you to use."

Mercadia broke her silence, "You must smell pretty bad."

Finn deliberately ignored the remark and accepted the room key from Patrick.

"Check out is at midday, but if you need longer we can extend it to two o'clock. There's a small charge of ten pounds if you do. I'll let you have the room tonight for thirty-five pounds. Breakfast is included and served between seven o'clock and eleven o'clock. Don't worry about paying me now. You can sort it in the morning." He pointed Finn towards the direction of the stairwell. "So that you know, lad, I have an eye for wrong un's and my gut is telling me I can trust you."

Finn nodded. "You can, and thank you again for your hospitality, and your trust."

He didn't miss Patrick's slight recoil as they shook hands. Mercadia sniggered and Finn quickly went up the stairs to the second floor, too tired and annoyed to pay any attention to his surroundings.

Heeding Patrick's warning, Finn crept silently past the other rooms. At the end of the corridor, he turned the key in the lock of room number four and closed the door behind him. Leaning back against the wood, Finn took a few brief moments to appreciate the quiet and pleasant odours of his surroundings.

He had not exaggerated when he told Patrick that this night had been the worst night of his life. Even the misadventure in Redwood Forrest, his descent into devil sand and an unfortunate rescue by his arch-rival Quinn, paled in comparison.

Fumbling along the wall, Finn located the switch, the room and the contents becoming visible in the soft light. His gaze fixed on the large bed and to the patchwork duvet and plump cushions. It looked warm and inviting, and he couldn't wait to climb under the covers, close his eyes, and put this whole sorry day behind him.

Shifting his position slightly to allow him to take in the rest of the room, Finn jumped at the sudden movement from the corner of his eye. Relief that it had only been his reflection in the mirror was short-lived. Mercadia howled in laughter as he continued to stare at himself in disbelief.

It had been no wonder that Patrick had hesitated to invite him inside. Finn's hair, now the ideal home for birds to roost, was matted with unidentifiable objects. His clothes, covered with an array of stains in varying colours, uncomfortably stuck to his skin. The tear in his trousers revealed his knee soaked in blood. Finn peered for a closer examination and observed with dismay the growth of hair on his face, far more coverage and length than he ever would have tolerated back home. His brown eyes, wild and bloodshot, stared woefully back.

With his face set like thunder, Finn marched to the bathroom and turned on the taps. He pushed the small device that would stop the water from continually disappearing, firmly into the hole. A lesson learned from his first experience of bathing in this strange world.

Studying the full complement of bottles on the shelf, Finn selected the one labelled 'Bath Foam' and followed the instructions, carefully dropping some of the liquid into the bath. He watched the effect of the potion as the water level rose, and an assortment of rainbow sphere shapes covered the surface. Fascinated he reached to pick one up. It burst in his hand.

Finn sensed this was only adding to Mercadia's amusement. "Are you planning on watching me bathe or have you seen enough now?"

"Oh, I've seen enough, thank you."

"Glad to have made your night," Finn bit back. The woman was infuriating.

"Come now, you need to learn to control that temper of yours."

"That's rich coming from you." His sarcasm was unleashed without any care as to who he was addressing. "Feel like throwing any more trees around?"

Surprisingly, Mercadia ignored his remark. Her tone had changed noticeably. Perhaps somewhere in there, an acknowledgement that she may have pushed him a little too far. "We will be watching you. Time is running out. You need to find the girl and quickly."

"I need to bathe and have a decent night's sleep." Finn slipped off his jacket and signalled, as far as he was concerned, the end of their conversation.

Mercadia paused, seemed to change her mind over what she had intended to say, and then remained blissfully quiet. Finn's muscles unknotted with the release of her connection. Good. He had not relished the idea of bathing with an audience.

He quickly peeled the remainder of his clothing from his skin and kicked the dirty pile into the corner. His hands swilled the water and confirmed a pleasant temperature. A gentle knock at the door interrupted before he could step foot into the bath. Muttering a curse under his breath, he grabbed the nearest item he could find, a large white cloth, and wrapped it around his torso.

Finn opened the door tentatively, one hand keeping a firm grip on the soft fabric. The petite woman in front of him smiled in greeting, Patrick's wife, he assumed. She offered him a bundle of clothing and a brown paper bag, smiling as he stared at her with mouth agape.

"You can thank me tomorrow," she chuckled as she walked away.

Touched by her kindness, Finn's mood lifted. The thought hadn't even occurred to him as to what he would wear in the morning. He scowled at the discarded pile of clothing on the floor. There was little chance of him wearing any of that again, even if he wanted to.

He examined the bundle she had pulled together for him. Blue trousers made of a thick material he couldn't quite recall the name of, a dark-blue shirt and a black jacket, very much like the one that Eddie, his first human friend, had given to him when he arrived through the portal.

Finn was careful to avoid contact with his skin, as he held the clothing out in front of him, surprised to find an almost if not perfect fit. Not bad. How had she guessed? Perhaps, she was a descendant of a dragon after all.

He peeped at the contents inside the brown paper bag, and almost howled in joy. It had been hours since he'd last eaten and although he was famished, the desire to wash away the leftover stench overruled his hunger. Reluctantly, Finn placed the bag on the bed and hurried to the bathroom.

A groan of sheer ecstasy escaped as he lowered himself into the water, and soothed what remained of his pain and embarrassment. Reaching for the containers, Finn read each one, in turn, identifying the bottle that would clean his hair and body. Using the contents as instructed, he washed the remnants of the storm free, and at last, felt like his old self.

One thing, however, obstructed his path back to normality. Finn scanned the bathroom in search of that miraculous item that Eddie had called a razor. Disappointed, he made a mental note to ask Patrick for one in the morning, and instead sank his body below the surface of the water. The heat had already eased his rigid muscles, and any tension that lingered slowly ebbed away in silence. Time passed by in a peaceful haze. Finn almost drifted to sleep, until the coolness of the water returned him to a semi-state of wakefulness.

Releasing the device, he emptied the bath and stepped out, wrapping the white cloth once again round his midriff. As Finn passed the mirror, his reflection beamed back an approval.

Satisfied, he shifted his attention towards the table that stood opposite the bed, the various contents piquing his interest. Picking up the metallic container, Finn searched the surfaces. Unlike the bottles in the bathroom, there were no instructions to enable him to understand its purpose. Tipping it upside down, he flinched at the small amount of water that spilt into a puddle. A realisation dawned, this was a boiling pot!

Finn's eyes eagerly searched the room for the stove, which frustratingly was found to be missing. Placing down the container, he noticed a small lever protruding from its base and hesitated for a brief moment before pressing it. To his astonishment, it lit and a faint rumble from the boiling pot could be heard. Finn recalled what Eddie had taught him about electricity, the boiling pot somehow connected, and again he marvelled that such a power existed.

Examining the assortment of baskets, Finn noticed a collection of herbs wrapped in a little white bag. Eddie had called it tea, boasting 'the British answer to all problems'. Finn failed to see the logic of this, but considered after today anything would be worth a shot. Dropping the tea bag into a cup, he waited for the boiling pot to calm and poured the water carefully.

Scrutinising the rest of the contents on the table, he gazed at the small brown container with an image of a cow. Milk that, 'no perfect cup of tea could be without', according to Eddie. Peeling the lid back, Finn tipped the contents and used the silver spoon, to 'swish and stir'. *Patrick and his wife were extremely thorough, Eddie would be impressed.*

Resting the cup on the surface of the small cabinet, Finn turned on the bedside lamp and crossed the room to switch off the light, his stomach somersaulting with excitement when finally, he could crawl into the welcoming warmth of the bed.

His hand dipped eagerly into the contents of the brown paper bag, the sandwich demolished in less than a minute. Hopeful of a further reward, Finn raked inside and triumphantly pulled out a sizeable mouth-watering slice of cake.

Fulfilled, he reached for the tea, a comforting ritual Finn

considered, sipping at the hot liquid. *Eddie right, as always.* When his quest completed, he would take some of the little white bags home and give them to his mother to try. Perhaps she would even be able to identify the herbs used and recreate her own.

With his thoughts turned to his mother, the memory of her tears haunted him as she begged for an explanation. Heartbroken, when Aaron vanished, the guilt of then taking her fragile heart, and crushing it further with his own departure, weighed heavy on Finn's mind.

He now understood the decision Aaron had taken to simply leave, although he'd cursed his brother at the time for the torment not knowing had caused. In truth, it had been the reason why Finn couldn't bring himself to do the same to her.

When the argument subsided, the house brought back from its state of disarray, their mother had eventually accepted his decision and promised for both their sakes, that she would not ask any further questions. Finn knew it had been difficult for her to do so, kissing her goodbye had been so much harder than he'd ever thought possible.

The morning Finn had travelled through the portal, he had risked one last opportunity to see her. She was standing outside, tending to her herbs in the Moon Garden that she loved so much and though she looked happy, Finn didn't miss the longing in her heart to reunite with both sons. His own heart had echoed in response.

Mercadia at least had fulfilled her promise and ensured that in exchange for Finn's services his mother was taken care of, and most importantly, kept safe from the enemies he had made. Enemies who now swore their allegiance to the Master, whose faction was growing considerably, along with his power. The Council's protection of the remaining three realms weakened, with each betrayal and battle that had been lost.

Finn contemplated the gamble they had taken tonight, using all of Mercadia's power to send the storm through the portal, and leaving themselves vulnerable to attack. *They must have deemed the prophecy to be of great importance, and worthy of taking such a risk?*

Finn knew little of the Council's two remaining Elders and prayed their powers were sufficient enough to maintain the Selensia barrier while Mercadia regenerated. The Master reportedly had been testing its boundaries since the discovery of the Silver Stag, and there was no doubt in Finn's mind that he would continue in doing so.

Switching off the bedside lamp, Finn stared into the darkness of the room, Mercadia's words repeating over and over again in his mind. "Find the girl, and quickly."

Hoping that tonight would bring him closer, he succumbed to his weariness, and slowly drifted towards slumber.

CHAPTER TWO

Middlesbrough, North East England

"Would you like another drink, Rowena?" he slurred, barely managing to retain his balance as the bar stool swayed precariously.

Cringing at the thought of another hour spent in his company, she shook her head emphatically. "It's Rowan and no thanks. I need to go." She rose quickly and gathered her belongings, grateful to have stayed on the mocktails all night.

Downing the last of his Jack Daniels, he swivelled towards her with an expectant look. The intention in his eyes was all too clear. "Your place or mine then? Either is good for me."

Her temper sparked at his sheer arrogance. *Do you honestly think I'd be so desperate for male attention, that I would allow you to rack up another meaningless notch on your bedpost?* The man's nerve knew no bounds.

All night she had listened to him drone on. His job, his house, his money, his cat, his previous conquests. Anything she had tried to share of her own life instantly had him turn the conversation back to himself so that he could carry on stroking his already over-inflated ego. He'd been utterly oblivious to the fact that she had drifted off into a much welcome daydream, paying no attention to anything she had eventually managed in conversation. The absolute breaking point, when she had observed him making 'come and get me' eyes at anything with a skirt and a pulse. The date had been a complete and utter disaster. The last hour spent waiting for an opportunity to make a polite and very swift exit.

"Neither, Philip," she said, hoping that the ice in her voice would send the message home.

"Aw, come on, Rachel, we had a good night, didn't we?" he persisted, gazing at her with puppy dog eyes.

Like this would somehow leave me suddenly wanting to rip your clothes off!

"No, Philip, you had a good night getting royally wasted and talking about you all night. I doubt very much that there is room for anyone else in your life." She pulled on her jacket and zipped it hastily. "Oh, and to spell it out again for you. My name is Rowan, not Rowena, not Rachel, but Rowan. R O W A N."

"Babe, there's no need to have a hissy fit," he drawled, trying to paw at her.

Recoiling, she swatted his hand away. "Look, I came out with you tonight as a favour to Jen, but seriously you're just not my type." *That should do it.*

"Well, you ain't exactly up to my usual standard either, love, but I am prepared to make an exception for you," Philip sneered and tumbled backwards off the stool, his arms flailing. He crashed to the ground, his face a mixture of shock and disbelief.

Rowan smothered the urge to laugh. Her mouth trembled violently as the rising hysterics persisted in their bid for freedom. Inwardly scolding herself for not feeling the least bit sorry for him, she turned away, biting down on her lip as she fought for composure.

A male voice called out, "Can someone fetch Stan for me?"

Rowan's gaze shifted to her brother, working behind the bar. He finished serving an elderly gentleman and turned his attention to her.

"I've been waiting for that idiot to do that all night," he smirked.

A snort escaped, and she clamped a hand over her mouth.

The older man chuckled, placing down his pint. "I'll go get Stan for you, Jake."

"Cheers, Pete." Her brother peered over the bar and shook his head. "I still can't believe you went out with him."

Colour seared her cheeks. "Well, you could have warned me about him earlier if you knew what he was like."

"He's a total tosser. The guy thinks he's been buying you Mojitos all night. A bloody good job I'm on shift otherwise he'd have succeeded in getting you as wasted as he is. I can imagine mum's face in the morning being greeted by that plank. She'd be overjoyed."

Rowan shuddered at the thought. "I don't know why I let Jen talk me into this. After the last blind date, I swore I wouldn't do it again. It isn't like I need a boyfriend right now."

They watched as a pair of giant hands dragged Philip roughly to his feet. "Think you've had enough, mate. On your way."

Jake nodded his approval.

Philip was glaring pure venom. "She did it. She set me up."

Rowan shrank towards the bar, moving away from Philip's accusing, jabbing finger. She reached for Jake's hand, and he pulled her aside.

Stan grabbed hold of Philip by the scruff of his collar. "Listen 'ere, mate, she didn't pour the booze down your neck, and you don't need any help to look like a prat."

Philip wrenched his upper body, attempting to break free. "Get off me."

The two men squared up to each other. Stan cracked his knuckles. "Now, we can do this the easy way or the hard way. Your choice, mate."

The pub fell silent, all eyes eagerly fixed on Philip, awaiting his next move. Philip, having weighed up his chances of success, turned and staggered towards the door, shouting threats of retribution.

Stan followed closely behind and grinned from ear to ear. "Come and see me when you grow a pair."

Philip was effortlessly ejected from the premises.

Rowan could see the disappointment that there would be no show. She heaved a sigh of relief, the night finally over. "Thank you."

"No problem, Rowan," Stan beamed at her. "Told you before, you can do much better for yourself."

She nodded, her thoughts drifting back to the daydream, and the memory of his touch, imagining how different tonight could have been, had it been him with her and not Philip. Blinking back the tears that threatened to spill, her heart yearned once again for the impossible. *Get a grip, Rowan.*

"Do you want me to get you a taxi?" Jake asked, his face full of concern.

She snapped her attention back to the harsh reality of the night and nodded. "Yes, please."

"Be back in a second."

Pretending not to notice the plethora of sympathetic looks from the other patrons, Rowan studied the bottles nestled at the back of the bar, and read each label in turn. A pitiful attempt to distract from her public humiliation.

Pete headed in the direction of the bathroom and patted her gently on the back. "He's gone now, love."

The heat in her cheeks blazed deeper.

Ten minutes later, Jake joined her on the other side of the bar, his coat on, and rucksack in hand. He arched a brow. "Are you suddenly training to be a wine connoisseur, or working out which one best to drown your sorrows with?"

"I was... oh, never mind. I thought you didn't finish your shift until eleven?"

Wrapping an arm around her shoulder, he hugged her close. "Gav said it was fine for me to get off early. He'll manage for the last half hour. Besides, I want to make sure that my little sis gets home safe."

"Really, or are you just after me buying you a parmo on the way home?"

"Well, I wouldn't say no to a hotshot, seeing as you're offering."

Okay, so I've pretty much walked straight into that one.

"What about the taxi?"

"I've already arranged for it to pick us up outside the Pizzeria."

She laughed, "Presumptuous, aren't we?"

"Nah, you just can't resist me."

Rowan shook her head and followed Jake outside, her eyes searching the street, thankful to note that Philip was nowhere in sight.

Seizing her hand, Jake dragged her across the road towards the Pizzeria. "Come on, I'm starving." He swung the door open, and grinned as he waved her enthusiastically inside.

"You know that a real gentleman would be buying the lady a parmo?"

"Yes, well, we are in the twenty-first century. And besides which, you did offer. You wouldn't want to disappoint your favourite brother, would you?"

"You're my only brother."

He batted his eyelashes. "This of course is true, but hey you adore me and I did rescue you tonight."

Rowan's mouth twitched at the corners despite her best efforts to control herself. Jake made it impossible to put up any further resistance. Grumbling, she pulled her purse free from her bag and approached the counter. "Hey Tony, can I get a hotshot parmo and a portion of cheesy chips to go?"

"No problem, Rowan, about ten minutes."

"I'll keep a lookout for the taxi. Thanks, Sis. You're a star." A quick peck on the cheek and Jake was out the door before she could object.

Rowan scowled at him through the glass as he pulled the e-cig from his jacket. He shrugged his shoulders and carried on regardless, plumes of smoke wafting into the night air.

The unexpected vibration from inside her bag soon distracted Rowan from her annoyance. She fumbled to retrieve her phone, groaning when the caller ID flashed with Jen Mobile. *Not what I need right now.* Bracing herself for the impact, she slid her finger right to accept the call.

"Hey Jen, what's up?" *...and there it was!*

"Did you ditch Philip? Seriously? I don't get it..."

Sensing her friend gearing up for yet another one of her famous lectures, she cut her short. "The guy couldn't even remember my name. He got wasted and ended up making a scene in the bar. Stan threw him out."

A brief silence followed and then, "Just a minute." Jen relayed the news to her boyfriend, Simon. He immediately leapt to the defence of his friend, clearly swallowing the pack of lies spouted by the hard done by Philip.

Holding the phone away from her ear, Rowan slowly counted to ten and resisted the temptation to join in the ensuing argument. Five minutes later and neither Jen nor Simon were willing to concede on the subject of Philip.

Rowan elevated her voice just enough to make herself heard. "Listen Jen, I've got a taxi waiting. We'll talk tomorrow. Oh, and for the record, Philip is a lying shit." She disconnected the call before either one could say anything in response to her last comment.

"Bad night, huh?" Tony said sympathetically and handed over the food.

"You could say that," she replied with a heavy sigh. "Thanks."

"No problem." He waved a quick goodbye and retreated once more to the kitchen.

Jake shoved the e-cig into his pocket, as soon as she joined him outside. "The taxi rang; they are about one minute away."

"Their definition of a minute or ours?"

"Your guess is as good as mine."

Shivering, she drew her coat closer, the night air bitter against her skin. "Well, for their sake, I hope it's our definition."

Jake eyed her choice of outfit. Strapless knee-length dress, bare legs and the killer heels she had bought a few days ago at the behest of Jen. "I'd have gone with outfit number two."

"Hindsight's a wonderful thing," she muttered, huddling close to him for warmth.

The taxi frustratingly arrived ten minutes later than promised. Jake, calling shotgun, automatically jumped into the front passenger seat. He beamed like an insane Cheshire cat. If it were any other day, Rowan would rise to the challenge. Tonight, however, she allowed him this small moment of victory and climbed into the back seat without complaint. *What did it matter?* They were en route home, and she could, at last, put this evening behind her, the lecture mentally prepared for the taxi driver, forgotten.

Attuned to her mood, Jake happily took the lead and chatted all things football. Settled against the seat, Rowan ignored their conversation, her thoughts preoccupied with Jen's phone call, her stomach twisted into knots. It was inevitable that Philip would call, and of course, make himself out to be the injured party. *But surely, he'd have picked a more civilised time to do it?* The amount of alcohol he had consumed would have most normal people passing out until late morning, giving her at least a fighting chance to speak to Jen first, and explain what had happened. She knew Simon and Philip were close. Quite possibly close enough to create a rift in her friendship with Jen. It was the last thing she wanted on top of everything else she had endured this evening.

The guilt continued to prick at her conscience for hanging up so quickly, her parting shot unlikely to have helped the situation or a case to plead with Simon. Running through possible scenarios and counter-arguments, Rowan completely missed the fact that Jake had suddenly stopped talking. An awareness that something was wrong only registered when Jake eventually spoke again. "Excuse me, mate, but you're going the wrong way."

Lifting her gaze to the mirror, she met the older man's stare. His eyes crinkled in the corners. "Now don't you be fretting, miss, I'm not planning on turning all crazy on you. The police blocked the main road off, that's all. Not sure if you know but there's been a gale force wind tonight."

Rowan heaved a huge sigh, relieved to note that the driver had no intention of taking them off to some abandoned cabin in the middle of nowhere, and chopping them into tiny pieces.

Studying her in the mirror, he chuckled softly. "You kids watch far too many horror movies."

Jake's shoulders shook vigorously up and down in his seat as he smothered his laughter. Rowan fought the urge to give him a swift kick. That was the last time her brother would be calling first dibs on their Saturday movie night in. No more of these grab and slash horrors. Tomorrow she would choose the film and the one she had in mind, a full-blown musical chick flick, would be guaranteed to make him suffer.

Ignoring her brother's continued sniggers, Rowan shifted her attention to the driver. "Has it done much damage?"

He shook his head. "No major incidents as far as I've heard. The worst of it seems to have focused on the outskirts of the village. They've been quite lucky really. You had nothing in the Boro?"

"It did get a bit windy earlier, but nothing that exciting."

Jake cleared his throat and turned to offer an apologetic smile. She could see his struggle for self-control, his mouth twitching as he met her gaze. Hiding her irritation, Rowan beamed back at him sweetly and waited. It took only a few moments before it finally dawned on him that she meant to pay him back. "Erm, how about a comedy instead?" he offered.

"I don't think so, do you?" Her smile widened further. "You'll go crazy for the one I have in mind."

Defeated, Jake slumped back in his chair. "Do you mind if we have the radio on?"

The older man laughed and switched on the stereo, the car blaring with sound. He reached quickly for the dial. "Sorry about that, I tend to turn it up when it's the Friday night club classics."

"It's okay," she reassured, the music bringing a small semblance of normality back.

Jake pulled his mobile phone from his pocket and signed into his social media account. "Nothing on my news feed. Wonder if there'll be any mention on the radio?"

"They did a report about an hour ago. It seems that the weather forecasters are completely baffled. I don't know why, it's not as though they always get it right, is it?" The driver chuckled.

Cold travelled down Rowan's spine. *Maybe not, but something tells me that their confusion this time is genuine.* Shifting her eyes to the darkness outside, the unfamiliarity of the road added to her increasing discomfort. Jake's mood almost echoed her own, as she watched him turn his head toward the window, confident that he'd sensed the same feeling of impending doom.

Oblivious to their unease, the older man hummed along to a song now playing on the radio, the volume cranked up a notch.

Finally, they exited onto a familiar stretch of road, and Jake visibly relaxed. Following his lead, Rowan allowed some of her tension to release. The driver respectfully switched off the stereo, as they passed through the centre of the village, eerily quiet for a Friday evening.

Pulling onto their street, he turned to Jake. "Whereabouts would you like?"

"A little further down, on the right."

The taxi came to a welcome stop. "That's fifteen pounds, mate."

Leaving her brother to settle the fare, Rowan called out a quick thank you and collected the food. Stepping free from the car, she almost stumbled over the broken remains of what looked to be the next-door neighbour's garden gnome. Her eyes swept across the drive, taking in the full extent of the destruction exposed by the streetlights. Hanging baskets, only recently purchased from the garden centre, thrown over the front lawn and beyond all hope of rescue. Wheelie bins toppled, their contents spewed across the drive. Rowan's nose wrinkled in disgust. *Perfect! No prizes for guessing who'd be cleaning that little lot up in the morning.*

Other than the varying degree of branches, wood, broken pottery and an assortment of litter scattered, she was relieved to find the house to be perfectly intact.

Jake gave a long whistle as the taxi pulled away. "I'm not cleaning that crap up."

"So, you're going to leave it to me to sort then?" she grumbled, navigating her way across the drive.

"Trade you, I'll do the cat litter tray, and you can do the bins," he offered, his foot accidentally kicking a tin can. She winced as it rattled across the drive and finally landed on the lawn. Jake shrugged and headed up the steps, although with a little more care as to where he placed his size nine feet. Following closely behind, Rowan pondered on both options, neither chore she found to be remotely appealing. Typically, Jake opted again for the one he considered to be far less time-consuming. *No surprises there really.*

Knowing her brother as well as she did, the likelihood of him surfacing out of bed this side of midday was extremely remote. Reluctantly she agreed to take the bins, unable to bear the thought of leaving the drive in its current state all morning. "Okay, it's a deal."

Jake smirked and turned the key in the lock. He pushed the front door open. Rowan hurried inside and resisted the urge to thump him. He released the door, and it creaked closed behind.

She rested the takeaway boxes on the stairs, while she slid off her jacket. "No need for you to look quite so smug."

Annoyingly, Jake leaned over her in his eagerness to get to the food. Snatching both boxes, he gave her a quick peck on the cheek. "It was my turn to do the litter tray anyway." Laughing, he proceeded to the kitchen.

Sighing at her stupidity, Rowan hung up her jacket, and paused for a few moments at the foot of the stairs, her ears straining for sound. Good. Their mother somehow managed to continue sleeping through Jake's noisy entrance. She followed him into the kitchen. "We'd better eat in here. We don't want the living room to stink of takeaway."

He nodded and dragged a chair out from underneath the table. It scraped across the floor, setting Rowan's teeth on edge. "Do you want mum to join us?"

Jake looked bemused. "Huh?"

Silently she pulled out a chair and sat. "Try and be a little quieter."

His tongue flicked out in response.

"Very mature."

Chuckling, he unwrapped the food, mischief written on his face as he waved the tray of cheesy chips under her nose. The scent of melted cheese was too tempting an invitation to ignore. "I really shouldn't be eating this."

Jake grinned. "I could always save you from yourself. There's some rabbit food left in the fridge if you prefer."

Rowan wrenched the box out of his hand. "After tonight I think I deserve this, don't you?"

"Yeah, 'cause if I had to spend more than five minutes in that plank's company, I'd be driven to cheesy chips too."

This time she didn't resist giving him a kick under the table. "Cheek."

Jake smiled and stuffed a large piece of parmo in his mouth. Helpless to resist, Rowan stabbed her fork into the mound of melted cheese. Her taste buds completed a victory dance after months of denial.

"Good?" He gave her a knowing wink.

She nodded and groaned in pleasure.

There was a sudden flash from above, the kitchen temporarily dimmed and then brightened. Fork paused in mid-air, Rowan stared at the ceiling and waited. Seconds later, the light flickered off and on again. Her gaze lowered and met Jake's.

"It's probably just one of those aftershock things."

"It was a storm not an earthquake, you idiot," she said.

Senses on full alert, Rowan's eyes searched every crevice of the kitchen. Nothing seemed out of the ordinary and yet a feeling of foreboding persisted. Another flash this time had Jake putting down his cutlery, and staring upwards.

"They're either having issues with the electricity supply, or that bulb is definitely on its way out."

She could hear the logic in his explanation but found herself unable to formulate a response, the words held captive in her throat, silenced by a sharp pain radiating from the centre of her forehead. Jake, oblivious to her rising panic, picked up his fork. His features rapidly fading from sight as the vision hit hard and devoured without warning.

Blinking furiously, Rowan attempted to focus through the haze. She was confused to find herself standing alone in the middle of nowhere. Jake, her home, even the village itself had disappeared entirely. Her feet kicked grit in the air as she spun full circle, searching for someone, anyone who could help. Desolation stretched out for miles in every direction faced. Rowan's mouth tasted copper as she bit down hard on her lip, praying the pain would be sufficient to jolt her free. Her mind, frustratingly uncooperative, remained locked in the vision's grip, leaving her with no alternative but to wait for it to unfold.

A sudden wind billowed dust around her feet, the particles lifting, blowing into her hair and face. She shivered in response, and turned in the opposite direction. Frantically, she rubbed the dirt clear from her sight, her hand instantly dropping to her side when a loud crack reverberated. The ground was rupturing and tearing itself open right in front of her.

Standing on the precipice, Rowan gazed at the horror below. A river of red filled with death and decay ran beneath her feet. Its foul scent permeated the air. Dozens of tortured voices, now alert to her presence, screamed out in agony, shattering the silence. Rowan fell to her knees, the tears pouring with each soul that called out, begging her for release. She squeezed her eyes shut and prepared herself. A voice shouted. "Rowan, no."

Jake's face instantly snapped back into view. Her relief at finding herself home was however short-lived. Something had followed her. Rowan sensed it wrap around the village and slither into the darkness. Her instincts warned that it wasn't alone.

Heart thumping, she attempted to call out. Her mouth, unbearably dry, had her coughing uncontrollably.

Jake dropped his fork and sprang from the kitchen table to fetch a glass of water. "Are you okay? Did you choke on a chip?"

She took a sip, her gaze darting around the kitchen. "You didn't feel anything?"

Jake shook his head. "Nothing."

"You're sure you didn't feel anything, just then?"

"No, did the light spook you or something?"

"Something…" Her voice trailed off.

He gestured upwards. "Well, it seems fine now."

The bulb remained illuminated. There were no further signs of interference. Rowan glanced to the kitchen window and scrutinised the darkness. She waited for that same feeling to return, but there was nothing. Whatever it was that hid in the shadows had gone.

Rowan rubbed her temples, her mind whirling in confusion as she struggled to decipher between reality and fiction.

Jake stared at her. "Are you alright?"

She gave a weak smile. "Yes."

He didn't look convinced. "You're sure? You know your face is white as a sheet?"

"It's probably the stress from tonight, and that bloody film you chose last week. Honestly, I'm fine now. I just got spooked, that's all."

It was enough to convince him if not herself.

Jake stared hungrily at the chips. "Are you going to finish those?"

Appetite lost, Rowan pushed the box across the table. "Fill your boots, I'm off up to bed."

Jake studied her face. "You're positive you're alright?"

"Yes, now don't you be waking mum when you come up."

Jake stabbed a fork into a pile of chips. "I won't and thanks again for the food. I do love you, Sis."

Surprised by the tears that welled, she rose quickly from her seat. "You're welcome, and I love you too, even if you are a muppet."

His grin imprinted to memory as she closed the kitchen door softly behind her. Tonight had not been the first occasion that her brother had told her that he loved her. For reasons unknown, this time Jake's words held more meaning.

Hesitating at the foot of the stairs, Rowan instinctively took several deep calming breaths, willing her anxiety to soothe before beginning her ascent. Her legs juddered disappointingly in warning as she reached halfway. The vision had impacted more than she realised. She lunged for the support of the bannister, slowly pulling herself upwards, and with relief reached the landing without further incident. Ignoring the temptation to head straight for the security of her room, Rowan instead turned in the direction of the main bathroom. The need to clean her teeth and scrub away the last remnants of the evening outweighed the desire to retreat and hide underneath her duvet.

Standing in the harsh light, Rowan appraised the girl staring back from the mirror. Her face was pale and fatigued, the events of the night having taken their toll. She grimaced and reached for the cleansing wipes, her night-time care routine providing a temporary distraction from the memory of the vision that persistently pushed at the edges of her mind.

A feather-like touch against her cheek brought a smile. Toothbrush paused in mid-air Rowan waited for a second confirmation that he had drawn close, pleased when he did not disappoint. Rinsing quickly, she patted her skin dry with a towel and again regarded the girl in the mirror. Although her skin was much paler, and the fatigue still evident in her features, her eyes at least seemed to hold a little less fear.

Leaving just enough light peeking through from the bathroom, Rowan tiptoed across the landing towards her bedroom, hesitating at the door. Her arm snuck through the small gap and fumbled for the light, a sigh of relief escaping when her fingers made instant contact. She flipped on the switch and stepped slowly inside, her gaze searching every nook before she could finally bring herself to close the door behind.

Dumping her clothes into the laundry hamper, she reached for the comfort of her pyjamas. A creak from the picture frame of the old Quaker cottage, above her bed, gave her the confidence she needed. Rowan turned off the light and climbed beneath the covers. "Hello, Charles."

He shimmered briefly into view, his smile warm and reassuring. A twinkle of mischief danced around his eyes, making her curious as she waited for him to approach. His arms wrapped around her shoulders, bathing her with strength and love. Their bond deepened further, as she allowed his energy to connect with hers.

"Are you alright? For a moment there, I wasn't sure you were going to make it upstairs."

She smiled, knowing that he would never have let her fall. "I'm fine. You're here now."

The room fell into sudden silence. Rowan sensed his regret and frustration. "Oh Charles, I didn't mean anything by that."

Although his voice was calm, she knew he struggled. "I should have been able to reach you. I'm so sorry to have let you down."

"It's alright," she said, knowing that her attempt to reassure him had failed miserably.

"No, it's not." He paused for a few moments before speaking again. "Forgive me, I know that you don't want to think about what happened, but I need to ask you about tonight, it's important."

She sighed. "Somehow, I had a feeling you would."

"I'm truly sorry, but the fact that I was unable to reach you or access the vision has concerned the Lightkeepers greatly, and me."

"They don't blame you, do they?"

"No, but they need to understand what happened."

"As long as they know you're not to blame. The vision isn't like anything I have had before. This time I felt as if I had been transported there, physically transported there."

"Where?"

"I honestly don't know. But it was cold and desolate and…" Rowan shuddered as the memory of the vision seized control.

"Tell me what you see, I must know."

Her skin broke into a clammy sweat, her hands reaching upwards to cover her ears. "I can still hear them screaming. Trapped, drowning in a river of blood, begging for my help. I almost did, but a voice warned me not to do so."

"Who?"

"I don't know who, but they are in so much pain."

He grasped her shoulders. "What else?"

"When the vision ended, I felt as though something had travelled back with me. It's hiding in the darkness. And it isn't alone. I keep trying to tell myself it's just the vision that's spooked me, but I can still feel it. They are connected somehow, to the vision, and the storm too."

Charles gently released his hold and pulled away.

"I'm right, aren't I? It's here in the village. Do you know what it is?"

"No, they are not from any plane of existence that we are aware of."

Rowan could hear the edge in his voice. "They? I knew it. So, it isn't alone. What do you think they want?"

"We don't know. But I do believe you are right about what you experienced tonight. The vision does appear connected to their arrival in the village. You need to be careful, and do what I say."

His stark warning filled her with dread. "Aren't you supposed to reassure me? Allow me to remain in blissful ignorance?" she joked, a lame attempt at humour.

"Would you rather I lie? Tell you it's just your imagination and that all is well with the world when both you and I know that it's not?"

Sensing her fear, Charles drew close and enveloped her in his arms once more. A surge of protective energy radiated through her. "I will keep you safe."

"I know you will, and I do trust you. Thank you for being there for me."

"Always," he replied.

Relaxing against the pillow, Rowan closed her eyes and drew from his strength, the last remnants of her fear released. Her vision, successfully locked away and no longer occupying her thoughts. Silence fell between them, and she slowly found herself drifting.

His sudden laughter pulled her back. Confused, Rowan attuned to his energy and detected the same mischief she had sensed earlier. She couldn't help but join in his amusement.

"What are we laughing about?" she managed, her sides aching with the effort of restraint.

"It was a real shame about that Philip."

The sudden realisation had a sobering effect. "It was you that knocked Philip off that stool."

Charles shimmered into view and gave a cheeky wink and bow before disappearing again. "I know, I shouldn't have done it, but honestly I couldn't stop myself. That was absolutely no way to speak to a lady. Even Tarwin had to admit he had it coming."

"Is Tarwin his guide?"

"Yes, although not for long. Philip is due to receive a guide change. From what Tarwin told me, one of the Sage Masters, Adeybo, I believe, has been assigned to try and straighten him out. Strayed well away from his path that one. Poor Tarwin, he's been battling for years, but the guy doesn't take a hint. Not much between the lugs if you ask me, despite his education."

"I completely agree. Will Tarwin be reassigned then?"

"Eventually. He's going to shadow one of the Sages for a time, needs to rebuild his confidence. Philip was his first assignment."

After a couple of hours spent in Philip's company, Rowan had a great deal of empathy and admiration for Tarwin. *I hope his next assignment proves to be more rewarding.*

She glanced at the clock and grimaced at the illuminated numbers. "Could you do me a favour, and check if Jake is in bed for me?"

In less than a minute, he returned chuckling softly. "Yes, he's snoring loudly. Amazingly Christine is still asleep too."

"How does she seem?"

"Her mind is at rest, don't worry. Aliyah mentioned that she was a little shaken by the storm, but she managed to calm her."

"Is Aliyah with her now?"

"Yes, all the guides are staying close tonight. Aliyah has cast a protection spell around the house."

"Thank her for me. I know mum has no awareness of her, but I do and I appreciate her being there for us."

"I'll speak to her when I know you've settled. Do you think you can sleep now?"

She yawned and snuggled beneath the duvet. "Goodnight, Charles."

"Goodnight, Rowan."

In the dream realm, he waited as she knew he would. His face broke into a grin the moment she crossed the doorway.

Brushing a lock of hair behind her ear, she took a step closer. Her heart raced, and legs trembled beneath as his eyes fixed on her, his hand reaching out to take hers. Rowan smiled and accepted without hesitation.

"You came back," he beamed.

As their fingers entwined, she was amazed to find her senses alive and bursting with need once more. Her aura thrummed, pulsing with an energy she had never experienced with anyone, other than him. The butterflies danced their joy in her abdomen, making her nauseous and excited at the same time.

Rowan found herself helplessly lost in the depths of his brown eyes as he searched her own, begging her to acknowledge their undeniable connection. She could only nod in response, unable to find the words to express the strength of her feelings.

"I need to find you. But something keeps blocking my vision."

Rowan sensed that something was Charles. Reluctantly she let go of his hand. "I don't know who you are."

"You have to trust me," he begged.

Tormented by the warning in her head and the yearning in her heart, she lifted her gaze to his. "How can I when I don't know you? I don't even know if any of this is real. It makes no sense to carry these feelings for a man I've never met, a man who lives in my dreams."

"What does your heart say to you?" His voice was raw with emotion.

"The same as yours, I imagine."

"Then let me find you, and tell me where you are. Please, I don't have much time."

"I don't understand. You've found me, haven't you?"

"I need to know where you live."

"Why, what difference would that make? This is just a dream."

"I promise, I'll explain everything to you, but not now, my time here is short."

Struggling with her feelings, Rowan turned away and called for Charles. He arrived within seconds, drawing her close. "What's wrong?"

"Can you see him?"

"No."

Her bottom lip trembled with disappointment. "Then, there is no hope."

"Rowan, I can't explain why I am unable to see his presence here, but there is meaning if he has come to you once more. Don't give up hope."

"He wants me to tell him where I am. What should I do?"

"Answer me one question, and be completely honest. Do you still feel the same way about him?" Charles asked.

She could no longer deny her heart. "Yes, I do."

"Then you must trust your feelings, and do what you know is right."

"But it doesn't make sense."

"Sometimes it is not for us to question what is, but instead to trust. Whatever you decide, know that I am standing by you, watching over you." Charles released his connection.

Alone she turned to face him, his look pleading her to trust. "Will you hold me first?"

He smiled and enfolded Rowan into his embrace. His lips pressed softly against her forehead. "How can I find you?"

The urgency in his words was all too clear. Decision made, and intuition guiding, Rowan visualised her home. Willing them both there together, as they stood now, locked in each other's arms. To her surprise and joy, the dreamscape immediately complied with her request. A blur of shape and colour finally manifesting into the image she had summoned. Lifting her head, she observed his reactions.

His eyes were seeming to take in every single detail of the house and its environment. "What road is this?"

"Sycamore, there's a sign at the bottom of the street."

Releasing her from his arms, he cupped her chin and raised her face to meet his.

"One last thing that I ask of you."

"What is it?"

"Stay out of the shadows."

His words shattered the dream and jolted her awake. "Charles?"

"I'm here, it's alright."

Sinking back against the pillow, Rowan closed her eyes, soothed by the touch of his hand as he tenderly stroked her hair. "Rest."

CHAPTER THREE

Guisborough, North East England

Gently releasing his energy from her sleeping form, Charles moved quickly to the raven-haired young woman entering the room, her face full of concern.

"What is it, Aliyah?"

"Something has changed."

"I know I sensed the shift too."

She walked to the window and peered outside into the darkness. "The others have been calling out all night, Charles. They are anxious."

"They have cause to be. We have not experienced this before."

"Have you spoken to the Lightkeepers since?"

"Briefly, they've instructed that we remain vigilant and report back with any concerns."

Aliyah glanced to Rowan, stirring in her sleep. Her voice lowered to a whisper. "It's not just these things that have gathered around the village. There's something else happening here too. Rowan is right at the heart of it."

His eyes flicked across to his ward. "I can't deny that they are connected."

"Did she see him again?"

"Yes, and you're right, Aliyah. There's a power at play here that none of us understands, not even the Lightkeepers. Our only solace is that Rowan has given her heart to him, so there must be light within."

"You and I both know that humans are capable of loving those who are not deserving," she reminded him gently.

"I have not forgotten. But I know Rowan to be different. I trust in her judgement, and you must trust in mine."

"I hope you are right, for all our sakes. Have you been able to connect with him at all?"

Charles shook his head. "The boy made contact through astral projection in the dreamscape. I do believe he has a physical presence, so there may yet be an opportunity."

"Do you know that for certain?"

"No, and neither does Rowan."

"Well, whoever this boy is, and whatever he wants, we must ensure Rowan's safety. Christine isn't strong enough to cope with another loss after David's transition."

Charles heaved a sigh. "I do understand what the consequences would be, Aliyah, the Lightkeepers have briefed me. Is the protection spell holding?"

Aliyah's gaze swept across to the window. "Yes, they are all safe here, hidden well within the light and away from the shadows."

Charles could not resist. "And how can you be so certain?"

She smiled, not rising to his bait. "Not to brag, brother, but it is the oldest magic. They're all under protection, I assure you."

"Even so, we need to remain on our guard. Rowan's vision is warning enough. I assume Harry is with Jake?"

"Yes, although he won't hear you calling over the top of Jake's snoring. How that boy manages to speak in the morning is a complete mystery."

Charles laughed. "Indeed, his stamina is to be admired."

Aliyah's eyes creased in the corners and a smile touched her lips. "Whose Jake's or Harry's?"

He didn't reply. Distracted by Rowan's soft groans, Charles hurried to her side. Laying a hand across her forehead, he soothed her brow, his senses alert to yet another shift of energy around her. "That's not her father."

Aliyah crossed to his side. "David was only granted time with Christine. Do you sense a threat?"

Charles shook his head. "Not at the moment."

"Then we'll talk later. It seems that tonight isn't quite finished with Rowan yet, and she may need you."

He nodded, staring down at the woman he had watched over since birth. "She's entered the dreamscape."

Curiosity followed disappointment as Rowan appraised the older woman who now stood in his place. She was dressed in black linen trousers and a soft cornflower sweater that emphasised the blue in her eyes. Her long silver hair tumbled loosely around her shoulders. When she smiled, it was with what seemed to Rowan as an honest affection. "I am sorry, dear, but I'm afraid it is just me now."

"I don't understand."

"I can see that, dear, but there isn't much time for me to explain and I do need to speed things up a little."

She turned with a quick clap of her hands. Their surroundings instantly dissolved. Rowan levitated into a cyclone of light before she could so much as utter a complaint.

"Hold on, dear, you're nearly there."

"Nearly where?" Rowan called, unable to bring her vision into focus through the persistent merry go round of colours and shapes.

"You must relax, dear, and let it come naturally."

"Easy for you to say. You're not the one sat on a bloody waltzer."

"A waltzer?"

"Oh, never mind."

"That's just as well, as we have no time for ballroom dancing. You need to trust me, dear."

Squeezing her eyes closed, Rowan slowly counted to ten. "Okay, I agree to trust you. Now could you just make it stop?"

"But it already has, see?"

Rowan gaped around the quaint little kitchen, its sandstone walls festooned with a curious assortment of bottles and jars.

A myriad of greenery decorated from the window to the floor. Large leafy tendrils swept out across the sparkling silver tops and warm oak cupboards. In the heart of the kitchen, a table covered in a simple white cloth and delicate blue china, set for two places. A jug of wildflowers adorned its centre, their fragrance divine.

The older woman smiled. "They are quite beautiful, my favourites in the garden."

Rowan nodded and inhaled the sweet fragrance. "I would love to see your garden."

"And you will, my dear, very soon."

A sudden movement from the fire hearth drew Rowan's attention as a rather excited small black Scottie dog leapt from its wicker basket and sprang in the direction of her legs.

"Now, Biscuit, where are your manners today?"

The little dog skidded to a stop, wagging his tail enthusiastically despite the scolding.

"I'm sorry, dear, it's just that we don't get many visitors."

Biscuit barked a response and the older woman stooped down to address him. "Well, yes. That's very true. But we must have patience. This is her first visit."

Rowan stared from woman to dog as they carried on their conversation. "I've completely and utterly lost the plot now." She rubbed her forehead.

The older woman rose, her expression serious. "I very much doubt that, dear. But you do look a little pale. Perhaps some tea will help."

"Sure, tea, why didn't I think of that?" Rowan muttered. Her words were met with a soft chuckle.

"It's good to see you haven't lost your sense of humour. You're going to need it, my dear."

Rowan heaved a huge sigh. "Okay, so if I am not completely insane, could you at least tell me who you are?"

"I'm Bessie, and you, of course, are Rowan."

"How is it you know my name?"

Bessie moved to switch on the kettle. "I just know, dear."

"Are you real?"

"As real as you are."

The little dog nudged Rowan's leg, and she bent to stroke him. "And, Biscuit, he's real too?"

"Yes, and my apologies, Biscuit, for the lack of introduction."

Biscuit rolled over to offer his tummy for Rowan to rub.

Smiling, Bessie turned towards the table, kettle in hand. She lifted the lid of the teapot and emptied the water inside. "He trusts you, dear, that's an excellent sign. I'm so very pleased."

Rowan rose to meet the older woman's gaze. "A good sign of what?"

"Of things to come. We must prepare." Returning the kettle, Bessie signalled for Rowan to join her at the table. "Please sit."

Biscuit curled around her feet as she accepted the tea offered. "Can I drink this?"

"Of course, it is your dream, after all," Bessie replied.

Rowan placed the teacup down and slumped into her chair. Disappointment had quenched her thirst. "So, none of this is real, then?"

"On the contrary, my dear, Biscuit, and I are very real."

"Then how is any of this possible?"

"It just is. We cannot question that, but instead must trust."

Rowan shook her head slowly. For the second time that night she'd been told to trust. Not easy to accomplish when logic and reasoning demanded an explanation.

"I know that you're not quite ready yet, but you will need to be very soon. Time grows short. You must come and find Biscuit and me. He will show you the way."

There it was again, another reference to time, and also to him.

"He?" Rowan asked innocently, although deep down she knew to whom Bessie referred.

"You know very well who," Bessie said.

"Yes, I do, but what I want to know is, how do you?"

"All will become clear. For now, he will find you and then together you must find your amulet."

"What amulet?"

"Your talisman, dear. You will need it for the journey ahead."

Rowan's frustration grew. "I really don't understand any of this."

"I know it has been rather an eventful night for you. All will become clear soon," Bessie reassured.

Biscuit barked from beneath the table.

"What did he say?"

Glancing to the silver carriage clock on the mantel, Bessie nodded. "You're right, of course, there is no time. Dawn approaches and Rowan has a hectic day ahead of her. My dear, I shall send for you tonight and we will talk some more."

"What do you mean? I have a hectic day ahead?"

"Off you go now. Say goodbye, Biscuit."

"No, wait…" Rowan cried.

Charles considered the exchange from a safe distance, his presence undetected. *Another piece of the puzzle.* However, unlike the other energy that had congregated around the village, he sensed no threat from the woman. She had in part spoken the truth. Both she and the dog held a physical presence in this world, although he found it somewhat odd that she had no guide with her. Charles waited until Rowan's energy released itself from the dreamscape, before returning to her bedside.

Rowan groaned and spun over, kicking a leg free from the duvet.

Soothing her brow with his hand. He settled her back into slumber, and called to Aliyah.

She shimmered into view and placed a hand gently on his shoulder. "What is it?"

"Can you keep watch? I must speak with the Lightkeepers."

"Is it the boy?"

"Not the boy. There is another who has contacted Rowan in the dreamscape. I sense she too has a part to play."

Aliyah nodded. "Then you must go."

"Thank you. I'll be back before she wakes."

With a final glance towards Rowan, Charles vanished from the room.

CHAPTER FOUR

North York Moors, North East England

Kane crossed his arms and leaned casually against the stump of the tree. It was indeed a calculated move, exuding an air of confidence that admittedly he didn't feel. The arch of the Master's brows was a positive sign as he continued to appraise him through the depths of the fire. Kane's eyes were resolute and unyielding, despite the coil of doubt that churned. He masked it well, having learned from the mistakes of others, as he'd watched them crumble under the Master's scrutiny and seal their fates.

It was a relief to note that his apparent arrogance had earned Kane some respect. The Master had relinquished his gaze and settled back into the flames.

Encouraged, Kane broke the silence. "I take it my news was to your satisfaction?"

The Master's lips curled into something closely resembling a smile. "Valoria will soon be mine."

Shifting his position, Kane leaned closer to the fire, his stomach somersaulting in anticipation. "Tell me."

"Jarrow is dead."

Kane sneered. "The fools, they sent their best warrior into battle."

"Yes. Your recommendation to strike tonight is most pleasing. However, don't be so quick to celebrate. We have not gone unscathed. My army was diminished, more than we anticipated. Jarrow proved to be a worthy adversary."

"Understood. And what of my premonition, and the scorpion's tail?"

The Master sneered. "It has fallen."

"Mercadia does not suspect?"

"No, or she would not have risked sending Jarrow into battle."

"Then the game has changed, Master. Your army will rebuild. Led by a worthy ally. How long do we have until the uprising?"

"The sun moves into position in four days."

"The twelfth sacrifice?"

The Master nodded, his pleasure evident. "Their blood has been spilt. The Waters of Samsara are turning."

"Then I shall return to complete the ritual."

"No, Aaron will complete the ritual."

Kane bit back his disappointment. "Do you trust him?"

"For now. He has proven himself to be loyal to me. You do not?"

Something about the sudden appearance of such a gifted mage filled Kane with suspicion. "Like you, I've had no call to question him. But I would urge you to remain cautious where he is concerned."

"Aaron is under close supervision. He serves me well enough. As for you, Kane, you will serve me by finding out why Mercadia took such a risk. Capture this girl and bring her to me, alive and unharmed."

"What of the Tracker?"

"He could be of use to us. After all he was the one to find the Silver Stag and obtain the first key. Not an easy feat for a man of his means. He may well be the one to find the others. Persuade him to join us."

"If I can't?"

"Then kill him. Speaking of which, where is that First Officer of yours? He wasn't with the others."

Kane stood and turned to the trees. The Fallen shrank back from sight, but were too late in their retreat. The Master's gaze had already locked onto the one he sought, the creature howling, as it was forced away from its brethren. Its claws scratched noisily into bark, a futile attempt Kane considered to brace itself against the sheer might of the Master's will. Despite the creature's bulk it hurtled effortlessly through the night air and landed with a loud thud in front of the flames, its leathery black skin slick with sweat as it scrambled onto all fours.

"You have failed me tonight, Irian," the Master said.

"Not I," the creature hissed, saliva dripping from its elongated snout.

"Then who?" the Master demanded.

Kane resisted the urge to snap its neck, as Irian's cold-blooded amber eyes met his.

"You dare to accuse your Commander? Miserable piece of filth, I shall kill you now," Kane said, his voice shaking with anger.

The Master shook his head in warning. Kane swallowed his temper and complied with the silent order to leave the matter with him.

The slits of Irian's eyes widened with renewed hope. He continued with his betrayal. "On the Commander's orders did we fail you. Please do not punish us further. We shall do better. I shall do better. He must do better," Irian announced.

Kane seethed, his hands twitching by his sides.

The Master smirked and met Irian's gaze. "You know that I expect complete loyalty."

"Yes," Irian hissed.

"Then where is yours?" the Master asked and raised his hand.

The creature dropped to the ground, writhing and clawing at its throat, unable to respond. The Master's vice-like grip continued to choke the life out of it. Kane stared without pity into its bulging eyes, no longer defiant, as blood continued to ooze from every orifice of the creature. A satisfying gurgling echoed through the forest. Kane sneered.

Irian, gasped for air one last time, before his flesh exploded, scattering pieces across the campsite.

"Let this be a lesson to all and don't fail me again."

Kane kicked a dismembered limb off his boot. "Understood."

The fire extinguished, signalling the Master's departure.

Sensing movement, Kane spun to face the six Fallen that had

now approached. Only one stepped forward. The others kept their distance.

"Any sign of him?" said Kane.

"No, Commander. We lost him after the storm."

Kane scowled. "And you are?"

"Barrock."

"Congratulations, Barrock, you're promoted to First Officer. Clean that up."

"Thank you, Commander."

With no appetite to watch, Kane strode purposefully in the opposite direction and away from the camp. The remaining Fallen moved quickly past him with eyes downcast, as they joined their brethren. Kane's lip twitched with pleasure, and he basked in their subservience.

Particular members had enjoyed the taste of their newfound freedom a little too much. They were unaware that Kane had heard their whispers during the night, as they retreated to their cocoons to plan ways in which to kill him. Kane knew of their desire to remain in this strange world with its plentiful supply of flesh and bone. They thought he had been sleeping and therefore oblivious to any attempts made to overthrow him. *Such fools!*

Alone in the forest, Kane laughed out loud at Irian's mistake. The obliteration of the first scout team had soon put an end to their plan for mutiny, their ringleader now scattered in several pieces across the camp, the main course for his brethren.

Although aggrieved that he had not been the one to end Irian's life, the night had concluded well for Kane, his favour with the Master redeemed after highlighting the tactical advantage the Council had inadvertently given the Master, and which happened to deflect from his own recent failure.

Navigating his way through the forest, Kane continued walking until the distance was sufficient enough to prevent him from hearing the sound of the Fallen tearing into flesh. He had seen enough for one night, and although it had been hours since he had last eaten, his stomach still churned with the memory. Focusing on the Master's news of Jarrow's demise provided a welcome distraction from the Fallen, and their pathetic attempts for supremacy.

Kane paused on the outskirts of the forest. Safely concealed within the shadows he watched with fascination the strange machines of this world move towards the glow of the distant village. Somewhere, hidden in its midst was the one he sought. Today had been close. The Tracker cornered and almost at the point of surrendering. Kane had sensed his defeat and relished in it. But then that glorious taste of victory had been snatched away by the Council's interference. Tomorrow would be another day, and he did not intend to fail.

Kane thought of Mercadia, so smug with her elemental spell, and demonstration of power. The same power that she had stolen from his family, and that he would soon claim back. Little did she realise this recent show of force would bring about her downfall. The uprising was no longer just a delusion of his crazy mother's mind. Kane had not forgotten. He would make damn sure that Mercadia didn't either.

The Selensia would breach, and Valoria would be taken, another realm surrendered to the Master's control, his plan seamless and helped along by the Council's misguided belief in the ramblings of some foolish mage. Though a sliver of doubt remained. Kane considered the risk that Mercadia had taken and questioned why she had chosen her best Tracker, sending him across time and space to find a human girl. *Why do they so fiercely protect him and leave themselves vulnerable to attack?* With only a small piece of the tapestry, the answers eluded him.

Kane silently berated himself. If he had just swallowed his anger and persevered a few more days, he may well have possessed the remaining pieces of the tapestry. The servant girl had been so besotted with him and eager to please in every way Kane demanded. Granted, he had enjoyed her for a short time. Such remarkable skills for one so young, and her access to the Council's records made her more than an appealing prospect. Kane had considered bestowing the honour of becoming his mistress, until she had bitterly disappointed him with her betrayal and stupidity.

The day she announced she was pregnant with his child, Kane had slit her throat. No whore would ever carry his firstborn son. He watched the light bleed out of her eyes, with no remorse for the mother, or child that died in her womb.

Deciphering the information contained on the small piece of cloth, stolen before her death, had made the Master nervous. Without the rest of the detail provided within the prophecy, neither of them could be entirely sure. They knew nothing of the human girl, only the world from which she came and the foretelling of a Tracker, who would show her the way. The Tracker would be born in Valoria, and he would be the protector of the keys.

Kane had known the minute the Silver Stag was found, that the one they called Finn, was the Tracker referred to in the prophecy. The day Finn had travelled through the portal, Kane had followed him, and his hunch had been correct.

He flinched as a sudden scream echoed around the forest. It was loud enough to alert anyone passing by of their presence. Temper erupting, Kane stormed back towards the camp. A fight had broken out amongst the Fallen, each arguing over the scattered carcasses of the first scout team. They snarled and wrestled at the scraps of meat.

Kane considered for a moment whether he should have given them an alternative form, one that didn't heighten their already bloodthirsty nature. He couldn't deny that this had brought certain advantages, including an enhanced ability to hunt their prey.

Sensing his arrival, the Fallen looked up.

"Any more fighting and I will rip the bloody lot of you apart myself."

Barrock turned and hissed to the others. The Fallen immediately withdrew into the shadows.

"I told you to clean up this mess," Kane said.

"We are, Commander," Barrock replied.

"Then do it without the squabbling. Have you set up my quarters?"

"Yes, and there is food ready for you too."

"Good. See to it that there is no further disturbance."

Barrock nodded and retreated in silence. Kane continued to his tent and was pleasantly surprised to find himself greeted with a large plate of spit-roasted deer, accompanied by an assortment of vegetables foraged from this world. The meal was much more fitting to his refined palate, and a significant improvement on Irian's pitiful offering of fish, Barrock's use of the Hymorius table much more developed.

Kane sneered, appeased by the thought of Irian's bones now being picked from his brethren's teeth. A befitting end for the miserable creature who had foolishly dared to mock his authority.

Whispering an intonation, Kane warmed the contents of the plate and slowly ate until nothing remained. Hunger slaked, he reached for the glass of wine and took a moment to savour the delicious bouquet of oak and spices from his home-world. The liquid warmed and soothed the last of his irritation. Pouring another glass, he contemplated his next move. Only when his plan was formulated, and the bottle drained, did Kane yield to his exhaustion and, fully clothed, stumble into bed.

CHAPTER FIVE

Pinchinthorpe, North East England

Finn groaned and rolled onto his side. He was far from impressed at having been yanked out of what had been, up to that point, a most enjoyable dream. Wrapping one end of the pillow firmly around his exposed ear, he snatched at the last remnants, hoping he could somehow find and pick up where he left off. He failed miserably.

"I know you can hear me." Mercadia's voice refused to leave him be, and continued with its annoying, and persistent drone.

The dream that he was so desperately trying to cling onto evaporated instantly. Finn turned onto his stomach and buried his face. Reaching for a second pillow, he swiftly dragged it over his head, attempting to stifle her voice as it continued berating.

"Don't you ever learn? I am not silenced that easily."

Cursing loudly, Finn hurled both pillows.

"Really?" she tutted, making him feel like a petulant child. Lying flat against the mattress, he folded his arms and glowered at the ceiling. He could sense her temper rising too.

"Oh, for pity's sake."

The curtains in his room tore apart, plunging Finn into daylight. Squinting from the sudden brightness, he kicked at the duvet repeatedly until it finally fell to the floor.

"Feel better?" Mercadia's voice dripped with sarcasm.

Finn swung his legs out of bed. "You're a complete pain in the neck, do you know that?" Stomping to the bathroom, he slammed the door behind, not caring a damn whether she happened to be watching or not.

"Have you finished behaving like a child now?" Mercadia enquired as soon as he emerged from the bathroom.

Reaching for the clothing Patrick's wife had given him, he pulled on the trousers.

"Can't you give a guy some peace?"

"Peace? What peace? Remember that you're here on the Council's orders. As I told you last night, time is of the essence. Please tell me that you found the girl?"

Finn acknowledged her with a grunt and continued to dress.

"Excellent news. You have at last, restored my faith in you."

Ignoring the remark, he searched around for his boots.

"Try the bathing room. I seem to recall that's where you removed your rags."

Muttering under his breath, Finn checked the bathroom as Mercadia suggested and could almost visualise her smug smile. His boots, covered in dirt, were nestled in the corner beneath the sink. He grimaced and ran the tap, washing the grime away.

"Have you ever considered that this quest isn't as easy as you seem to think it is? Particularly with the Master's minions on my tail."

"Why do you think we chose you? It certainly wasn't for your charm!"

"Even with my ability, I am one man."

"One man you may be. But you're not alone. The Council is with you, keeping a close watch."

Finn rolled his eyes. "Don't I know it."

"May I remind you what could have happened last night, had we not been watching?" Mercadia said.

Finn had to concede on that point. He dried his boots and pulled them on. "I am grateful to you."

"I'm glad. Now, the girl you must contact immediately."

"That was my intention," Finn grumbled, scooping up the discarded remains of his torn and still sodden clothing, and dropping them into the wicker bin. Returning to the bedroom, he heaved a sigh and collected the bedding he had thrown onto the floor. Sensing her impatience, Finn continued with his efforts to straighten the room rather belligerently, grinning as she huffed loudly.

"Did I not mention before about the sheer importance of time?" Mercadia said.

"It's a few minutes, and Patrick has been kind to me. Besides which I need money to pay him for the room, and also for food and transport. I can't leave the poor man high and dry when he has shown me much kindness."

"Very well. Go to the mirror. My power, as you know, is still regenerating, but I can manage this. I will need your help though."

Finn did as she requested. "What is it that you need from me?"

"I want you to focus on the mirror and listen to my voice. Put aside all other thoughts and feelings. Nothing else exists but my voice. Use your senses and reach your way forward through the glass. Every ripple brings you closer. Know that you will find me, my voice your guide."

The mirror brightened, breaking free from the constraint of its frame and continued to grow in size, consuming his vision. Finn stepped closer, drawn like a moth to a flame.

"That's it, follow my voice. Allow all of your senses to let go. Trust me."

Taking a deep breath, Finn relinquished the last shred of doubt and propelled forward, passing through his reflection with a shudder. Light shimmered around him, and his body surged with an unexplained power. Holding his arms out in front of him, he watched as luminous waves rippled outwards with each searching sweep. The effect suddenly brought reminiscences of his childhood and the long days spent with Aaron casting coins across the waters of Tahlia in exchange for wishes granted.

The brightness of the mirror evaporated with the memory. The room as it was before, except that the reflection staring back at him was no longer his own. "What is this?"

"It is called the Lemure." Mercadia was too slow to conceal her surprise.

"You weren't sure I could pull this off, were you?"

"I admit I wasn't altogether confident."

Finn sensed something else behind her answer, and could almost feel her battling to bury it beneath the surface. "What are you hiding from me?"

She shook her head quickly. "Nothing."

Finn wasn't convinced. Mercadia's eyes shifted past him, as though she had detected something of interest, and yet desperately tried to ignore it. He decided against another argument, for now.

Delving into her robe pocket, Mercadia retrieved a small yellow crystal and offered it to him. Tentatively he reached his hand forward, eyes widening when it slipped through the glass with ease. A contrast of temperature felt against his skin, the coolness of the glass and the warmth of Mercadia's brief touch, as she dropped the crystal into his hand.

Finn ran a finger across its smooth surface. "What is it?"

"Citrine, it will provide you with what you need."

Removing his hand from the pane, he stared at the crystal resting in his palm. "How do I use it in this world?"

"Take the Citrine, and visualise what you need. When you see this firmly in your mind, then place it in your right pocket, and reach into your left. Be careful though, the crystal only has so much magic stored before it needs to return to our world and recharge. Use it wisely," Mercadia said.

Finn followed her instructions and visualised the currency he had observed exchanged in this world. Taking care not to manifest too much, and avoid attracting unwanted attention to himself, he placed the crystal into his right pocket and waited for a few moments. A heaviness dropped into his left trouser pocket. Slowly he reached inside, almost stumbling backwards as he pulled out a roll of paper notes.

Mercadia chuckled. "There are limits as to what you can manifest. The crystal will let you know if you ask too much of it."

"I understand." Finn returned the money to his pocket. "I need to eat now, and you, I sense need to rest. I assume the Selensia is holding up?" He observed the pain in her eyes. "What else haven't you told me?"

Mercadia lowered her gaze. "As we feared, the Master attacked last night. He took advantage of the fact that I was weak."

Finn gave a sharp intake of breath. "How bad is it?"

Mercadia raised her eyes to meet his. Her voice shook as she spoke. "He succeeded in fracturing the Selensia. The damage was enough to send three of his assassins into Valoria. We've repaired the rift in the veil, but they are free to move within the realm."

Finn sank to his knees. "It's all my fault."

"No, we knew the risk we were taking when we created the storm through the portal. Gregor has sent all the men he can spare into Valoria to help Elisha."

Finn's stomach was in knots. "Which assassins?" he asked, although he was not sure he wanted the answer.

Mercadia tugged at the collar of her robe. "We do not know who the other two are."

"But you do know of the third?" Finn asked.

She nodded, her gaze sliding away from his and her bottom lip trembling.

Finn watched her fingers play with the Sapphire ring on her hand. "Drey's alive, isn't he?"

Tears glistened in Mercadia's eyes. It was the first time Finn had seen her look so vulnerable.

"Yes," she said quietly.

"You let him go?"

"I couldn't do it," she said miserably. "I had hoped instead to reach him and bring him back before it was too late. I thought his love for me was strong enough."

Finn observed the regret in her eyes. "You know that Drey's soul is lost, don't you? He killed innocent people."

"I know that, now. I should have destroyed him when I had the chance." The guilt was evident in Mercadia's eyes.

"What else is there?" Finn asked.

"Jarrow is dead."

"Drey?"

Mercadia nodded, her voice full of sorrow. "Jarrow fought

bravely, but his wounds were too much. The Selensia's repair left him nothing to regenerate with."

Finn sensed her struggle to regain composure.

"The man I loved is truly dead. The Drey who attacked last night was something unrecognisable. The power he consumed in the void..." She took a deep breath in. "He's completely deformed, malevolent. Jarrow didn't stand a chance."

A realisation occurred. "With Jarrow gone that only leaves one other Elder on the Council besides you," Finn said.

"The Master won't attempt another attack before my power has regenerated. Jarrow struck his blow too before he died and the Selensia sealed. He fought bravely and with honour."

Finn's blood ran cold, the gravity of Mercadia's words sinking in. *If the Master's assassins had access to the Valoria border that could mean that...* "My mother?"

"Safe, and under the Council's immediate protection here in the Castle. Gregor has ensured that she has everything she needs. We have a cloaking spell around Riverwood," Mercadia assured.

Finn felt his fear subside a little.

"Gregor has sent his second guard to Moon Dell. We cannot take the risk of Drey and the others crossing the borders and discovering the White Stallion."

"Is Spirit safe?" Finn asked.

"The Fae have him under their protection. Thankfully, that's one secret Melissa didn't manage to share in her throws of passion with the Master's second in command."

A familiar churn of anger stirred in his gut. "So much betrayal. What are you going to do about Drey?"

Mercadia's voice barely a whisper. "I must kill him. He too will see that I am not the same as I once was."

"Be careful. The Council is vulnerable. Now may not be the time to fight."

"I will be. You should know that your mother has been of great service. Her knowledge of herbs is incredible. Many of Gregor's men survived the night and are recovering swiftly from their wounds. She has earned the full respect of the Council, and your King. That will go a long way for both of you."

"I appreciate you taking care of her, and I am pleased that she has been of service to Gregor. But understand that she is not working for the Council, and under no circumstances is she to be sent to the frontline as Gregor's next healing mage. Do you hear me? If anything happens to her you can forget the prophecy and I won't give a damn how many trees you hurl."

Mercadia sighed. "Understood. We need to release the Lemure. I have to rest, there is much both of us need to do."

"How?"

"Let go. Allow my voice to drift away until it is no more. Release me now."

The connection cut, Mercadia's thoughts no longer linked to his own.

Alone, Finn faced his reflection, unable to mask the internal conflict raging inside. In a furious haze, he headed to the bathroom and splashed cold water on his face. His hands gripped the basin tightly, jaw repeatedly clenching with each thought that whirled back and forth. The Master had sent assassins into Valoria, Jarrow was dead, and Drey alive to seek his revenge. His mother safe, and Riverwood cloaked, but for how long? Only two Council Elders remained, and what of Spirit? Finn knew about the Fae but not of the magic that Mercadia spoke of. *Is it strong enough to protect my friend?*

Finn's stomach continued to churn. Torn between telling Mercadia that he was coming home right now and staying to find the woman that he loved. The woman whom the Council believed was worth fighting for, even dying for. Finn exhaled profoundly, releasing some of the anger. Grabbing his jacket and room key, he sprinted down the stairs towards the reception of the B&B.

"Good morning, lad. You are looking so much better," Patrick smiled warmly. "Have you had your breakfast? There's still time."

"No, I haven't yet, but thank you." Finn followed Patrick into the dining area, a petite woman coming out from the kitchen.

She wiped her hands on her apron. "You're the last one, so you can take your pick of seats," she said.

Finn chose the table nearest the window and peered through the glass. The garden, although in a state of disarray from the previous night's storm, still managed to retain its beauty.

He smiled and turned his head in time to see Patrick kiss his wife fondly on the cheek. "I'll settle up with you after your breakfast, lad. I need to do my paperwork. I'll leave you in the capable hands of the Mrs, she'll take good care of you."

Patrick disappeared with a grin, leaving the two of them alone.

"Thank you so much for the clothes and the food last night…" Finn hesitated.

She chuckled. "Edith, and you're welcome. Help yourself to fresh juice. I'll fetch your cooked breakfast. The full works?"

"I'm not sure what the full works are but as I'm starving, yes please."

"Coming right up, one belly buster breakfast on its way."

Finn smiled and placed his jacket on the back of the chair. He waited until Edith returned to the kitchen before heading to the long, pine table to inspect its contents. Reading the label marked 'Orange', Finn raised the jug, took a quick sniff, and then poured himself a small glass of juice. The sharp taste had him smacking his lips in pleasure. Admittedly it had a slight tang to it but proved incredibly refreshing. He gulped the full glass and took the liberty of pouring himself another, before sauntering back to the table.

Staring through the window, Finn moved his senses across the garden and completed a quick sweep of the surrounding grounds. He scanned beyond the B&B and travelled towards the centre of the main village. Finally, he traced a path to Sycamore Road and searched the shadows for any threat, pleased to note that Kane and the Fallen were nowhere in sight. Bringing his attention back to the room, Finn relaxed into the chair, his stomach growling with excitement as the kitchen door swung open, and Edith appeared with a plate of steaming food. She set it down in front of him.

"Eggs, bacon, mushrooms, sausages, beans, grilled tomato,

black pudding and fried bread. That should certainly keep you going," she winked at him.

Finn stared at the plate salivating. A feast fit, for a King. "This is all for me?"

Edith laughed. "Tea or coffee?"

"Tea please."

She left him, returning seconds later with a teapot and milk jug. Finn was still gawping at the plate.

"Tuck in before it gets cold."

He picked up his knife and fork and took a bite of sausage, groaning with appreciation as his taste buds burst with sensation. Edith beamed her approval before heading back to the kitchen.

Finn devoured the food with great enthusiasm, and didn't stop until an empty plate remained. Remembering Eddie's constant drilling over table etiquette, he placed his cutlery together on his plate and reluctantly signalled that he had finished his meal.

Having worked up quite a thirst, he guzzled the last of his orange juice and then poured his tea, sipping at the hot liquid while he watched a small group of birds outside search for their next meal. One sensed his attention and looked up from the group. It flew away from its companions and to the ledge. Finn placed his cup down and raised the window. The little bird ventured inside and cocked its head at his open hand. After a few minutes, it hopped into his palm. Finn whistled a melody from his home-world, the bird joining in the chorus. Together they finished the song.

"Thank you, little one, now back to your brothers, and stay away from the South Fence. West of the house is best for the worms."

The bird chirruped its thanks and departed. Finn laughed as the small flock headed West. Sensing movement from the kitchen, he closed the window quickly.

"How was it?" Edith asked. She gathered his empty plate and glass.

"Delicious, thank you so much."

Her smile warmed, and she spoke with affection. "Come

back again soon, Finn. It's been a pleasure to have you stay with us."

"I will, I promise."

Edith's joy radiated from her as she retreated to the kitchen, with a bounce in her step. Finn collected his jacket and headed for the reception area.

Patrick grinned. "A bloody good cook that Mrs of mine."

"I agree. Her breakfast was truly a feast for a King. My friend Gregor would be envious," Finn said.

"Well, you get your friend over for a visit. He'll be shown the same hospitality."

"Thanks, Patrick. I know you've done so much for me already but could I trouble you for one last favour before I leave?"

"What can I do for you, lad?"

"Have you any chance a razor I may borrow?"

Patrick laughed. "Aye, lad, one moment." He returned a few seconds later with a razor and a tin of shaving foam.

"I won't take long." Finn bounded up the stairs and back to his room. Reading the instructions on the tin he applied the foam to his face, and picking up the razor he eagerly set to work.

Ten minutes later, the old Finn grinned back at him from the mirror. Leaving the razor and the shaving foam in the bathroom, he completed a last appraisal of the room, making sure he had left nothing of value behind, before making his way downstairs.

"An improvement, lad," Patrick acknowledged as Finn approached the desk.

"Thanks. You and Edith have been truly amazing. I don't know what I would have done last night without your kindness."

"You're welcome, it has been our pleasure. You remind us so much of our son, Thomas." Patrick's voice broke. He stopped talking and fumbled behind the desk for some papers. Finn read the sadness in the older man's eyes and knew that the son Patrick spoke of was no longer with them. Reaching inside his pocket, Finn's hand wrapped around the roll of cash. He took it out and flicked through the notes, handing across thirty-five pounds to Patrick.

"I hope that you will accept this also." Finn gave him a further handful of cash. "I will be moving on today, and I very much want to thank you for the kindness you have shown to a stranger."

Patrick stared at the volume of money in his hand. "I can't accept this, lad. It's way too generous."

"Please take it. Use it to repair the fence and restore the garden."

Patrick swallowed hard. "Thank you."

Finn offered his hand. "Take care of that beautiful dragon of yours."

The older man roared with laughter and grasped Finn's hand. "Aye, lad, that I will, that I most certainly will."

As Finn turned to take one last look, Edith had joined her husband behind the desk. "What was that?"

"Nothing, dear!" Patrick responded.

Finn chuckled and with a genuine affection, waved the couple goodbye.

CHAPTER SIX

Guisborough, North East England

Rowan heaved a sigh as the hot water assaulted her skin, and battered her aching body into submission. Although the night had been a revelation, it still left her with more unanswered questions and a war that raged between her head and her heart.

How could she possibly have feelings for a man she had never met? A man she wasn't altogether sure existed? Even her guide in spirit couldn't see him, so what did that tell her? You're in love with the Invisible Man, an Alien, or had she finally boarded that train to Crazy Town? And just when she thought it couldn't get any worse, she had drunk tea with an old woman called Bessie and her talking dog. Yes, that's right, a talking dog, such an utterly regular occurrence, nothing to worry about at all.

"So why on earth would you contemplate packing your bags, leaving your boss in the lurch, while you go off in search of some hocus pocus talisman, that you have no idea what, or where to look?" her head challenged. *"Are you completely insane? What possible excuse would you give to your boss? To your mum? Sorry but I need a few days to find myself? I blame the cheese, it always gives people nightmares."* Her head concluded its rant.

"Absolute rubbish and you know it," her heart retorted. As much as she tried to rationalise the events of last night, she couldn't deny her feelings. *"Have you forgotten the way he looked at you? The way you felt in his arms? And what of his kiss?"*

Rowan fought to catch her breath, her heart drumming in her chest as she recalled the heat from his lips brushing against her skin. She shuddered with need.

"You see?" her heart argued, *"there can be no denial. He calls to every*

part of your being and wakens the fire within. What you feel for him is real. This is the truth."

Sighing, she switched off the water. Her head had admitted defeat in the sudden silence of the bathroom. There was no escape from the impossible truth and the fact that, yes, she had indeed boarded that train.

Shivering, she stepped quickly from the shower, and narrowly missed standing on Angus, who had curled himself into a fluffy ball on the thick pile bathmat. Her arms automatically flung forward to steady her balance. "Silly cat," she scolded.

Angus, unperturbed, stretched and yawned lazily. Cursing, she snatched the nearest towel from the rail and wrapped it around her. "Well, stay there if you must, but if you're still here when Jake gets in the shower, you'll be one sorry kitty cat."

Angus slowly licked his paw, paying no heed at all to her warning.

"I mean it, kitty, you best scoot before you end up resembling what we humans would call, a drowned rat."

With a casual flick of his tail, he turned his back and lay down to snooze, a deliberate snub. Rowan resisted the temptation to drag the bathmat right out from underneath his furry backside. With a huff, she left him to it, stomping barefoot across the landing.

Pausing outside her mother's room, she pressed an ear against the door, and waited, relieved when only silence bid a greeting in return. Senses alert, she attuned to the vibrations of their home, searching for additional confirmation, all was still with no sound of movement from below. Rowan smiled, her temper dissipating. It seemed that her mother had finally followed her advice, days of nagging at long last paying off. A small weight lifted from her shoulders and boosted her forward.

With a renewed vigour, she dressed in jeans, an old t-shirt, and trainers. An impressive effort, she considered, catching sight of her reflection in the bedroom mirror, and all in less than ten minutes! Her chestnut hair towelled dry and pulled back into a ponytail. A few tendrils escaped, softening her features. Absent of makeup, her skin flushed with a healthy glow. The sheer simplicity of her appearance complemented by the fire that he had stoked within. Rowan exuded confidence, and felt on top of the world, practically strutting down the stairs. Bring on the day, she was ready for anything. Her stomach rumbled its discord... well, almost.

Sipping at her coffee, she surveyed the damage outside from the kitchen window, a mental checklist forming of tasks ahead. The back garden sadly had fared no better than the front. Ornaments smashed, plant debris and an assortment of rubbish scattered across the lawn. Placing her mug down, she leaned closer to the glass, her eyes locked on the object at the far end. Rowan's heart sank. A loose fence panel had blown free and now rested in the adjoining garden along with, mortifyingly she noted, their parasol. She deliberated whether her newfound confidence would be enough to enable her to tackle the delights of 'Miserable George'. Inwardly cringing, she registered the fence panel's position. She had absolutely no doubt in her mind that it had crushed some, if not all, of George's azalea flower bed. Her gaze flicked to the parasol lodged dangerously close to his pond and prized Koi carp. The verbal ear-bashing was most definitely a given, although the degree could vary, depending on the mood she caught him in.

She considered whether to get it over and done with now or wait until he had completed his usual lunchtime visit to the local. If she delayed, there would at least be a fifty-fifty chance that his mood mellowed sufficiently to attempt a civilised conversation. Biting down on her bottom lip, she mulled the options over. The sudden ping of the toaster was a welcome distraction from the problem.

Temporarily pushing all thoughts of George aside, she savoured the hot buttered toast, a rarity for a Saturday morning, given that her brother had an incredibly annoying habit of raiding the cupboards the night before 'Shopping Day', and consuming the last of everything. She barely managed to scrape enough milk out of the carton for her tea and keep just enough for her mother.

Jake, however, she chuckled, would be out of luck, and would have to wait for the shopping to arrive. Although annoyingly he would likely surface around the same time.

With her hunger abated, she drank the last remnants from her mug and stacked it in the dishwasher. Jake, not so considerate, had left evidence of last night's feast on the counter along with a small collection of bowls and glasses that had miraculously managed to brave their way from his room.

Rowan worked quickly to clear the mess that her brother had left in his wake, her thoughts every so often drifting back to George. She explored the possible apologies and counter-arguments that she could put forward to lessen the tongue-lashing that was inevitably coming. George, notorious on the estate for his miserly ways and lack of goodwill, refused to let anyone retrieve any possessions that accidentally found their way into his precious garden. The local children had nicknamed him 'Miserable George'. It had quickly stuck with the adults too.

Rowan couldn't help but snigger at a memory unlocked from last Autumn. The expression on dear old Elsie's face, who relayed the tale of the only occasion that George had been so embarrassed, as to stun him into silence. An unfortunate incident, which hailed the arrival of some oversized knickers and bra in his gooseberry bushes. Elsie had successfully retrieved her rogue underwear. However, George now avoided her like the plague, which Elsie advised she was more than happy about. It had come as no surprise to Rowan, that Elsie had rarely pegged her smalls out on the washing line, particularly on blustery days.

Head aching with the effort, Rowan finally concluded it best to wait and lessen the sting. There was no risk of George approaching her directly in the interim. He would much prefer to argue from the comfort of his doorstep, and of course, he knew he had something that she wanted.

With the decision made, she pushed George firmly from her mind and turned her attention to the top of her task list. Armed with everything that she would need, she stepped outside and appraised the full extent of the damage. In the broad light of day, it looked considerably worse than she had recalled from the previous night. The lawn was littered with rubbish from both bins, one overturned on the drive, the other on the main street, its contents spilt out. Ornaments and plant pots were smashed to bits. Hanging baskets wholly obliterated, their materials decorating the driveway.

The sound of a brush sweeping from across the road drew her attention momentarily away. Their neighbour, Duncan Peterson cast a sympathetic look and shook his head. "'Tis a sad sight. My Nora would be turning in her grave."

"I can give you a hand over there, once I've finished up here?"

"Lassie, that's very kind of you, but it looks like you already have your hands full."

Rowan grimaced. "It would seem so."

"Where's that brother of yours? He should be out here helping you."

"If only. No chance of him surfacing till at least mid-afternoon."

"Aye well, make sure you leave something for him to do."

"Oh, there'll be plenty, I'm sure."

Duncan laughed and gave her a wave. "I best get on. Good luck, lassie."

Immersing herself in the task at hand, Rowan gradually lost all track of time as she bent, swept, and sifted. A couple of the neighbours stopped to chat in empathy, comparing the damage with their gardens. She listened politely, careful not to ask too many questions, and keep the conversations brief. Rowan didn't want to appear rude, but there was a lot to do, and as the morning wore on, she grew hotter, and admittedly somewhat cranky.

"You didn't need to do all of that, I could have sorted it."

Sweat beading her forehead, Rowan turned and forced a smile. Her mother offered a glass. The ice chinked, and she gratefully accepted, downing half of its contents in one steady gulp. She wiped her mouth. "I'd hoped I would have it all cleared before you got up. Did you enjoy your lie in?"

"You were right. I needed it. You've done a good job."

"Thanks. Maybe after I finish here, we can take a trip to the garden centre? Replace some of the hanging baskets and ornaments?"

"I'd like that. I could do with the distraction, to be honest."

Rowan sensed she wanted to say more. "What is it?"

Her mother took a seat on the step and patted the space beside her. "I dreamed of your father last night. It felt so real."

Rowan lowered herself quickly and placed the glass to one side. "Maybe it was, mum."

Taking some tissue from her pocket, she dabbed at the corner of her eyes. "I would love to think your dad was there, watching over us all. I miss him so much."

"I'm sure he is. Did he say anything to you, in your dream, I mean?"

She nodded slowly. "It was very bizarre. He mentioned you, and when the time comes, I must trust and let you go."

"Did he say anything about Jake?"

"Only for me to not give up on him."

Rowan fell silent for a few minutes, reflecting on her mother's words. It was evident that she'd received a visitation, the messages from her father were of importance.

Placing an arm around her, Rowan snuggled closer. "Did dad say anything else?"

"He gave me some ideas for the garden, and asked me to keep some rosemary by the front, and back door," she laughed.

Again, something in the request suggested her father had a specific purpose, or reason in mind. What that was, Rowan couldn't be sure. "We can pick up some rosemary from the garden centre if you like?"

Her mother clapped her hands together. "That's a wonderful idea. Shall we grab lunch out too? Your brother can sort the shopping since he has eaten the last of the food."

"Sounds like a plan. Give me an hour. I should hopefully finish then."

"I don't know what I would do without you." Giving Rowan a quick hug, she retreated inside.

The promise of lunch and her mother's good mood gave Rowan the incentive she needed. She swiftly drained the last contents of the glass and turned back to the task in hand. Picking up the brush, Rowan swept with a little more enthusiasm, determined to finish within the hour as promised. Head bent and absorbed in her work, she didn't see anyone approach.

"Need a hand with that?"

Her gaze lifted slowly, not quite believing what she had heard. The colour instantly drained from her cheeks. Brush clattering to the ground, Rowan stumbled backwards and shook her head, her mind swimming in a fog of confusion.

"It's not possible," she whispered.

He smiled, and her knees buckled beneath her. Before she hit the ground, he was there, sweeping her into his arms. Rowan breathed in his scent as he held her close to his chest and carried her to the doorstep. Gently he placed her down, and sat next to her, his eyes full of concern as he took her hand in his.

Rowan stuttered for the words, "I... I..."

He squeezed her hand. "I know."

"But how?"

"I told you that I would find you."

"You're real?"

"Yes."

"I honestly believed I was going crazy."

He hugged her close. "Never."

"I don't even know your name."

He kissed her forehead, and her heart exploded. "Finn, and yours?"

"Rowan."

"Of course, that makes sense."

Rowan pulled back and searched his face. "What does?"

Finn released her from his embrace and stood. Sliding his hand gently underneath her arm, he lifted her to her feet. "Another time. Right now, we need to go."

"Go where? You still haven't explained how it is that you are here."

Finn frowned. "Do you trust me?"

Rowan took a moment to study him. "I shouldn't. We hardly know each other."

"But do you?"

"Yes, I believe I do."

"Then come with me now," he insisted, taking hold of her hand.

Rowan freed herself gently from his grip and cringed as she noted the flicker of hurt passing over his face. Her head and her heart locked horns once more.

"*Are you completely nuts?*" her head scolded. "*You know nothing of this man. He could be a total psychopath.*" Her heart immediately leapt to his defence. "*You need to trust your feelings. You know the truth.*"

Rowan rubbed her temples slowly, an attempt to relieve the pressure building as the argument continued and pulled her in opposite directions. "I'm sorry," she said.

"I don't understand."

"I need time to think about this."

Finn looked away, his gaze in search of, she wasn't entirely sure, but something instinctively told her it wasn't good.

"I'm afraid time is a commodity that we don't have. We need to leave, and now."

"Why? What's the urgency?"

Finn met her eyes. "It's not safe here for you."

The vision from last night reared its ugly head again. Ice crept across Rowan's skin, and she shivered involuntarily. "What do you mean, it's not safe?"

Finn sighed and ran a hand through his hair. "I mean that others are looking for you, right now."

"Who?"

Finn searched her face. "Somehow, I think you already know."

"Then why?"

"To stop the prophecy from being fulfilled."

"What are you talking about? What prophecy?"

"It foretells of a woman born in your world who is destined to save mine."

"And you think that woman is me?"

"I know that woman is you."

"You're wrong."

"Am I?"

"Even if I were to believe you, my mother and brother are here. What about them? I can't just go. They'll be worried."

"If we leave now, they'll be safe, I promise you. I can't make the same promise though if the others find you here. Whether you believe me or not about the prophecy, you know they're coming for you."

"I'm not leaving my mother without so much as an explanation. She will be worried sick, and believe me when I say that she, and my brother, will come looking for me. They'd still be in danger," she argued.

Finn closed his eyes and fell silent for a few moments.

Rowan pressed her point further. "Please, at least let me do this my way and keep my family safe. If I don't, I'll never forgive myself, or you. Plus, I need to pack a bag. I assume we won't be coming back tonight?"

He opened his eyes, his expression serious. "Not for a while at least."

Nausea churned in Rowan's stomach. *This can't be happening.*

Calling out for Charles, she almost sobbed in relief when a firm hand took her shoulder.

"I take it this is him?" Charles said calmly.

"Yes," she responded silently.

Finn, oblivious to Charles presence, continued to search Rowan's face for a response.

She nodded slowly as Charles enveloped her in his energy. "What does he want?"

"He told me that I'm part of some prophecy and others are looking for me. Is he lying?"

"Wait a minute," Charles instructed.

Finn flinched and looked nervously around. "What was that?"

"It's okay," Rowan reassured, "something I can explain, but as you said, let's keep it for another time."

"It would seem that there is much we need to learn about each other," Finn answered.

"Then you understand why I need to think about this?"

The expression on Finn's face indicated he did. "I know I am asking a lot turning up like this, but please, you have to trust me. There isn't time to debate this. We need to leave, and soon."

Rowan turned her attention back to the man that had guided her since birth. "Charles?"

"I do believe the threat is real, and until we know more about what happened the other night, I suggest that you do what he asks, at least for now," Charles said.

Rowan nodded. "I'll leave with you, but first I need you to follow my lead and play along."

"Play along?" Finn asked.

"Act? Do you have a theatre where you come from?"

"Theatre?"

"Storytellers, playwrights, a show, performance?" Rowan took a deep breath.

"We call them fable keepers. The ones who recreate stories of the past, present and future," Finn said.

"Close enough, just watch what I do and then follow me."

"As long as we are quick. Some of the fable keepers I know take an entire day."

Rowan hurried inside the house, Finn following behind. She found her mother sitting at the kitchen table, nursing a glass of water. Her eyes looked lost, although the hint of a smile formed on her lips.

"Mum, is everything alright?"

The spell of the daydream broke as her mother's eyes drew towards her voice and immediately fell on Finn. She frowned. "I didn't know we were expecting visitors."

Rowan pulled a chair free from the table and sat. She indicated for Finn to do the same. *Here goes, I hope he understands the concept of work wherever it is that he comes from or I'm in serious trouble.* Rowan steeled herself for the lie to come.

"This is Finn. We work together. Finn, this is my mother, Christine."

"Oh, you've never mentioned him before."

Finn flashed her a smile. "Lovely to meet you, Christine."

So far, so good. If I keep the word work in there, we might have a chance of pulling this off. Rowan considered her next words.

Her mother's posture visibly relaxed. "It's nice to meet you too."

"I haven't mentioned him before as he is fairly new to the company. Finn's only been working with us for about a couple of weeks." The lie sat uneasily in Rowan's stomach.

"Are you enjoying it, Finn?"

"Oh yes, people are very friendly, and Rowan has been amazing, such great support to me while I've been here." Finn turned and gave her a wink.

Rowan could feel the sting of heat in her cheeks, as her mother's mouth twitched with amusement.

"Really? Well, she is a brilliant assistant. It's such a shame that boss of hers doesn't truly appreciate her worth."

Finn beamed. "Well, please be assured that I certainly do appreciate her."

Rowan's face burned furiously as his gaze met hers.

"I see. That's good to know. Although not to be rude, but this is Saturday and Rowan's day off. Was there a particular reason for your visit?"

"Yes, my apologies, I appreciate this is your day off, but I need to leave today, and wondered whether you had thought any more on my offer?"

Rowan took his cue. "I'm flattered that you thought of me. As I already explained, I'm just not sure I can go right now."

"Oh, what's this?" her mother asked.

Rowan intervened before Finn could speak. "They need some help developing their London branch. It's one of the reasons they brought him in. Finn's travelling down there this evening to complete an initial survey and pull together a development plan. He asked me to assist him, but I said I couldn't go. As you can see, he doesn't seem to take no for an answer. I guess that's why the company hired him."

Her mother's eyes lit with excitement. "You never said anything?"

"How could I leave you and Jake? Besides, I didn't think Finn was serious. There are others in the company far more skilled than me." *Please let him understand and not blow this.*

Finn studied her face for a moment and after what felt like the longest minute spoke. "I'm perfectly serious, and as Christine has quite rightly stated, you are the company's best assistant. I need you." Their eyes locked, and the kitchen fell into silence.

Her mother cleared her throat. "This is amazing. Of course, you must go."

"Are you sure? I could be gone for a few weeks. There's quite a lot that needs sorting down there," Rowan said.

"Jake and I will manage. He can take me to the garden centre tomorrow. Oh, Rowan, opportunities like this don't come that often. You have to seize them when you get the chance." Her mother's eyes sparkled. "This is what your father meant when he told me to let you go."

"I promise you, I'll take good care of her. Your daughter is important to the company, and to me," Finn reassured.

"You damn well better. She's my world."

Rowan heaved a sigh. It had worked. "I guess that's settled then. I'd better pack."

Her mother stood. "I'll get you a case. I think I still have one in the spare room. Excuse me, Finn." She gave Rowan a quick thumbs up and left the kitchen.

As soon as they were alone, Finn reached for her hand.

"I hate lying to her."

"I can see that. But it's a necessary lie, and one that will keep your family safe."

"Jake doesn't even know that I'm leaving."

"Christine will explain it to him."

"You're sure about this? There's no other way?"

Finn shook his head. "We need to get away from this village before the sun sets."

"They're real? Those things that live in the darkness?"

"Yes. How is it that you know of the Fallen?"

"The Fallen? Is that what you call them? I sensed them in the village." Rowan noted the confused look on Finn's face. "Again, something for me to explain later. Are they hunting me? Why?"

"They travel with the one who is. They do his bidding. He serves another. That's why we don't have time to delay. The fact that you've sensed them means they are close to finding you."

"I'll be quick, I promise," she reassured.

Finn released her hand.

Rowan hurried from the kitchen, her heart pounding as she sprinted up the stairs, Finn's words ringing loudly in her ears.

Moving swiftly around her bedroom, she gathered both casual and work clothing from her drawers and tossed them onto the bed. Toiletries could always be bought once they had set off, and were away from the village, although she would pack her toothbrush at least. Staring at the random selection in front of her, Rowan bit down on her bottom lip. *What do you pack when you have no idea where you are going, or how long for?*

Her mother entered the room quietly and handed her a suitcase. "Have you got everything you need? He's not given you much time."

"I think so, and anything else I can always buy. Are you sure you're alright with this? I could tell him no."

"Yes, I'm sure and your father is right. As much as I know I will miss you, I need to let you go."

The timing of her father's message was indeed far too much of a coincidence.

"It's only for a few weeks. I'm sure Jake and I will cope without you."

Rowan's eyes slid to the bedroom door. *What would Jake say about all this? Would he understand, try to stop me? Perhaps I should wake him and at least tell him that I'm leaving.*

As if she had read Rowan's mind, her mother shook her head. "Don't you be worried about Jake. I can explain once he surfaces, and you can always give him a call later. Besides which, I don't think that young man downstairs is quite ready for a grilling. Although it strikes me that he could easily charm the honey from a bee." She perched on the end of the bed and grinned impishly.

Rowan eyed her suspiciously. "What are you grinning at?"

"Finn's extremely good looking too, did you not notice?" she teased.

Rowan concentrated on folding the last of her clothing into the suitcase. "I would be lying if I said I didn't."

"I can tell that he likes you, and judging by your reaction downstairs, I'm betting that the feeling is mutual."

Rowan banged the case firmly shut. "It's early days so please don't go getting ahead of yourself."

Her mother's eyes were dreamy. "I remember how I first felt when I met your father. Every time he looked at me, he took my breath away."

Rowan sighed. "It scares me how strongly I do feel."

"I know, darling, but if you allow your fear to rule, you'll never find happiness. Is that why you didn't tell me about the trip? Why you didn't want to go?"

"I guess. At first, I thought it wasn't real, that I imagined it. But he's here, and no matter how much I try, I can't deny how he makes me feel." Not quite the truth, but it was close enough.

"Then go on this trip with him. Take a chance, what have you got to lose?"

Rowan kissed her softly on the cheek. "Will you tell Finn I'll be down in a minute? I need to get changed out of these clothes."

"I will, and I'm glad for you. It's about time you found someone who makes you as happy as your father made me."

The bedroom door closed gently behind her, leaving Rowan alone with her guilt. A necessary lie to keep her family safe, Finn had told her. It still didn't sit well, yet she understood that the alternative would be far worse. Dumping her clothes into the laundry hamper, Rowan changed swiftly into a fresh set of clothing. Reaching for her handbag she retrieved her mobile phone and quickly fired an email to her manager, tendering her resignation with immediate effect due to unforeseeable personal circumstances. Sighing, she collected her handbag and the suitcase from the bed, and taking one last look around, said goodbye.

Her mother was laughing as she entered the kitchen.

"What's so funny?"

"Let's just say Miserable George won't be making a nuisance of himself. Look…" Her mother pointed over to the window.

Rowan stared in disbelief as George waved a hand in greeting before lifting the fence panel back into position. Their parasol, she noted, was returned and lying on the lawn. Eyes wide, she turned to Finn who merely grinned at her.

"As I said before, he could charm the honey from a bee," her mother giggled.

"He knocked while you were both upstairs," Finn explained.

"But how?"

"I have my ways," he said.

Composure regained, her mother turned and beamed. "Thank you again. I haven't laughed this much for ages."

"You're welcome and you should do it more often. It suits you."

"Oh Finn, you can encroach on our weekend any time."

Rowan smiled. "Mum, would you mind grabbing my car keys. I think they're in the living room."

"No problem, I won't be a minute." She patted Finn's arm affectionately and left the two of them alone.

Any doubts that Rowan had were gone in that moment.

"Are you alright?" Finn asked, searching her face.

"I am now. What you did with George was pretty amazing. My mum too. It's been a long time since she truly laughed."

"I can see how important she is to you and believe me when I say that I understand how difficult it is for you to leave. Anything I can do to ease that for you, I will."

"So, you do care about me?" Rowan's breath quickened as Finn drew her into his arms.

Lowering his lips to hers, he kissed her softly. "More than you know."

She pulled away, desperately trying to hide the effects of his kiss.

Finn picked up her suitcase. "What have you got in here?"

Rowan detected a slight unsteadiness in his voice. "The bare essentials."

"Somehow, I doubt that," he teased.

"Don't be cheeky, a girl has to pack for all eventualities. Isn't that right, mum?" Rowan asked as her mother entered the kitchen and handed over the car keys.

"It is indeed."

"I'll wait outside, leave you to say goodbye in privacy." Finn extended his hand.

"Don't be silly, Finn. You've earned a hug from me."

Raw emotion briefly flickered across his face as the two embraced. He quickly masked it with a grin and picked up the suitcase. "See you in a few weeks."

"I hope so and good luck with the project, Finn."

"Thanks." He waved and left them alone.

Rowan turned to face her mother. "I have my mobile, so if you need me, give me a call. If I don't answer straight away, maybe I am driving, in a meeting or have lost a signal. Drop me a quick text, and I will ring you as soon as I can."

"Okay," her mother sniffed.

"You're sure you're alright about this?"

She nodded and hugged Rowan. "Now that I've met him, I am."

"Are you going to come outside and wave us off?"

She shook her head. "If you don't mind, honey, I won't. Just give me a call tonight, let me know you've arrived safely, or if it's too late you can drop me a text."

"Will do. I love you."

"I love you too. Oh, and Rowan?"

"Yes?"

"He's a keeper."

Rowan smiled and turned before her mother could see the tears that welled in her eyes. She quickly headed outside.

Finn was waiting on the front steps, her suitcase in his hand.

"We'll take my car."

"Car?" Finn asked.

Rowan laughed and took hold of his hand, leading him to the garage at the side of the house. Finn stared as she popped the boot open and gestured for him to place her suitcase inside.

"I've seen these machines, but never one this close up."

She opened the passenger door. "Well now, you're going to be riding in one. Get in."

Finn ducked his head and sat, his hands fidgeting in his lap as she closed the door. Climbing in beside him, Rowan switched on the engine, the car roaring into life.

"Follow what I do and put your seat belt on."

"Why do we need a restraining leash?"

"If the car should crash..." She caught his anxious look. "Not that I plan for that to happen, but if the worst should happen it will spare us both from ploughing headfirst through the glass."

"I'm all for safety," Finn replied and quickly copied her movement. His seatbelt clicked into place.

Releasing the hand brake, she edged the car slowly forward, driving free from the garage and onto the street. "Where do you want me to head?"

Finn closed his eyes for a moment. "Onto the main road that takes us out of the village. I'll let you know when you need to turn. We have to get as far away from here as possible."

"And then what?"

"Then we wait for further instructions."

CHAPTER SEVEN

Middlesbrough, North East England

Awakened by the darkness, Kane prised himself free from her flesh and threw back the covers. Marching to the window, he scoured the street below and caught a sudden movement from the shadows, the Fallen slipping un-noticed into the building. Cursing that he had so foolishly lingered with the girl longer than he had intended, Kane gathered his clothing from the floor and dressed.

"Going somewhere, gorgeous?" She lifted from the pillow, the sheet falling away to expose her breasts. Her voice was soft and teasing as she added, "I thought you had more stamina than that."

He laughed at her attempt to lure him back into bed. "I do for the right woman; however, I have no taste for corpses."

She shook her head, her confusion evident. "What's that supposed to mean? Are you saying that you didn't enjoy it?"

Kane lowered to the edge of the bed and gave a cold hard stare. Without warning, he seized a handful of her hair and dragged her face towards his. She struggled for release as his mouth crushed against hers. Finally, he relinquished his grip. His lips pulled back into a cruel smile. "Oh, I enjoyed it." He noted with pleasure the tears that brimmed and threatened to spill down her cheeks.

"Then why are you so cruel? I thought you liked me? We were supposed to be going for dinner."

Kane's gaze flicked across to the corner of the room, and he raised a hand. The Fallen stilled in the darkness and waited. "I have more important matters to attend to."

Her face flushed a deep shade of red. "You're seriously doing this to me? After we've just slept together?"

"Girl, you were merely entertainment."

Eyes blazing fire, she vaulted from the bed and snatched her dress from the floor. "I can't believe I fell for it. How stupid am I? To think you might be different than the other jokers around here."

"Yes, indeed, how stupid are you? Falling into bed with a stranger on the promise of romance and a fine meal."

"You bastard, get out! Find whichever rock you crawled out of, and bury yourself beneath it."

"Not just yet, my girl."

"I ain't your damned girl." She yanked at the zip on her dress and turned frantically, searching the floor. "Where the hell are my boots?"

Kane's eyes shifted to the doorway of the bathing room. The shadows halted in response to his unspoken command.

She followed his stare and flounced across the room to retrieve them. "Well, thanks for nothing," she muttered, pulling on a boot.

Kane's gaze skimmed to the creature lurking behind, and he gave the nod. The Fallen released a low growl, its mouth salivating.

Eyes wide and cheeks drained of colour, she spun to face him. The other boot slipped from her grasp and dropped to the floor. "What was that?"

Euphoria pumped through his veins. "That, my girl, is your fate."

She retreated towards the door. "You're insane."

Kane moved forward. "And where do you think you're going?"

"Getting the hell out of here!" She turned to run but was too late.

The Fallen sprang from the shadows and knocked her to the ground.

He laughed. "You're going nowhere, girl."

"I'm sorry, oh god, please no, stop, help me…"

Kane leaned against the wall, his nose wrinkled as the scent of death filled the air. The Fallen continued its frenzied feast.

Kane turned his attention away from her body and whispered an incantation. Time to attend to another matter, having lost the opportunity the previous night.

Unperturbed by the eyes that watched him from the darkness, Kane's consciousness slipped free from his physical body and descended into the void, travelling deeper through the blackness and towards her. Moments later, Kane emerged into the great hallway. He glanced towards the sealed chamber doors. The guardian rose from its seat and approached. "What do you want?"

"I need an audience."

"It's not time, young apprentice."

"I must speak with her, Morbae. We've had interference."

"What sort of interference?"

"The kind that requires me to seek counsel."

Morbae studied him closely. "Were we wrong about you?"

Kane was careful to keep his temper in check. "Have I not already proven myself?"

"So far, yes, but this is just the beginning and already you falter."

"What you ask of me has not been easy, surely even you know that."

"You are aware of the consequences of your failure?"

Kane nodded. "I am fully aware. I would not be here if it weren't important."

"Very well, young apprentice, I shall request an audience."

Morbae evaporated, leaving Kane alone in the great hall. He could hear muffled voices through the door. *Perhaps it was a risk for me to attempt contact so soon, and yet, she has to know.*

The chamber doors creaked open. Morbae waved him inside. "Be careful, young apprentice. She is most displeased."

Exuding more confidence then he felt, Kane walked towards the slender figure standing next to the open fire. She didn't look up or acknowledge his presence but continued staring into the flames, her expression distant.

Kane broke the silence. "Forgive the intrusion…"

She cut him off. "Why have you come?"

"We've lost trace of the Tracker. All scent wiped out by a storm sent by the Elders. The Master grows impatient. I fear his trust is diminishing."

"Was it she?"

"I believe so."

"I see. Such an elemental spell will have come at quite the cost to her. You must use this to your advantage. Reaffirm his trust."

"Word has already been sent. The Master has taken action."

"Good, and was this to our advantage?"

"The scorpion's tail has dropped."

"Which one of them has fallen?"

"Jarrow."

Her laughter sent a chill down his spine. "Most pleasing news. For a moment there, my apprentice, I wondered whether my trust would diminish too."

"My soul belongs to you. I would never give you cause to question my loyalty."

"That may be. As much as this news is welcome, you still took a risk contacting me so soon."

"I need to know what to do about the Tracker. This world is vast. You know that I cannot fail the Master's orders."

"I do. The prophecy must be allowed to come to pass."

"I understand. But how am I to proceed?"

"Lift your shirt."

Kane obeyed, his teeth gritted to suppress the pain of the black fingernail cutting deep into his chest. His skin scorched as the sigil buried below the surface, leaving nothing but a black mole. "You will show no one." She reached into her robe and withdrew a small vial of dark liquid.

"What is it?"

"The blood of a descendant."

"The Tracker's?"

"Yes."

"How did you come by this?" The words had left his lips before he could stop them. Kane immediately lowered his eyes. He was surprised when nothing happened, his question dismissed. *Unusual for her not to react and silence my curiosity.*

"Drink one drop," she instructed.

"Then what?"

"Then, you shall see."

He placed the vial into his pocket. "I shall not fail you."

"I sincerely hope not. Now you must leave me." She turned her back to him.

Morbae appeared and ushered Kane through the chamber doors. "Remember your oath, young apprentice, and do not fail us."

Kane released his consciousness, hurtling back into the void. Something dared to move closer as he travelled, and he swatted it away, wincing slightly from the claw that scratched his hand. Kane turned and caught the creature's eye, the others he noted circling close. Raising his injured hand, Kane drew his fingers into a fist and watched with satisfaction the creature choke, and claw at its throat. His other hand raised to engulf his own throat and he fought against the sudden compression. *How could this creature retaliate?*

Kane released his hold, and the pressure eased, allowing him to draw breath. The warning delivered, however, had been enough for it to slink back into the darkness with the others and leave him be. *Strange that this time they should choose to attack.* Kane did not dwell on this further, a familiar, and welcome, weight in the centre of his abdomen, indicating the convergence of body and spirit.

Adjusting his focus, he gauged that only minutes had passed. The Fallen were continuing to devour the girl's corpse. Tiny hairs lifted on the back of his neck, as the last of her bones snapped and crunched between teeth.

Barrock entered the room, and Kane's hand instinctively clasped around the vial. The Fallen paused to sniff the air. "Something is different about you."

Releasing the vial, Kane waved Barrock away. "I don't exactly relish the feed."

"That's not what I meant."

"Then get to the point of what you did mean, Barrock, before I lose my patience."

"Forgive me, Commander. I thought I smelled… blood on you."

The injury inflicted by the creature in the void smarted on the back of Kane's hand. "The girl scratched me with those talons of hers."

Barrock stepped forward and inhaled the wound. "It has a strange scent."

"We know little of this world, or these humans, Barrock. Everything has a strange scent."

"Then forgive me, Commander, for pointing this out, but perhaps you need to take more care as to what you lay with."

"Perhaps, but it occupied the time, and she was quite a pleasurable experience."

A growl interrupted from behind. Kane's anger rose as Barrock continued to converse with his First Officer in their foreign tongue.

"Have I not warned you before, Barrock, about speaking another language in my presence?"

The Fallen shrank back into the shadows with a hiss. Barrock spun to meet Kane's gaze. "My apologies, Commander, we have just fed, it is natural for my brethren to revert to their tongue."

Eager to change the line of questioning, Kane swallowed his temper. "I shall let it go this time, but see to it that you remind your brethren. Now tell me what did he say?"

"He requested permission to dispatch the scout team to the village. The others, of course, are waiting for further orders."

"Yes, he can dispatch them, although I want you to lead the scout team personally. Search every inch of that village. The Tracker is hiding somewhere."

"What about yourself, Commander, do you not require me?"

"Not right now. I need to clean up here first. But I will join you very soon. Station two of your best officers outside. They can escort me to the village. The others can return to camp."

"Very well, Commander." Barrock turned to issue the relevant command, the Fallen instantly retreating, before giving Kane one last look. "Are you sure all is well with you?"

"Of course, I'm sure. Now go."

"Yes, Commander."

Alone, Kane switched on the light and turned his attention to the floor. He had to admit the Fallen had indeed ensured nothing was left behind. The only evidence a deep red stain on the carpet, and the one remaining boot.

Kane crouched to the stain and considered for a few moments before whispering the incantation. A dark mist released from his fingers and hovered over the congealed pool. Tendrils of black spun from its centre and coiled around the fibres dragging her blood from the carpet's surface and rising into the air. Kane clicked his fingers and engulfed the substance in blue flames. The room filled with the scent of sulphur as it burned. The remaining ash drifted gently into Kane's outstretched palms. He stared at the boot and repeated the chant. Memories of Melissa stirred.

Kane strode to the bathroom and searched for the water source. With a quick turn of the tap, it spilt into the bowl. He tipped the collection of ash and smiled as it dissolved within the clear liquid and disappeared down the hole. He had learned his lesson a long time ago and would not repeat his past mistakes.

The wound throbbed as he washed his hands. Kane turned off the taps and patted his skin dry with the cloth that hung nearby. A healing rune would easily remove it, and yet he found it strange that he had no apparent desire to summon this. His fingers instead ran back and forth over the deep scratch, stirring an emotional response, a feeling of protectiveness.

There is no harm in leaving it for now. I can take care of it later should it prove to be troublesome.

Completing a final surveillance of the room, Kane satisfied himself that there were no other signs of anything amiss and left. He closed the door behind him, and strode silently through the corridor, avoiding the lifts and instead using the main stairwell.

The young woman behind the desk looked up and flushed as he caught her appreciation.

"Like what you see?"

"Yes… I mean, no. I mean, I'm sorry," she flushed.

His gaze skimmed over the ample cleavage that strained behind the buttons on her blouse and he smiled. "I like what I see, another time perhaps."

Kane swaggered to the exit of the hotel, very much aware of her eyes following and boring into the back of him. He laughed as he stepped into the fresh night air. Indeed, he may save her for another time, that's if he did not have any better prospects.

Signalling to the Fallen, stationed in the shadows, Kane walked away from the hotel in search of somewhere a little less conspicuous. Oblivious to the admiring looks and curious stares, he left the hive of human activity behind and turned into a dark alleyway. Out of sight, he ordered the largest of the Fallen to step closer. "Your name?"

"Gallo."

"Your comrade?"

"Rivik."

Kane summoned Rivik closer. "Prove yourselves loyal to me, and only me, and I will reward you both."

"Yes, Commander," they replied.

Kane closed his eyes and reached his hands forward. Gallo and Rivik turned without hesitation, allowing the mark to burn into their thick hide.

"You understand what this means?"

"Yes, Commander, we are aware," Gallo responded.

Kane smiled. "You are promoted to my guardians and take your instructions from me alone."

"What of Barrock? He won't like this," Rivik hissed.

"Leave Barrock to me. You will serve him only because I wish it. When the time comes, you will kill him."

"Yes, Commander."

"Do not share any of this with the others. What you see now, you will not speak of."

Kane smiled, empowered by their complete obedience as each lowered before him. Taking the vial from his pocket, he opened the bottle and gently tipped it forward. A single drop of blood fell into his mouth. He placed it back into his pocket, ignoring Gallo's questioning look, and mounted. "Now take me to the village."

Kane's eyes sparkled with interest. Rivik had deliberately positioned himself as an equal at their side.

"Yes, Commander," Gallo replied.

Together they ran, keeping to the shadows and out of sight. Rivik matched pace for pace and headed away from the lights of the main town. They moved past the forest and towards the outskirts of the village. Kane's excitement grew as they neared the border. Tonight, he would not fail. The Master's faith in him would be fully restored, enabling Kane to move forward with his plan and secure the success he so badly craved.

Distracted with his musings, Kane narrowly avoided catapulting headfirst as both Gallo and Rivik skidded to a sudden halt. Neither of the Fallen would move despite the demand for total obedience that burned into their hide. Gallo, shaking his head vigorously, spun away from the village, refusing to cross its border. Rivik followed suit. Annoyed and bewildered by their reaction, Kane dismounted and glared at each in turn. "Why?"

Their eyes darted back and forth, Gallo released a whimper and Rivik licked his lips. They slowly inched away from him, and the village border. Kane knew that they feared his reaction, and of course, they would be fools not to, given that he was seconds away from obliterating one or both. Their continued defiance and sudden change of behaviour suggested something else was influencing them.

Suppressing his anger, he turned to Rivik. "I gave you both a direct order."

Head hung low, Rivik refused to meet his gaze and instead dug his claws into the earth. A further act of defiance as far as Kane was concerned. Another warning scorched deeper into Rivik's hide, and he sneered as Rivik let out a whine. The Fallen's eyes a flame of fury.

Gallo snarled. "Punish us if you must, Commander, but we are unable to cross the perimeter."

"You haven't answered my question. Why?"

Gallo gestured his head towards the village. "Can you not feel it, Commander?"

Kane reached with his power towards the village. The darkness held no reply. "Feel what?"

"Sorcery," Rivik spat out.

Kane turned and waved a hand over the perimeter line. "I sense nothing."

"Perhaps your potion has made you immune," Gallo replied.

He considered for a few moments. "If you cannot enter the village, then where are the others?"

Gallo sniffed the air. "They are close, on the other side."

"Searching for an entry point?" Rivik asked.

Gallo nodded. "That would be my guess, although if Barrock hasn't been able to find a way in by now, I doubt he will, at least not this night."

Kane held up his hand, silencing them both as something niggled. Stepping across the perimeter line, he turned his concentration inward, focusing on his breath. A spark ignited, his thoughts turning to the vial, the blood now fully integrated with his own. With each beat of his heart, he felt a change.

The blood pumping in his veins heated his skin, neurons of power surged, illuminating him from the inside. The air around him shifted as he moved his fingers in a playful dance. All anger forgotten, as the energy continued to grow in strength and force. An electrical discharge fired from the tips of his fingers. The ground smouldered beneath.

"Come and face me, if you dare." Kane waited for the response he instinctively knew would come.

He smiled when a voice, carried along by a breeze, answered his own. "You have no right to be here, Warlock."

Slowly Kane scanned the horizon of the village in search of its owner. "Who are you?"

"Who are we?"

"We?"

"Call your creatures away, Warlock."

"You haven't answered my question."

"This village is under our protection. Leave now."

"Answer me!"

"You have no sway over us."

A serpent slowly uncoiled in his gut. "Do you have any idea who I am?"

"We know that you do not belong in this world," the voice replied.

"Then, the fact that I am here is a testament to my power."

"We will not allow those creatures entry to this village."

"You cannot stop us."

A howl answered from across the village. Kane turned to face Gallo. "What was that?"

"One of our brethren," Gallo replied.

"Dead," Rivik snarled.

"You, perhaps not. But the darkness cannot withstand our light. Now take your creatures while you still breathe and be gone from this village."

"Not without that for which I came."

"And what is that, Warlock?"

"The Tracker and the girl."

"Both under our protection. You have no rightful claim."

Kane's anger unleashed and shattered an overhead light. "Your interference in a matter that does not concern you is a declaration of war."

"So be it, Warlock. But to quote your own foolishness, you have no idea who we are."

Ice bit deeper into Kane's skin, and he pulled his clothing tighter. Gallo and Rivik whimpered, backing further away from Kane and the village borderline. Kane's attempts to call forth his power failed as the cold continued to furrow its way deeper. He spun in a desperate attempt to locate and confront the unseen presence that had suddenly approached. Words failed him, the cold gnawing at his body, his throat constricted by the sheer force of its grip. For the first time, the fear that Kane sensed was his own. Shaking uncontrollably, he retreated, his muscles screamed in protest, the cold sinking through his core and into his bones.

"A testament of our power," the voice affirmed, "now call off your creatures."

Kane sank to the ground as the unseen presence abruptly relinquished its hold.

"Commander?" Gallo ventured.

All waited for his next move. Although it stuck in the back of his throat, Kane had little choice but to comply. Rising to his feet, he reluctantly gave the signal for the Fallen to retreat. Gallo nodded and howled in the direction of the others. Barrock immediately responded to the call.

"Instruct the others to meet us back at the camp, Gallo."

"Yes, Commander."

"A wise decision, Warlock, you're not as foolish as you look," the voice confirmed.

Kane's eyes flashed fire. Rivik shook his head in warning and gave a low growl.

Teeth gritted, Kane addressed the unseen presence one last time. "We shall leave, but know this, the Tracker and the girl are, and will be mine."

"We shall see, Warlock," the voice responded.

Kane's body betrayed him as he mounted Rivik, and he cursed inwardly at such a pitiful display of weakness. Rivik, however was smart enough to keep his own counsel.

"Go," Kane ordered. At his instruction, both Fallen broke into a run, Gallo following at a close distance. He waited for a few minutes to pass then stole a glance behind.

"It does not follow. Gallo has checked," Rivik hissed.

"Even so, I do not trust it. Have you encountered such a presence before, Rivik?"

"No, Commander, not one such as that."

Kane shifted his position and released the ache in his back. "Perhaps the Master may know of its existence."

Rivik's voice lowered. "If the Master did, then surely, Commander, he would have better prepared you."

Kane considered. "We shall soon find out."

"You're telling him?"

"It is foolish to keep anything from him."

Rivik slowed as they approached the entrance of the forest. "The Master does not take defeat lightly, as well you know."

"Yes, and yet this is not something we have encountered before. As you have already noted, had the Master been aware of its presence then he would have better prepared us."

"May I suggest that you take some time to consider your decision. Or at least as to how to relay such news to the Master. A third failure will enrage him."

Gallo spun his head. "I would rather not be shredded and have my brethren feed upon me, Commander. Rivik makes a good point."

Kane could not deny the validity of their argument and yet to withhold information from the Master would be futile and equally as dangerous. "I cannot avoid such news. The Master would see through any attempt. His punishment will be all the more severe."

"There isn't anything more severe than being ripped apart and eaten," Gallo growled.

Kane smirked. "You are wrong, Gallo. At least death would be instant. There would be no memory of your brethren, consuming your remains as you would cease to exist. But imagine a lifetime of suffering and pain. The Master's methods are excruciating, even for the likes of you."

"You speak as one with experience," Rivik replied.

"I have witnessed many suffer at the hands of the Master. He is without pity. If it comes to a choice, I would rather die instantly, than have the Master's pets burrow holes into me."

"The Weavers are not too dissimilar from us. Our power surely matched?" Gallo said.

Kane shook his head. *Such bold and foolish words, little doth the creature know.*

"You are gravely mistaken, brother. The Weavers are not born from the same place as us. They bear no resemblance to the power we hold."

Rivik's words surprised him. *Such insight for a Fallen who had never shared the same proximity as a Weaver.* "And how is it you know of them, Rivik?"

The Fallen tensed beneath him. "Like you, Commander, I watch, and I listen."

Kane was unconvinced by the response. Something instinctively told him that Rivik's experience was much more than that. *But why does he hide it? How does he have the means to survive such contact?*

As they entered the forest, the two Fallen increased their pace and sprinted towards camp. "I still don't want to be fodder for my brethren," Gallo growled. "For all our sakes, I trust you know what you are doing, Commander."

CHAPTER EIGHT

Outside of Pitlochry, Scotland

Finn sensed her tiredness as Rowan shifted uncomfortably in her seat. The effects of the last cup of coffee had worn off, and he noted, in less than an hour of them leaving the tiny village she called a 'service station'. He wasn't particularly surprised by this, despite her insistence that the coffee was all she needed. He remained unconvinced by such a disgusting looking substance, and its miraculous cure for fatigue. Even as Rowan had passed him the cup, offering for him to taste and see for himself its hidden magical properties, he doubted. His nose wrinkled at the memory of the strange scent she wafted underneath his nostrils. It was not one that remotely appealed, and immediately reminded him of the Gylliac reed that grew along the shoreline of Tahlia.

Finn scrunched up his face, recalling how his mother, who was so convinced by the healing properties of the grass, had chosen to blend this in practically every one of her topical healing remedies. Often covered in cuts and scrapes from his adventures in the forest, Finn had the sheer misfortune of having the Gylliac reed lotion applied daily. He had been over the moon the day his father had confirmed there would be no further need as Finn was old enough to learn the healing runes. The only lesson he had paid close attention to and had worked diligently at, even surpassing his father's expectations.

Rowan yawned loudly and rubbed her eyes, breaking him from the memories that stirred. Finn gently placed a hand on her shoulder. "Take the next road from here. There's somewhere close we can spend the night."

She nodded. "You were right about the coffee."

"I'm glad you agree. Hopefully, I've put you off drinking that stuff," he laughed.

"I wouldn't quite go that far. But its taste is not for everyone, and if the smell bothers you that much, I won't drink it." She smiled and flicked the lever at the side of the wheel. The car turned from the main road as she followed his instructions to the building he had sensed earlier.

Rowan switched off the engine and turned to him. "You know you still haven't given me any idea as to where we are going, and we've been driving for hours."

"In all honesty, I don't know myself yet."

"I can't just keep driving aimlessly, Finn. We need a plan. I mean, how long do I have to stay away from home?"

"It was important to get you as far away as possible from the village. Isn't that enough for now?" he asked. "Can't we talk about this in the morning when we've both had a chance to rest?"

"I guess," she said with a sigh.

They got out and went around the back of the car. Finn retrieved her case from the boot and carried it as they walked towards the building.

Rowan paused outside the entrance and began fumbling in her bag.

"What are you looking for?"

"My purse. I know it's here somewhere… aha!"

Laughing, she followed him into the building. The man behind the desk stood in greeting.

"Welcome to Norbrook Hotel. My name is Richard. Checking in?"

Rowan flashed him a smile. "Hi Richard, I don't have a booking confirmed but we're hoping you would be an absolute star and have a room free tonight? It's been a long drive, and we need to rest."

Finn didn't miss the appreciation in Richard's eyes as he

beamed back at her. "Your luck is definitely in. I have one twin available."

Rowan passed him a small piece of plastic. "Fabulous. I'll pay for the room now."

Richard tapped on something hidden below the desk, a machine whirred from behind and churned out a piece of paper. He passed it to Rowan. "If you could just sign here for me."

His gaze flicked momentarily to Rowan's chest. "Here is your room key. Is there anything else I can do for you?"

Finn took the key card out of his hand. "She has everything she needs from me. Thank you. I would, however, advise that you do yourself a service and practice some manners."

The smile fell away from Richard's face. "I'm sorry, sir. I don't understand?"

Finn ignored Rowan's stare. "Eye to eye contact may avoid such misunderstandings in future."

A deep shade of red stained the young man's cheeks, and he nodded. "Enjoy your stay, sir."

Finn picked up the suitcase and reached for Rowan's hand. She gripped his fingers tightly and walked stiffly beside him to the lifts. Finn prepared himself for the explosion he sensed coming. They stepped inside together, Rowan immediately pulling free, and pressing the button for the fourth floor. She turned and glared at him as soon as the doors slid shut.

"What the hell was that all about? Are you trying to get us thrown out?"

"Where I come from a man should have a little bit more respect for a lady."

"He was doing his job. Are you going to insult every man who smiles at me?"

Finn's temper flicked. "Not when their intentions are honourable. However, a man who leers at the breasts of the woman I care for, well let's just say that Richard was lucky I considered his youthful ignorance. Otherwise, he'd be nursing a bruised face."

Rowan's lips twitched at the corners. "While I appreciate that you were looking out for me, I can handle myself. Richard isn't the first guy to take a sneak peek at a woman's breasts."

Finn sighed and forced himself to admit the truth, that his reaction in part had been the result of jealousy. He reached forward to stroke her face, relieved when she drew closer to him and nestled her cheek against his palm.

"I didn't like the way he looked at you. I'm sorry, I wasn't prepared for this."

She smiled. "Neither was I."

The doors of the lift slid open, and he followed her out. They turned left along the corridor and stood outside of room 406. Finn passed her the key card, and she slipped it quickly in and out of the small box attached to the door.

The room was pleasant enough, although Finn felt a twinge of disappointment to see the two separate beds. He placed the suitcase down and sat on the one nearest the window. "Do you mind if I take this side?"

"Of course. I'm sensing you're disappointed?"

"I'd be lying if I said I wasn't a little, but I understand."

Rowan sat beside him and kissed him softly on the cheek. "I knew you would, but it's our first day together, and as much as I want to share your bed, I need to take the time to get to know you and get used to us."

He nodded. "Take whatever time you need."

Rowan gestured towards the bathing room. "Seeing as you called first dibs on the bed, do you mind if I use the bathroom first?"

"Dibs?"

"It means choice."

"Oh, yes," Finn said.

She reached for her suitcase and placed it on the bed. He watched her unzip and fumble through its contents. "What are you looking for?"

She waggled a small brush at him. "I need to clean my fangs."

"Erm fangs?"

Rowan laughed. "It's just a joke. I need to clean my teeth."

She collected some clothing and disappeared into the

bathroom. Finn resisted the urge to study the rest of the contents of her case. Instead, he zipped it up and placed it on the floor away from the bed.

Lying back against the pillows, Finn waited for her to emerge. A familiar tap of energy signalled Mercadia's connection to his mind once more.

"I'm amazed you've taken this long."

"It's been a testing day."

Finn could sense the weariness in her voice. "What's happened?"

"Jarrow was laid to rest."

"I'm so sorry. You must feel his loss greatly."

"Thank you. I had so foolishly hoped that the Master would as a mark of respect allow us one day's peace to bury our dead, and he couldn't even find it in him to give us that."

"He attacked during the ceremony?"

Mercadia's voice trembled with anger. "Drey and the others attacked the village of Eloria while the Master's first army made a further attempt on the Selensia."

Finn's stomach tightened. "Did they succeed?"

"The Selensia is intact, but Elios is exhausted, your mother is attending to him. Nothing remains of Eloria. Drey killed them all, before Gregor's men could get to them."

"You need to stop him." Finn could sense her pain.

"He's coming for me."

"And taking countless lives in the process," Finn said.

"What would you have me do?" she snapped. "If I leave now Elios will be alone, and the Selensia will fall. Everyone will die."

"Surely there's a way to stop this?"

"The girl. She is our only hope at fulfilling the prophecy and putting an end to this."

Finn ran a hand through his hair. "But we can't sacrifice innocent people while waiting for the prophecy to fulfil."

Mercadia sighed. "Gregor is sending as many men as he can to the other villages, and escorting them to the sanctuary of the Castle. Elios and I must work to strengthen the Selensia."

"Rowan is with me now. Tell me what you need us to do? Will you be sending the coordinates for the portal?"

"Not just yet, she is to be guided by another. Rowan will need to fulfil the requirements of the prophecy before you both can return to our world. You need to await their orders and do what they request."

"Who?"

"I cannot tell you. I need to be very careful what I say."

"Then how do we get in touch with this other person?"

"The girl already has."

Finn frowned. "She hasn't said anything to me."

"She may not be aware yet. This isn't something you or I can control. We are in the hands of the prophecy."

"I hope you're right."

"I must go, Elios is calling me. I will be in contact with you soon."

Mercadia released her connection, leaving Finn in a torrent of pain, anger and confusion.

The bathroom lock released and he glanced in Rowan's direction. She paused in the doorway. "What is it?"

Finn shook his head and swallowed the huge lump in his throat.

Rowan hurried towards him and knelt, her eyes searching his face. "What's happened? You're shaking."

"My world, people are dying, and there's not a damn thing I can do to stop it," he replied gruffly.

Rowan drew him into her arms and held him tightly for a few moments. "Talk to me," she whispered.

Finn released himself from her embrace and lifted her chin to give a brief kiss. "You're tired. I don't want to burden you with all this now."

"If it's hurting you, then you must. I can't sleep knowing that you're in pain. Talking about it will help and they say a problem shared is a problem halved. I am a good listener."

She moved to the opposite bed and waited for him to begin.

Finn chuckled. "Do you mind if I undress first?"

"I thought we were going to talk?"

"We are, although I wouldn't mind doing it in comfort."

Rowan raised her hands to obscure her vision. "Go on then."

"You can look, I wouldn't be at all upset."

"I'm not doing it for you. I am doing it for me," she teased.

Finn slipped his clothes off and jumped underneath the duvet. "I'm done. You're safe now." He wiggled his brows up and down. "Aren't you going to ask me to do the same?"

"These are my pyjamas. There is no need to avert your eyes." Rowan climbed beneath the covers and turned towards him, her head propped in her hand.

Finn smiled. "You're amazing."

"No, I'm not," she protested.

"Yes, you are," he argued. "Being here with you, and knowing how much you care, it eases the pain."

"Tell me, I want to help."

"There's so much I need to say to you but I don't even know where to begin with it all."

"Why don't you start with what upset you tonight?"

Finn nodded and explained his connection to Mercadia and the Council of Elders, the risk they had taken sending the storm through the portal to protect him. The Master's attempts made on the Selensia and the breach that allowed his assassins into Valoria and... he paused.

"What is it?" Rowan asked, sitting up.

"Your face... I've said too much, haven't I?"

"No. I'm sorry, it's just that it is an awful lot for me to understand."

"How can I make it easier for you?"

"Tell me what the Selensia is. You've mentioned it a couple of times."

"The Selensia is a veil of energy that runs along the border of Valoria and prevents the Master from crossing into the realm."

"So, a force field of sorts that no one can pass through?"

"That's right."

"And the Council of Elders created it?"

"Yes, but when Mercadia used her power to send the storm into your world, the other two Elders couldn't protect it. The Master's assassins were able to pass through it. Jarrow died defending it."

"He's a Council Elder like Mercadia?"

"Was. He is no more, thanks to me. Now the Master's assassins have slaughtered the entire village of Eloria. They're free to travel around the realm and…" Finn's voice trailed off and he shook his head sadly.

"I'm so sorry. I can't even begin to imagine how you are feeling," Rowan said softly.

Finn flopped down onto his back and stared at the ceiling. "I feel helpless and guilty."

"Has Mercadia said that she blames you?" she asked.

"No."

"And she hasn't because she knows you're a good man. She chose you for your strength and your kindness. There is no way she would have protected you if she didn't feel that you were worthy."

"She protected me, because of you. Mercadia knew you wouldn't come without me."

Rowan slumped against her pillow. "Back to this prophecy again. I don't understand why I'm so important to the people in your world, or how they think I can save it?"

"I wish I could explain, but I don't fully understand everything myself."

"You said before we were to await instructions, who from? Mercadia?"

"No. Mercadia spoke of another. She said that they will approach you."

"Did she say when?"

Finn sighed. "No, but then I didn't ask."

"Helpful," Rowan muttered.

"How about we wait and see what tomorrow brings?" he suggested.

"Fine," she huffed and reached to the bedside lamp. It gave a soft click, the room plunging into darkness.

An awkward silence fell between them, the minutes passing by.

Finn had almost drifted into sleep, until murmuring from outside their room nudged him awake. His eyes glanced towards the door and he waited, relaxing when the couple's voices eventually faded.

Rowan shuffled restlessly underneath the covers and released a loud sigh.

Finn waited to see if she would speak first, biting back his amusement when instead she took all of her frustrations out on the pillow. After several beatings later, the cushion having seemed to relent to her demands, Rowan lay down her head and released another sigh. Finn sensed her desire for him to acknowledge that they were both still awake, but there were no words that he could offer. None that would bring any reassurance as to who it was that Mercadia spoke of, and what message they would deliver.

When his silence continued, Rowan turned away from him, her breathing finally settling into a slow and steady rhythm.

Finn understood that it had been a lot for her to take in, finding out about his world, the creatures that stalked her, and being asked to leave her family and all that she knew behind. Rowan had remained calm throughout, and had accepted his explanations that this was the way it must be. Had their positions been reversed, Finn wasn't sure he would have taken the news quite so well.

He smiled and compared all that he had discovered about her with the attributes of the Rowan tree itself. Finn could see their likeness, Rowan demonstrating all of the same qualities, her courage, resilience, and wisdom evident. He had witnessed her protective instinct, in the way that she had challenged him, and had sought to secure her family's safety before her own.

Finn knew for certain that Rowan was indeed the one the prophecy referred to, and who would help him and the Council of Elders to save their world.

Yawning, Finn closed his eyes, pushing his thoughts aside and allowing his exhaustion to take over. Tomorrow was a new day, and one that would hopefully bring the answers they were seeking.

CHAPTER NINE

Pitlochry, Scotland

Charles knew by Rowan's reaction that she had not truly accepted the reality of the conversation from the previous night. Her head tilted to one side and brow furrowed as the images swirled and gathered, once more manifesting the small cottage. Ignoring the figure who waved insistently from the doorway, Rowan turned her back and instead searched the dreamscape.

The guilt weighed heavily on Charles's heart as she called for him to come. Nicolai's orders, however, were clear.

When he failed to respond, she shuffled her feet and heaved a sigh, her gaze returning to the cottage. Charles sensed her disappointment, and his cheeks burned with shame. The knowledge that Nicolai would not have asked this lightly brought him little comfort.

Silently he willed her forward and hoped that Rowan would instinctively hear his words of encouragement, the connection they shared, giving her the courage to step into the unknown and trust her intuition.

The figure waved again and shouted, "I haven't got all day, dear."

To his relief, Rowan pulled herself tall and strode purposefully towards the cottage. "I'm sorry. I didn't believe I would see you again," she answered.

Heart swollen with pride, Charles followed at a safe distance, keeping his energy masked within the dreamscape's rays and avoiding alerting either woman to his presence.

Rowan entered the cottage, stepping immediately into the

kitchen. Charles noted the change of appearance and the introduction of two floral armchairs resting by the open fireplace. Logs blazed and crackled noisily in the hearth. The sound instantly transported him back through time.

The memories flooded uncontrollably, despite his best efforts to push them back, reminding him of Rowan's previous incarnation as his beloved wife, Anna. Heart aching, Charles recalled the many nights they had shared in front of an open fire, eating popcorn and laughing the hours away, until the embers glowed and he took her in his arms and made love to her. The days spent riding through the valley she had once called home. Horses tethered, they lay together on the soft blanket in Anna's glade of enchantment and shared their hopes and dreams for the child that was growing in her womb.

Rowan took a seat in one of the armchairs and momentarily closed her eyes. Her chest lifted as she inhaled the scent of the wood burning. A smile touched her lips, and she released a soft sigh. Charles desperately wished he could see into the memory that had stirred and share the experience. He knew that it was frowned upon by the Lightkeepers, yet his soul yearned for a single moment spent with his Anna.

A sudden movement broke Rowan's reverie. The little dog rose from its basket and gently curled itself around her feet.

The older woman seated herself opposite. "A part of you still believed this to be a dream."

Rowan nodded slowly. Charles sensed her struggle to decipher between reality and fiction, her turmoil transmuted and becoming his own. Although he wanted to reach out and reassure her, he was duty-bound to ignore the overarching need to protect his ward. Nicolai's directive was not to interfere, but to observe the exchange anticipated and report back the findings.

Distracting herself, Rowan reached down to pet the little dog. A few minutes passed before she finally acknowledged the older woman's words. "You're right, I had thought last night was a dream, Bessie."

"It was, dear."

"Then this too is a dream?" Rowan asked.

Charles didn't mistake the disappointment in her tone and wondered at the connection forming between the two women.

"Yes, and no."

Rowan's brows furrowed. "I don't understand."

Bessie leaned forward. "I know it's a lot to take in, but Biscuit and I will do all we can to help you."

On cue, Biscuit rolled onto his back and exposed his stomach. Laughing, Rowan reached to give him a playful rub. Charles noted with fascination, the energy cord that had anchored itself between girl and dog. His interest peaked as something gleamed from within the animal's essence, and he fought the overwhelming urge to move closer. Bessie gave a slight cough, and Biscuit spun back onto his feet, preventing Charles from examining the energy cord further. *Had she known? Could she sense him watching?*

Charles studied the older woman carefully, but she made no other signs that she was aware of his presence. His attention shifted back to Rowan.

"He likes you, dear." Bessie's eyes crinkled in the corner.

"He's cute," Rowan replied.

The little dog instantly sprang to his feet. Bessie gave another cough. "I'm not quite sure he likes the word, 'cute', dear."

Rowan's eyes glanced to Biscuit, who sat on his haunches and stared. "Sorry, Biscuit, I didn't mean to offend you." She extended her hand without hesitation.

The little dog gave it a lick before returning to his basket. Charles caught the glint of green in the animal's eye before Biscuit curled back into a ball and buried his head beneath fur.

Rowan turned her gaze to Bessie. "Am I forgiven?"

The older woman chuckled. "Yes, dear."

Charles sensed Rowan's genuine relief and reflected on the bond that had developed so quickly. Biscuit continued to snooze, oblivious to the other presence in the room.

"Why don't you tell me about him?"

Charles immediately snapped his attention to the conversation. Bessie visibly relaxed in her chair, and reached for one of the two teacups that appeared on the stone hearth. She gestured to Rowan to take the other before sipping at the steaming liquid.

"You mean Finn?" Rowan asked, reaching for the drink.

Charles, equally surprised by the question, considered the extent of the older woman's abilities. *How indeed had she known? Had she sensed the boy's arrival too?*

Bessie smiled and nodded. Charles could not be sure whether her reply was in response to Rowan's or his unspoken question.

"I thought I had dreamt him too, yet how is it possible? For me to be in love with a man who really shouldn't exist, and yet he does... I just don't understand."

"The heart always knows the truth, dear."

Rowan considered for a moment. "If that's true, then I believe I have the answer to my earlier question."

"Which is?"

"You and Biscuit are real."

Pulling a tissue from her pocket, Bessie quickly dabbed at her eyes. "I am so pleased that Biscuit and I have both found a way into your heart. I hope you know that we do echo your feelings. We've waited a long time for you."

Of that, Charles could be confident. There was no hint of a lie in the woman's words.

Rowan frowned. "I know you're real, but I still don't understand how any of this is possible."

Bessie remained quiet.

Rowan glanced towards the little dog and shrugged. "Perhaps I need to accept that somehow it is."

Charles smiled. Rowan's intuition was now guiding her.

Bessie returned the small cup to the hearth. "Good, then I would say that we are making progress. Now tell me about him, what's he like?"

"Finn, you mean? Well, he's different from other men I have known. He's strong, funny, charming and yet intense at the same time. The way he looks at me, how he makes me feel, I almost stop breathing."

Bessie gave a loud sigh. "Yes, I too have known that feeling.

Amazing, isn't it, to know that one person can have such an effect."

Charles sensed the undercurrent of loss and regret in her words. He knew Rowan had picked up on this too.

"What happened?" she probed gently.

A dark shadow crossed the older woman's face, and she shifted uncomfortably in her seat. "Perhaps another time," she responded. Tears formed in her eyes, and she turned her head from Rowan's gaze.

"I'm sorry, I didn't mean to stir up such painful memories for you."

The older woman took a few moments to compose herself. "You didn't, dear. Not many people find a love like that in their lifetime, and so I count myself fortunate that I did, regardless of how it ended."

Charles sensed Rowan itched to know more. In truth, he was curious too, yet he knew she wouldn't push Bessie and risk causing further pain. Pride in his ward swelled when Rowan deliberately changed the subject. "Finn said that others were looking for me?"

"I'm afraid he's right. Listen to him, you must remain safe."

"Why is it so important?"

Bessie shook her head. "I cannot answer that."

"But you know, don't you?"

"I won't lie to you, dear. But my hands are tied, as are yours."

"Why are they? What is stopping you from saying what you really mean?"

"My dear, I do not govern fate, or the order of what is and what must be. I cannot give you all the answers. To grow and to learn you must discover them for yourself."

"What is it you expect me to do?"

The older woman picked up a small silver bell from the floor and rang it gently. *Had it been there all along or had she suddenly manifested it, and to what purpose?* Charles didn't have long to wait. He stared open-mouthed at the brown hare that bounded into the kitchen, a small piece of yellow parchment tied to its green necktie. Rowan's mouth fell agape too while Bessie quickly released the paper.

"Thank you, Mortimus."

The hare gave a little bow in response and disappeared from the room. It had been many centuries since Charles had witnessed such interaction with the animal kingdom.

"Now I know I am dreaming," Rowan whispered.

Bessie passed her the parchment in silence.

"What is this?"

"Read it and memorise the address, dear. You must tell Finn to take you here. Don't delay."

Charles did not need to see the paper to know to whom the address belonged. He watched with interest as the older woman raised her hand in the air and signalled to something or someone else. "There's just one more thing, my dear."

"Wh… wh… what is it?" Rowan stuttered, still appearing to be in shock. She had failed to notice the gentle hum and a flicker of movement.

With a slight adjustment of energy, Charles focused his vision to the disturbance he had sensed and finally caught sight of the small winged creature fluttering in front of Rowan. Her eyes widened as it settled onto her.

"Albion, if you would please," instructed Bessie.

From his current position, it was difficult to see what exactly Albion was doing although there was a faint shimmer from Rowan's lap. Charles inched a little bit closer, careful to ensure his presence remained undetected. He could see the gold dust taking shape into a strange pattern, a light emanating from its centre.

"What is it?" Rowan asked.

Bessie chuckled. "A dragonfly."

Rowan shook her head. "No, I meant what is the symbol?"

"It's called a rune. You must show this to Finn, as soon as you wake. It's important, dear."

"What if I don't remember it?"

Bessie raised her hand once more in the air. "You will, dear. Thank you, Albion."

Rowan returned her gaze to her lap and gasped. The symbol, along with the dragonfly, had vanished. Charles appraised Bessie carefully. He flinched when she suddenly cast a glance in his direction and then looked away. *Has she sensed my presence? Or is it a coincidence that she so happened to look across to where I am standing?*

If she had sensed him, she gave no further indication of this, her focus once more on Rowan. "We've run out of time again, my dear. You must go and speak to Finn. Show him the rune and tell him to take you to the address I have given you."

"Will you explain any of this to me when we meet?"

"I will tell you only what you need to know. Now you must leave," Bessie said.

Charles sensed Rowan's reconnection to her physical body and prepared to depart. The older woman stood abruptly and cleared her throat. Charles paused as she turned in his direction. "Before you go. I must ask that you do allow her to trust him. To trust us."

She disappeared before he could utter a reply.

Releasing his connection from the dream realm, Charles travelled quickly towards the Lightkeepers, reflecting on her words. At his sudden arrival into the Great Library, Nicolai rose. "Well?"

"Your perception is correct, brother."

The others murmured amongst themselves as Charles approached the table.

Nicolai raised his hand, the library falling into silence. He gestured for Charles to take a seat beside him. "And so, it begins."

CHAPTER TEN

North York Moors, North East England

The surviving members of the Fallen howled and scattered in all directions as the Master continued his rampage. Scrambling past the charred and torn remains of their brethren, they fled into the trees, the Master clearly in no mood to be reckoned with, following their Commander's latest report.

Alone and with Rivik's previous words of warning still ringing in his ears, Kane turned towards the fire and swallowed the temper that threatened to rise. "We were unprepared for this enemy. It is unlike anything I have come across before."

The Master glowered at him and, without any warning, broke free from the flames, a long silver staff gripped tightly in his hand, pointing accusingly. "Your failure to deal with this so-called enemy is inexcusable. Give me one good reason why I should not kill you now."

Standing his ground, Kane gathered his thoughts quickly and with a nonchalant flick of his hand, replied, "It was a minor setback, I assure you. We shall be…"

He had not registered the attack until pain seared through his core and forced him to his knees. Gritting his teeth, he clutched the wound inflicted. *How is it even possible and with just one strike?*

The staff, dripping in blood, edged dangerously close to his face. "I do not care for your tone," the Master hissed.

Kane batted it away. "You do not care for weakness either, which is why you appointed me and why I can assure you that this is nothing more than a minor setback. You asked for a reason why you should not kill me, and I give you that reason… time."

He forced himself to his feet. "There is no time to replace me, and no one in your kingdom strong enough. I'm the only one who can give you what you desire."

"Be careful, Kane. You are not as indispensable as you think." The Master spun and marched into the fire. "Deal with this new enemy, and if you fail me again you know what the consequences will be."

The flames abruptly extinguished.

Anger punched hard in Kane's gut as he considered the Master's parting words. This had not been the reaction he was expecting and was utterly unwarranted given that little had been known of this world and the unseen force that had attacked that night. The Master's dismissive wave of a new threat and his reproach of Kane was as foolish as his attempts to challenge.

'Know thy enemy', the words had been ingrained since commencing his training. Kane inwardly kicked himself at just how swiftly he had forgotten that very first lesson. A fundamental mistake and one which had cost him severely. The Master's attack on him was a clear warning that their relationship, tenuous at best since the night of the storm, now hung by a single thread.

Stepping from the safety of the trees, Barrock gave a low growl. "If he keeps that up there will be none of us left to hunt."

Kane wrinkled his nose and surveyed the carnage. The twisted and scorched remnants of the Fallen scattered in all directions. "How many this time?"

Barrock surveyed the camp and licked his lips instinctively. "It was enough to cause the rest to flee, Gallo and Rivik included."

Kane ignored the hint of glee in the Fallen's voice. "They will earn no favour by acting like cowards."

"Yet their cowardice has ensured their survival. The Master was in no mood to reason."

"That may be, but the Master will not look on this favourably, nor will I."

"With respect, Commander, none of us hold any favour with the Master, including yourself."

The Fallen's eyes slid down to Kane's waist, and the wound

inflicted from the Master's staff. "You really should attend to that. The cut looks deep."

"A mere graze, Barrock," Kane deflected.

"For a mere graze, it bleeds well."

He narrowed his eyes, Barrock immediately taking a step back in retreat. "I suggest you focus on finding your brethren if we are to avoid our heads being served on a platter to the Weavers."

Barrock hissed and turned his nose to the East, scenting the air once more. "Understood."

"Once you have found your brethren, clean up the camp and get rid of the filth. I want you to report back to me with Gallo and Rivik, if they are still alive, in two hours."

Barrock sprinted into the darkness of the forest, without so much as a backward glance.

Grateful to be alone, Kane set off in the direction of his tent. With each step taken, the injury inflicted by the Master smarted and caused him to stumble. Wincing, he leaned against a tree and fought to steady his balance. The pain had reached a crescendo now his shock and anger had dissipated.

He could see that his tent was almost in touching distance, and yet he lacked the physical strength to walk towards it. Fumbling around in his pocket, Kane drew out a dagger and carved a healing rune into the air. The energy from the rune seeped into his skin, bringing momentary relief, but not enough to heal him. Seizing his opportunity, Kane pushed forward with everything he had left in him, crying out in agony as the pain peaked once more and sent him crashing through the canvas doorway.

On the ground, he lay with sweat beading his brow and the sound of his blood rushing through his ears. Kane wondered whether this was the beginning of his demise. He had no strength left to call upon; the rune's effects had failed to remove the wound that had been inflicted.

The ceiling spun in and out of focus, making Kane nauseous. With little option remaining, he allowed the darkness to consume and release him from his physical body.

Passing through time and space, he was vaguely aware of the

creatures, watching from a distance. The scratch on his hand throbbed a reminder as he felt it draw closer to him, and yet surprisingly made no further move to attack. Given his current predicament, Kane didn't slow to consider the reasons why, instead propelling his consciousness forward, an overwhelming sense of relief spreading through him when the chamber doors came into focus. Pushing all thoughts of the creature to the back of his mind, he careered into the Great Hall. The guardian, Morbae, caught hold of him, and both toppled to the ground.

"You're hurt," Morbae grunted.

"The wound will not heal," Kane gasped.

"The Master's handiwork?"

"Yes, he was none too pleased by my recent report."

"Show me."

Kane lifted his shirt grimacing with the effort.

Morbae nodded. "A Lyboria bite."

"Lyboria?"

"Serpents used to keep prey submissive. The wound itself will heal in two days, but the venom will have taken its effect by then."

Kane shook his head. "I did not see any serpents."

"How did you come by the injury then?"

"I was struck with the Master's staff."

"A staff?"

Morbae fell silent and re-examined the wound. "Given your current predicament, I am confident it had a serpent's head. No doubt masked from you when the Master attacked."

Kane nodded his head. "The staff was covered in my blood, I did not see any serpent's head."

"A wound such as this can only be from a Lyboria bite, and if I am right, then this is yet another betrayal. Rest, young apprentice, I must seek urgent counsel."

"Can I not have an audience myself?"

Morbae eased Kane into the chair. "You're in a weakened state, and the venom is spreading. There is no time."

Although exhausted Kane fought against the urge to sleep, fearful of losing the connection. Instead, he kept one eye on the chamber door while focusing all his energy internally to the rising sea of anger. The increase of adrenaline pumped through his veins, preventing him from slipping. Kane continued to seethe at the Master's cruel attempt to turn him into a mindless puppet.

With his attention firmly fixed on the chamber doors, Kane failed to notice the reappearance of Morbae until he dragged him to his feet and turned him away. Struggling within Morbae's grip, Kane attempted to spin the guardian around.

A crash of the chamber doors from behind and swish of robes across the floor had Kane pause in his efforts. She was by his side in a matter of seconds, lifting his shirt. Morbae tightened his grip as black fingernails thrust without any warning into Kane's wound. He screamed as she twisted and dug her nails, scraping deeper and deeper at his core despite his pleas to stop. Tears coursed down his face when her hand finally emerged victorious holding onto an illuminous substance. Pulling a bottle from her robe, she pressed it inside.

"Give me your hand quickly," she ordered, reaching once again into her robes, this time to retrieve a large bronze dagger.

Kane noted the ancient scribing running the length of its blade. He held out his hand and gave a sharp intake of breath as she cut into his palm. Blood instantly spilling, she motioned for him to hold his hand over the bottle and allow it instead to fall inside. Kane's eyes met her own, and she shook her head refusing to answer his unspoken question. He remained silent and waited.

"That's enough," she told him.

Retrieving a cork from her robes, she pushed it firmly into the bottle. Morbae released his hold and accepted the bottle offered, exchanging this for a piece of white cloth. She smiled and passed it to Kane. He wrapped it around the wound on his hand. Although he had lost a lot of blood, surprisingly he felt much better.

"In the Arvantis, Mistress?" Morbae asked.

She nodded, then pointed towards the chair. "Sit, my young apprentice."

Morbae disappeared, leaving them alone.

"Disappointing that he has lost his faith in you, yet not much of surprise. He never was one to trust."

"His actions tonight would suggest not," Kane agreed.

"It would seem, and a complication indeed. But nothing that will prevent me from fulfilling my plan. I have removed the poison from the Lyboria. The wound will heal as expected in a couple of days. Do nothing to escalate the healing and draw suspicion. He must believe that you are still infected. The blood magic that I have completed will ensure this but do not give him any cause to doubt. Follow his instructions."

"How can I avoid raising his suspicions?"

"He knows that you do not have the knowledge of the Lyboria and have no inkling of what he has done, therefore nothing to make him think it wouldn't have worked."

"Surely he can tell from my words or my behaviour?"

She smirked. "Don't worry, my young apprentice, the venom of the Lyboria doesn't turn you into one of his mindless minions. It only guarantees your complete and utter compliance. You would still be expected to act otherwise and behave as normal, however be aware that whatever he orders you to do, you must immediately obey regardless of the consequences. You cannot hesitate in your actions or you will raise his suspicion."

"But what if that goes against the plan? Lately, he has been unpredictable."

"Then we shall have to cross that bridge when we come to it. The Master knows you are the best chance he has for success. The use of the Lyboria was a cheap and desperate attempt to keep you under his control, especially as he knows that your power is growing. He must believe that it worked. Otherwise, the consequences for you I guarantee will be fatal."

"Do you know of the entity that attacked me?"

"I am not familiar with these entities you speak of. However, I have connections within the other dimensional planes which may know more. For now, I would advise you to stay away from the village until we know how to defeat this enemy."

"That will be difficult. The Master expects me to bring the Tracker and girl to him. He will not tolerate a further delay and his patience is thin."

"A dilemma, I agree. But you must maintain the pretence of your weakened state. That in itself will give you some protection. The Master himself knows that your wound will not heal for two days. Although the venom cannot infect you, the wound is still open, and you do remain at risk of infection. I trust you have medical supplies?"

"Yes, but I must fulfil the Master's orders. The Tracker so far has evaded the Fallen, and I'm confident he now has the girl, a two-day delay is too much time lost. We know little of the girl or the prophecy. Even with the form and capabilities I have given to the Fallen, we are limited in our ability to track them. The Fallen cannot travel in direct sunlight."

She summoned Morbae with a click of her finger. "The brooch," she ordered.

"Of course, Mistress, a wise choice."

"The Fallen as you are aware are born from the darkness. In the light they lose their power. But in the girl's world, shadows are cast, darkness lingers and night is almost of equal time."

Kane appraised her features as she spoke, her voice weary. He noted the hard lines of her face and the slight stoop of her frame. Her hair was tinged with grey and the depths of her eyes consumed by shards of ice. The war of the ancients had undoubtedly taken its toll on her.

"I hear your thoughts. You should know that if I am to succeed, there are certain sacrifices to be made," she explained.

"Let me give you some of my power," Kane offered.

"The time will come when I will need it. For now, I will bear this loss."

Morbae re-appeared and dropped the brooch into Kane's palm.

"What shall I do with this?"

She smiled. "Choose one of the Fallen, your most trusted, and pin this brooch to them. It will merge into their form so there will be no risk of the others or the Master seeing this. The brooch has the power to transform their bite. It is also Lyboria."

"And then what?"

"Come now, my young apprentice, time spent in a strange world. Surely you must have found those open to manipulation and control? Use their weakness to aid you and if they do resist, the Lyboria bite will ensure their complete compliance. You need allies in this world to fulfil the Master's plan and avoid attention to ours. I trust you still have the vial?"

The memory of the power he consumed from ingesting a single drop stirred and his thoughts drifted. *What would happen if I were to drink all of the blood? Would that give me the strength to stand against this new foe?*

Aware that she was studying him, Kane pushed the thoughts to the back of his mind.

She moved closer to him, her lips briefly brushing against his. Kane noted the suspicion in her eyes as she drew back.

"There is something else you have not told me."

Kane sighed. It would be pointless to deny it. "The blood had an unexpected effect on me."

"Really? And how much did you consume?"

"Only the one drop as you instructed."

Her brows furrowed. "I must see this for myself."

Kane did not resist her arms as they slipped around his neck. She brought him close and kissed him, her lips teasing the memory of that night forward and something else. Parting his mouth with her tongue, she explored further. The kiss strengthened, and to Kane's surprise, desire stirred. He attempted to pull away.

"Don't," she ordered and seized his mouth once more, probing deeper.

His mind surged with different visions, and ones which he had no wish to share. Using what little power was restored to him, Kane erected walls around the secrets he must protect.

She released her hold and met his gaze. "What is it that you are guarding, my apprentice?"

"Nothing you need concern yourself with. Some memories remain sacred."

She loosened the lace of her gown. Kane averted his eyes away from the swell of her breasts. She laughed and pressed her body tightly against his. "Don't resist me," she purred.

"Mistress, you go too far."

Morbae's warning was met with a hiss.

Kane groaned, her mouth taking his once more, her tongue plunging deeper, sending fire to his groin. She continued to search into the furthest recesses of his subconscious, for what, he could not be sure. Kane's stomach churned with dread. Not all the walls he erected had survived her attack.

Satisfied with the discovery she had made, she released him and glanced down towards his bulging erection. "A reminder that you are mine."

Kane cursed, allowing his anger to take control and dampen the swell below. "You had no right. Have I not served you well?"

She ignored his question. "Morbae, I have chosen my apprentice well."

"You could have destroyed him, Mistress."

Kane glared. *Unbelievable, twice this night, my life threatened by the ones I have given nothing but loyal service to. I shall not forget, and neither shall I forgive.*

"A small risk given his abilities. Now that I possess a Nyrvallia, we cannot fail."

Morbae's eyes widened. "A rarity indeed. But if you have discovered this, so too can the Master, if he hasn't already."

"Too absorbed with his power to even scratch below the surface of those who serve him," she scoffed. "The Master failed to seek out the ancient texts before he destroyed the Moren. He has lost the knowledge, but I have not and as soon as I am free…"

"What is a Nyrvallia?" Kane demanded.

She smiled and stroked his cheek tenderly. "A conversation for another time. Now my apprentice, heed my words, for if you disobey me, know that your suffering will be greater by my hand than anything the Master can bestow. Under no circumstances

121

mention the Nyrvallia to the Master or the creatures you travel with."

"When will you tell me what it is? What I am?"

"As soon as the prophecy fulfils, and I am released. Only then will I share the secret of your heritage."

Kane fumed. "I have no choice but to obey."

"Wise words," Morbae replied.

"You are not to consume any more of the blood I gave you or indeed you will risk the Master's discovery. He must not know that the Lyboria failed."

"Understood."

She kissed him briefly on his cheek. "We will speak again in a few days."

Kane nodded as she took her leave, the chamber doors closing quietly behind her.

"Do not fail us, apprentice."

Morbae's words echoed in the void as Kane released his connection and searched for that familiar pull, catapulting him forward. The creature drew closer but did not attack. It merely followed behind as far as its abilities would allow it to travel. When Kane no longer sensed its presence, he instinctively rubbed the scratch on his hand, confused by the physical reaction and his emotional response to it.

A judder in his body signalled he had reconnected. The transition was much quicker than before. Kane swept all thoughts of the creature to one side, concerned as to how much time had passed while he had lain unconscious on the floor. Rising, he noted with relief the brooch still clutched in his hand and shoved it inside his pocket.

Pulling the door of the tent aside, Kane completed his surveillance. If the Fallen grieved for their brethren, it wasn't evident, given how they tussled over the remains that littered the ground.

Kane caught sight of Barrock hunched over in the distance, Gallo and Rivik at his side, their heads bowed and raw flesh dripping from their mouths. *Good, at least I have time to regain my composure and consider the choice.*

Kane repositioned the Hymorius table to the furthest corner of the tent and murmured an incantation. A bottle appeared with the cork removed, accompanied by a large crystal goblet. Kane seated himself and poured. He swilled the red liquid and took a moment to inhale its fragrance, the last of his reserves from home. A necessity following the betrayals that he had tolerated. His fingers drummed on the table as he sipped slowly. The liquid warmed his throat and travelled to greet the fire that blazed within.

Had the Master's plan succeeded, Kane would have endured hours of unnecessary torture. For that, he would not forgive.

Neither would he forgive her intrusion of his mind, the breaking down of his memories and secrets of the past. Her refusal to divulge the Nyrvallia, unacceptable.

Kane swallowed the last of the liquid, an attempt to curb the monster that raged within. He vowed the two would suffer, their desire to reign defeated by his hand. *I will take control of all four realms, and they will kneel or die.*

He considered the three Fallen outside. Barrock his second in command prone to challenging him. More than likely Kane would raise suspicion if Barrock was to become completely subservient, although the Master's latest display of temper may be enough to convince the others.

Gallo and Rivik swore to be his protectors, and yet disappointingly fled at the first sign of trouble. Kane considered which of the two Fallen would be the better choice. Gallo far more obedient than Rivik… and yet.

Kane reflected on his exchanges with Rivik. Each time something within the abyss of Rivik's eyes stirred. Kane could not quite put his finger on what that was. The Lyboria would indeed help him to uncover the truth and use it to his advantage. With the decision made, Kane poured another large glass and waited. They didn't keep him long.

"Commander?"

He drained the contents of the bottle before summoning the Fallen inside. His lips curled into a sneer as he noted Gallo and

Rivik, keeping their distance behind Barrock. Rising from his chair, Kane approached and studied the two carefully. Gallo struck a more submissive position. Rivik stood his ground. *There it is again, slithering in the depths of his eyes. What is it that this creature hides?*

Kane turned his attention to Gallo. "You were both sworn to protect me, were you not?"

"Yes, Commander."

"And yet at the first sign of trouble, you turn tail and run like cowards."

Rivik snarled. *A challenge?*

Barrock spun to silence his brethren with a warning look. Kane watched with interest as Rivik refused to meet his gaze. *Does he know I suspect?*

"If you're going to do it, Commander, I suggest you get on with it."

"What is that you think I am going to do to you, Rivik?"

"That's why you summoned us. To finish what the Master started."

"Silence, Rivik," Gallo snapped.

Barrock glared at them both. "Forgive him, Commander, it's been a difficult night for our brethren. Rivik sorely regrets his actions."

"Do you indeed?"

Rivik continued to look away. "Yes, Commander."

"We will not fail you again," Gallo reassured.

"I expect not or you will suffer the same fate. Now leave me."

Barrock gestured for the others to leave. "Yes, Commander."

"Not you, Rivik."

The Fallen stopped in its tracks and turned to face him. "Is there something you need from me, Commander?"

"You will remain here. There is something I wish to discuss."

Kane smothered the urge to laugh at the look exchanged between all three. "If I were going to kill him, I would have done it by now."

Giving his brethren one last glance, Barrock quickly ushered Gallo out of the tent.

"So, you have no intention of killing me?" Rivik asked once they were alone.

"No, but torture isn't out of the realm of possibilities," Kane smirked.

"I'd rather you kill me and have done with it. I grow tired of all this."

"You are unlike the others, and that intrigues me. I have no intention of killing you. Nor will I torture you. It seems you have done enough of that yourself."

"Then what?"

"A choice and a chance for you to be different, set yourself apart from the others, make yourself indispensable to me."

"Doesn't sound like much of a choice," Rivik muttered.

Kane reached into his pocket. "I gave you form, power in this world. Now I can give you more. In return for your total allegiance to me."

"Your mark burns in my hide, you already have my allegiance, whether I like it or not."

"Yes, but I don't have you, do I? I can see it in your eyes. There is something you hold back from me. I want to know what that is."

Rivik shifted uncomfortably. "I have no idea what you speak of, Commander. Perhaps you have suffered a blow to the head."

Kane studied him closely. "No Fallen would dare speak to me like that, and yet you do, despite my mark."

"Forgive me, Commander. It must have been the effects of this night."

"I am no fool, I sense there is more to you, and that is the only reason you live."

"If there is, Commander, it is not something I am aware of."

"Yet you sense a difference, don't you? Something that sets you slightly apart from the others."

Rivik sighed and met his gaze. "What is it that you think you know, Commander?"

Kane considered the question. What indeed?

Although the answer still eluded him, Kane knew he was close.

Rivik looked all the more uncomfortable under his scrutiny. "Accept my offer and we shall together discover your secret."

"And what if that secret is something neither you or I may like? Can you still guarantee my life?"

"If you accept my offer, your life is guaranteed, of that I can assure you. The power you shall have will be more than that of your brethren. You will be stronger. As to what hides behind your eyes, I sense it will only enhance our purpose. I intend to unlock it, and in return reward you."

Kane felt the sweet taste of victory as Rivik met his gaze and slowly nodded his head.

"I accept your offer, Commander. But do not forget your oath to me."

Pulling the brooch free from his pocket, Kane pinned it to Rivik's chest. "You have my word."

The gold melted into Rivik's skin. Kane's stomach churned as a foul smell assaulted his nostrils. He placed a hand over his mouth to stifle the rising vomit. Rivik wailed and dropped to the floor, eyes wild and body convulsing. A forked tongue lashed out at Kane and caused him to flinch. The wailing reduced to a hiss. The convulsions finally slowed and stopped.

At last, there was silence. Unable to tell whether the Fallen was dead or unconscious, Kane shifted closer. Something wriggled free from Rivik's body. Kane froze, not quite believing what he was seeing. The dark mass climbed on top of the Fallen's frame. It forced entry to Kane's mind. "You know what I am?"

Kane nodded slowly, unable to formulate the words.

It laughed. "Not quite the transformation you were expecting."

"How is it possible?" he asked, regaining some of his composure.

"Not possible until now."

"Will you remain in that form?"

"No, like the Fallen, I need a body to inhabit, to enable my survival in this world."

"Are you Rivik?"

"I am Rivik."

"You recall that you gave your allegiance to me?"

"You have released me, Commander. My allegiance is yours without question. My reward, however, I will decide. You will repay me for my services when the time comes."

"What is it that you desire?"

"Revenge."

"On who?"

"A conversation for another time. The others have sensed something is wrong." The dark mass dissipated into Rivik's body.

"Commander, is everything alright?" Barrock called from outside the tent.

Rising from the floor, Rivik quietly took his place at Kane's side. Sensing that Barrock required proof, Kane signalled for him to enter. "An understanding reached as you can see," he replied, gesturing to Rivik standing close.

"Forgive me, Commander. We cannot lose any more of our brethren. Our numbers have dwindled, and the others grow restless."

Rivik growled. "I have accepted my fate, Barrock. There shall be no further challenge."

Kane sensed Barrock's suspicion, the Fallen scenting the air. "Something smells strange."

"Remnants of my power, a punishment for Rivik's disobedience."

"And what of Gallo? He ran too. You cannot blame Rivik in isolation?"

"You will find as we speak the mark removed from Gallo's hide. He is demoted and will receive no extra favours from you or I. Rivik, however, will retain his position having proved himself, this night, to me."

"Very well, Commander. Will you take another of my brethren to join Rivik?"

"I have neither time nor patience to replace Gallo. Rivik will stand alone and serve me or else face the consequences."

The two Fallen were silent for a moment, each studying the other. "Do you accept your fate, brother?" Barrock asked.

"I do, and there is no need to fear, I shall not be the one to fail again," Rivik hissed.

Barrock nodded slowly. "Then so be it, brother. You alone will now bear the responsibility. There is nowhere for you to hide."

Kane smiled. "Indeed."

"What are your orders, Commander?"

"Take me back to the place the darkness is at its strongest, where there is no resistance to greed and temptation. Such a place will have a clear energy signature, one that we can easily track. Remember the girl we found in the town? Her scent as she willingly gave in to her desires before you tasted her flesh? I want more like her, Barrock. Find and take me to them."

Barrock lowered in front of him.

Rivik nodded his agreement. "I shall follow, Commander."

Kane's mouth curved into a smile. "Lead the way and find what I desire."

They exited the tent, heading in the direction of the town, Rivik following close behind. Kane's mind raced with the possibilities of the Fallen's true nature as they moved from street to street, keeping hidden amongst the shadows. *A night of revelations and one of possibilities.*

Barrock paused occasionally to scent the air, his excitement palpable. The two Fallen broke into a run, stopping outside of a drinking tavern.

Kane dismounted. "Do not reveal yourselves."

"Yes, Commander." Barrock slunk back into the shadows.

"Summon us if you have a need," Rivik replied.

Kane nodded and entered the tavern. A brief silence greeted him. He stared around the occupants of the dimly lit room and smiled once he found the one he had been seeking, the drone of conversation resuming as he strode to the mahogany counter and waited. He sensed at least a dozen pairs of eyes boring into his back and turned his head, his gaze meeting the sultry glance of the brunette sitting in the centre of the room, the man who accompanied her oblivious to the lack of interest in his conversation. Kane's eyes flicked appreciatively across the swell of her breasts, and he smiled. She averted her gaze and brought her attention back to her companion. Kane drummed his fingers on the mahogany counter and waited.

"What can I get you?" A dishevelled-looking male approached, lifting a rag from his shoulders to wipe a glass.

Kane gestured to the couple in the corner. "What is the lady drinking?" he asked.

The tavern keeper followed his gaze and smirked. "Vodka and coke."

"I shall have the same, and another for the lady."

"Listen, mate, I'm happy to take your money from you, but a friendly word of warning seeing as you're new here and I don't like blood in my carpet. Stay clear of that one, she's Ronan's skirt."

"Is that Ronan?" Kane asked, studying the man in the corner.

"No, that's Jimmy, Nicki's brother. But I wouldn't be messing with him either."

"And why is that?"

"He works for Ronan and he's just been released from prison for GBH."

Kane frowned. "What is this GBH?"

"Grievous Bodily Harm. Got a nasty temper on him that one. The last idiot to start a fight with him is in a wheelchair. He's lucky it wasn't a body bag." The tavern keeper turned away to pour the drinks.

Kane studied the couple and smiled to himself as the man stood up and walked quickly past him, disappearing through another door.

He shifted his attention to the brunette. She met his eyes and ran a hand seductively through her hair before picking up her glass and taking a long drink.

Kane whispered an incantation and pulled a crisp note from his trouser pocket. "Thanks for the warning, you can keep the change," he instructed, collecting the two glasses. He sauntered to the table and placed a drink in front of her.

"Why, thank you, sugar, but you really shouldn't have."

Kane stroked a finger down her cheek and brushed her lips gently. "I think I should." He lowered himself into the man's seat and took a sip of the liquid. It had a strange taste yet was not completely unpleasant to the palate.

"I haven't seen you before, do you live locally?" she asked.

"No, I'm just looking for someone."

"Who are you looking for, sugar?"

Kane gave a slow smile. "You."

She laughed and leaned forward, her ample cleavage exposed further as she studied him with interest. "Why me, sugar?"

"I like what I see."

"Really? Well I..." Her gaze slid past him. "Shit," she muttered.

Kane smiled and leaned back in his chair, aware of the man storming towards them.

"Thanks for the drink but some other time. You need to leave," she said quickly.

Kane picked up his drink. "Oh, why the rush? I was just enjoying our conversation." Languidly, he raised his glass and took another swallow of the liquid.

"Who's this guy, Nicki?"

"No one, he was just looking for his blind date and thought I might be her."

"Yeah, well you're out of luck, mate, this one is taken and if you know what's good for you, you'll stay clear."

Kane placed down his empty glass and rose from his seat. He appraised her companion. "A shame, I was starting to enjoy our conversation."

"Time to piss off, mate," the man said and took his seat.

Kane sneered and strode to the door, turning to give her a wink before exiting.

"Did you find what you were looking for?" asked Barrock.

Kane mounted Rivik's back. "Exactly what I was seeking. Now return to camp, dawn will soon approach and you must regenerate with the others."

Rivik shuddered beneath him.

"Is something wrong?" Kane asked.

"I sense…" His voice trailed off as Kane leaned in close to Rivik's ear. "Whatever you think you have detected, keep your counsel."

Barrock approached. "What is it, brother?"

"I thought I sensed something, but the feeling is gone, brother," Rivik said.

Barrock sniffed the air. "There is a residue of something. It lingers close to you."

Kane met the Fallen's eyes. "For a second time, you seem to insinuate something, Barrock."

"Forgive me, Commander. I imply nothing. Perhaps the scent comes from your wound?" he offered quickly.

Kane deliberately softened his expression. He had almost forgotten about her warning. "You are right, Barrock. The injury inflicted by the Master was deep. The scent, a sign that the magic I have used to heal is failing." He clutched his hand to his side and grimaced.

"All the more reason for us to get back to camp," Rivik growled.

Barrock nodded and faced the direction of the forest. Rivik leading the way as the Fallen ran swiftly through the shadows. Kane slid his body low to Rivik's skin, maintaining his pretence.

He remained oblivious to the darkness that shifted beneath him and the two black cords that broke free from the Fallen's skin.

Kane grunted, suddenly feeling nauseous.

"Nearly there, Commander," Rivik called and picked up his pace.

Barrock joined alongside him. "He doesn't look well, brother."

"I'm not dying," Kane spat out.

"No, but your injury, Commander," Barrock argued.

"My magic has faded. I must rest."

Kane's stomach lurched as Rivik weaved in and out of the trees. He almost cried his relief as they broke free into the small clearing, the camp silent and empty of activity. Kane slipped from Rivik's back and staggered towards his tent.

"Sleep well, Commander."

The Fallen turned to the trees to join the others. "Do you think he will survive the night?" asked Barrock.

"The Master will not have killed him. We do not possess the girl or the Tracker, and there isn't time to send another Commanding officer in his place," Rivik replied.

Barrock nodded. "I don't believe the Tracker is in the village, brother."

Rivik was silent a moment. "How close did you get before the entity attacked?"

"One claw over the border."

"And the others?"

"The same." Barrock retreated into his cocoon.

Rivik cast a final glance towards Kane's tent. *The Nyrvallia will indeed awaken, I have made sure of that.* Encased in his shell, Rivik released his physical body and began his regeneration.

CHAPTER ELEVEN

Pitlochry, Scotland

Finn rubbed the sleep free from his eyes, the room now bathed in soft light. "What is it?" he asked, focusing his gaze on her face.

She passed him a piece of paper, her hands trembling. "Do you recognise this?"

Ice travelled his spine as he studied the image, his mind propelling back through time in search of the memory suppressed. "Where did you see this?"

Rowan shook her head. "First tell me what it means."

His fingers traced the lines she had drawn on the piece of paper, a lump catching in his throat, the memory of his father's death resurfacing. He struggled for the words to explain, his stomach churning with conflicting emotions.

She reached for his hand and squeezed it gently. "Finn?"

His gaze met hers. "It's my father's sigil."

"I don't understand," she whispered.

Finn returned the piece of paper. "Neither do I."

She bit down on her bottom lip and stared at the rune. "This doesn't make sense."

Mind whirring, he fell against the pillows. *How is it possible? How can she know of its existence? That rune was hidden for years. Its secrets buried the day my father died.*

"Are you mad with me?" she asked.

Finn reached to pull her down beside him, brushing his lips gently against her forehead. "No, it's just that I never expected to see that rune again."

"What does it mean?"

Finn sighed with the pain of the memory released. "It is the Morvantia Crest. My father was the last surviving member of the Order that served the Crest. When he died, we lost the protection of the Morvantia. There was no one to wield its power."

"Not even Mercadia or the other Elders you spoke of?"

"Only those born into the Order are pure enough to carry the Morvantia."

"Can't the Council of Elders resurrect the Order? Aren't they powerful enough?"

"It's not that simple. The Morvantia is living energy. It chooses who shares its power. My father was the last born with its Crest. When he died, it died too. My mother believes it's the reason the Master was able to penetrate our world and infect the Moren."

"The Moren?"

"There are four realms within my world: the Moren, Valoria, Elyssia and the Astylliss. The Moren was the first realm that the Master invaded. He destroyed it and everything that dwelled. Nothing but ash remains. He wants control over the other realms now."

Rowan's breath hitched. Shifting his position, he turned to study her. She was shivering.

"Climb under the duvet," he whispered. He sensed her hesitate. "It's fine, I'll stay below the sheet," he reassured.

She lifted the duvet and settled herself beneath. Her eyes glistened with tears as he stroked her cheek softly. "What is it, Rowan?"

"I've seen the Moren, in my vision. Those people that the Master killed, he's left their souls trapped beneath the earth. They need help."

Finn raised himself and swallowed the rising bile. "The Master has consumed the Moren's life force, it's feeding his magic. That's how he must be doing it."

"Doing what?"

"Tearing holes in the Selensia. How many souls did you see?"

"There were too many of them to be sure," Rowan said and bit her bottom lip.

"But you heard them?"

"Yes, I heard them. They're in so much pain."

"Will you tell me of this vision of yours?"

She lifted and pulled her knees to her chest, her arms hugging her legs.

"Rowan?"

"Please don't ask me, at least not right now. It hurts to think about it. Oh god, I feel as though my head is going to burst with all of this."

Not wanting to cause her distress, Finn didn't pursue the vision further. "At least tell me about the Crest. Where did you see it?"

Rowan sighed and reached into her pyjama pocket. She handed Finn another piece of paper. "You need to take me to this address."

"Who lives at this address?"

"The woman who showed me the rune. Like you, she's visited me in my dreams, and told me that I must show you the rune."

"Who is she?"

"I only know that she is called Bessie. I don't know anything else about her. All I can tell you is that I trust her."

Finn considered for a moment. "She must be who Mercadia spoke of. Yes, we'll go there as soon as it gets light."

"Mercadia knows of her? But how?"

"I don't know. I guess we'll find out soon."

Enveloping her in his arms, he kissed her softly. "Think you can manage a few more hours sleep?"

Rowan freed her hand from his embrace and reached to switch off the bedside lamp. The room returned to darkness. "As long as you hold me," she whispered.

"I will," he reassured.

Silence fell between them. Finn stared at the ceiling and waited for her to drift.

"I don't want to dream," she mumbled.

"Then don't," he whispered.

"Thank you, Charles."

Charles? Who was Charles?

"Rowan?"

She didn't respond. Her breathing settled into the gentle rhythm of sleep.

Reaching out with his senses, Finn scanned the room. They were alone and safe, no other presence detected. *Could it be that Charles was like Bessie? Another who had appeared to Rowan in her dream, but for what purpose? What is going on? Why hasn't Mercadia mentioned Charles or Bessie?*

Finn closed his eyes, his thoughts continuing to tumble back and forth. If Bessie was indeed the one that Mercadia had spoken of, then she must have known about the rune.

Damn it, Mercadia, you have no right to spring this on me, do you hear me, woman?

"Whether you believe me or not, I did not know about the rune, Finn. It is as much a surprise to me as it is to you," Mercadia replied.

"So, you were listening in to our conversation?"

"No, I was sleeping when you rudely called out my name and disturbed me. Do you have any idea what the hour is?"

"I don't care at this moment. I take it you have read my thoughts and are aware?"

"Yes, I am."

"Then tell me how does this woman Bessie know of it?"

"You will have to ask her that question, but perhaps at a more civilised time."

"And what of this Charles?"

"I have no idea. I suggest you speak to the girl about that. Goodnight, Finn."

Grinding his teeth together, he said, "Could you give me a little help?"

Mercadia gave a huff. "Very well."

Heat emanated at the centre of his forehead, thoughts of his father, the Crest and the mysterious Charles temporarily pushed to the furthest corner of his mind.

Mercadia released her connection as soon as Finn stumbled into slumber.

CHAPTER TWELVE

Scottish Highlands

"Are you okay, Rowan?" Charles asked, his hand gently brushing her cheek.

She glanced towards Finn and frowned. "He's been different with me this morning. Colder somehow. I don't understand it. Did you notice anything at all last night?"

"No, although he did spend a great deal of time staring up at the ceiling, and I wouldn't have said he looked particularly happy then. He fell asleep much later than you."

Rowan considered for a moment. "He does communicate telepathically with this Mercadia. She could have said something last night that upset him."

"It's a possibility, although by his behaviour at breakfast, I did have the distinct impression it was more you he was upset with."

"I felt that too. Although I'm not sure why, did I talk in my sleep? Say anything that might have upset him?"

"Not that I can recall," Charles reassured.

Rowan's gaze flicked momentarily to Finn as a soft snore escaped.

"Perhaps he didn't get enough rest?" Charles offered.

She stared at the road ahead, her mind whirring. *Can it be as simple as that? Finn's sudden bad mood caused by lack of sleep? Is tiredness the reason behind him snapping at my questions this morning, and then ignoring me over breakfast? Would it justify why he had barely said two words in the car, and then gone straight to sleep when I attempted a conversation? Even the cup of tea at the last service station had not been enough to keep him awake and make him civil towards me.*

Rowan's stomach lurched in response, confirming what she had feared to be true. "I'm pretty sure he is mad with me, although I don't honestly know the reason why. Maybe he's regretting his decision to find me. Maybe it's because I am a disappointment and not the heroine he was expecting."

"He's an idiot if he thinks that," Charles muttered.

She smiled. "I don't understand. Why me?"

"Why not you?"

Rowan shook her head. Her hands gripped more tightly to the steering wheel. "I mean, this sort of thing doesn't happen in the real world. Here I am driving miles from home with a man I barely know, a man who comes from another world, in search of an old woman and her talking dog. I feel as though I am completely losing my mind."

Charles laid a hand briefly on her shoulder. "I cannot explain Finn's arrival to you, any more than I can explain Bessie or the dog. But it's real, and you are not losing your mind. Whether or not you believe this, you are special. I have always known that about you."

"Thank you, for believing in me so much." She changed the subject. "Do you know if mum and Jake are okay?"

"Jake has calmed from his initial anger. Harry did say that he was keen to talk to you, he needs to hear for himself that you're well. Your mum seems happy that you've found someone and Aliyah allowed David a further visitation last night."

"Did my dad say anything else? Any messages for me?"

"Only for your mother. He's eased her mind, so she doesn't worry about you."

"That's good, although I do wish he had been allowed to contact me. I miss him."

"I know, Rowan. The Lightkeepers have their reasons. I cannot question them further on that."

A tear slid down her cheek, and she wiped it away. "I appreciate the fact that you tried. I'll give mum and Jake a call when we get to Bessie's. We're only a few miles away."

Charles squeezed her shoulder gently. "He's waking. I think it best if I leave you two alone to talk things through. We can speak later tonight."

Rowan felt the gentle release of his energy as Finn yawned loudly. "Where are we?"

"About five miles outside of Latheron."

"How long was I asleep?"

"Most of the journey," she replied and cringed at the bitterness in her voice.

Finn remained silent for a few minutes. "I guess I deserved that. I am sorry about this morning. I didn't mean to take my mood out on you."

She sighed. "It would help if I knew the reason you were in a mood. Did I do something wrong?"

"I don't know, that depends on whether you have feelings for another. Last night you spoke of a man, Charles. Who is he?"

Rowan could feel his eyes burn into her skin. Her hands were suddenly clammy as they gripped the steering wheel. "Is that what's been bothering you? Why you were so cold this morning?"

"Is he your lover?" Finn demanded.

"No," she snapped.

"I need to know who he is. Is he important to you?"

"Yes, he is, very much so."

Finn's tone was dejected as he mumbled, "I see."

"I don't think that you do. I can hear it in your voice, you assume the worst."

Finn shuffled in his seat. "What am I expected to think? You're going to have to give me more to go on here. I'm struggling to understand what he is to you."

She shook her head. *How am I supposed to do that? It isn't something I can explain easily to a layperson, so how the hell do I explain it to a man from another world?*

The *Sat Nav* system distracted her from her thoughts, as it signalled their arrival into Latheron and delivered the next set of instructions. Rowan, acutely aware that she still had not given him any explanation, focused her attention on the directions given.

Finn fell into a stony silence, the tension in his body beside her.

Driving into the village, Rowan paid little attention to its sights. The atmosphere in the car was becoming increasingly uncomfortable. She considered the various ways in which to explain Charles's existence to Finn and ran possible conversations through her head.

A thought suddenly occurred, and without warning, she erupted into laughter.

"I fail to see what's so funny," Finn huffed.

Rowan wiped the tears away and attempted composure. She failed miserably, unable to keep a straight face.

Here I am completely stressing how to explain who Charles is, and to a man who technically doesn't exist in this world either. A man who stepped out of my dream. It makes perfect sense!

"This isn't a joke. I left my world for you," Finn said angrily.

"I'm sorry, it's just that I've been so worried that you will think I'm completely crazy and yet, the funny thing is that you're not supposed to exist either. It's ironic that I am sitting here struggling to find the words to explain who and what Charles is."

"You're not making sense."

"Charles is my spirit guide, not my lover. He doesn't have a physical presence in my world, and I am the only one who can see him, and others like him. Charles and I communicate in the same way that Mercadia communicates telepathically with you. I am not sure what you heard, but it wouldn't have been the full conversation and so very easy for you to jump to conclusions."

"What's a spirit guide?"

Rowan sighed. "That's the part I'm not sure how to explain to you. I don't know if spirits exist in your world. What do you believe about life after death?"

"I don't understand. Is Charles a human like you?"

"He was a long time ago, but when his physical body died, his consciousness ascended. He is what we call spirit energy. I don't know if you can understand any of this or not, all I can tell you is that he's important to me and a big part of who I am. I need you to accept that and trust me."

Finn covered her hand briefly with his. "If he means that much to you, then yes."

A small weight lifted from Rowan's shoulders. "Thank you, and for the record, I left my home and family behind too, and I did that for you."

Rowan's gaze flicked to the map on the dashboard. They had passed through the village and were less than ten minutes from their destination, the road leading them back into countryside. The landscape stretching out ahead was breathtaking, with lush green hills to either side of the way. Rowan imagined herself standing at the summit, the wind blowing her cobwebs free, the sun on her face and the earth's energy coursing through her soul.

The *Sat Nav* or *Daft Nav* as she often referred to it had soon destroyed her daydream when it insisted she take the next turn down a narrow lane littered with potholes. She breathed a sigh of relief when it guided her off and along the gravel driveway that led to the cottage. Finally, she brought the car to a stop and switched off the engine. "I hope Bessie has plenty of hot water," she groaned and rubbed the back of her neck.

Finn leaned across and kissed her cheek. "Let me make it up to you."

Rowan couldn't resist. "Oh, and how are you going to do that?"

For the first time that day, he grinned and wiggled his fingers in front of her. "Did I mention that I have magic hands?"

"Really?"

"Yes, and I can assure you that you won't be disappointed."

"Well, I shall look forward to seeing what your magic hands can do," she teased.

Finn winked. "Now there's a challenge I can't refuse."

She stepped out of the car quickly before he could notice the slight heat in her cheeks.

He glanced around. "Are you sure this is the right place?"

Rowan stared towards the cottage, reassured by the familiar sight of the grey stone hare standing on the little porch, and the dragonfly sun catcher hanging in the window. Excitement danced in her stomach, the cottage precisely as she remembered from her dreams. "I'm sure." A breeze ruffled her hair, and she inhaled the fragrant scent of blossoms. "Can you smell them, Finn?"

His gaze wistful. "Yes, I can."

"What is it?" she asked gently.

"They remind me of my home," Finn said.

Rowan reached for his hand and pulled him forward. "Come with me. I want to introduce you to Bessie, and Biscuit too of course."

Finn nodded and laughed as she bounded up the steps and squealed in delight when the door sprang open.

"Well, it's about time. I thought you two were going to stand outside all afternoon," Bessie scolded.

Finn shook hands with Bessie. "Nice to meet you."

"And you, Finn. I have heard so much about you."

"All good, I hope?"

"If not, then you wouldn't be here," Bessie chuckled. She turned to Rowan and gave her an affectionate hug. "You made it, at last, my dear. I have been looking forward to this day for such a long time." Taking a hankie out of her pocket, she gave her eyes a quick dab.

Rowan felt the lump catch in her throat. "Me too," she managed.

There was a little bark and the sound of feet skittering towards her.

Bessie smiled. "And of course, I am not alone, someone else has also been looking forward to today."

Rowan giggled and knelt, Biscuit showering her with kisses. Surprised by how much affection she felt for the little dog, she scooped him into her arms. He nuzzled her chin and snuggled closer. Finn's expression was unreadable as he watched them both together.

Bessie shook her head and motioned for them all to go inside. "Warms my heart, seeing you both together at last."

Rowan smiled and without hesitation, headed into the kitchen.

Placing Biscuit on the floor, she stood open-mouthed and stared around her. The kitchen was everything she remembered from her dreams and more. "I can't believe I'm here, and this time it's for real. But where are the two armchairs?"

Bessie gave her a wink. "We don't need them just yet, dear. Sit, both of you. I have a pot of tea made and scones freshly baked."

A crisp white linen cloth covered the kitchen table, and three places were set with delicate blue china. In the centre, a silver stand filled with Bessie's baking and two small pots containing jam and cream. Rowan couldn't help but grin as Bessie poured the tea. Finn reached his hand across the table to pick up a scone and sniff it.

"May I?" Rowan asked.

He nodded and watched as she placed it onto a side plate and cut it in half. She gestured to the accompaniments on the table. "You can try it with jam and cream, or you can eat it on its own."

Raising half the scone to his mouth, Finn tentatively took a bite, his eyes widened. There was no hesitation in taking a second taste. "This is good, Bessie," he mumbled in between mouthfuls.

Eager to try, Rowan picked up her own, and buttered both halves. Adding a small amount of jam, she groaned in pleasure, her taste buds responding enthusiastically to the combination of warmth and sweetness. "I honestly didn't realise how hungry I was," Rowan acknowledged after the last crumb was demolished.

Finn, she noted, was already helping himself to another. Rowan caught his gaze.

"What?" he shrugged innocently and took a large bite, rolling his eyes upwards.

Bessie chuckled. "So, how was the journey?"

Rowan covered her mouth and yawned. "Tiring."

"Yes, you do look exhausted, dear. Why don't you finish your tea and then go upstairs and draw yourself a nice bath?"

"That sounds lovely, but I'm afraid if I did, I would want to sleep after that."

"Supper won't be for a few hours yet, so there would be no harm if you did, dear."

Finn reached across and squeezed her hand gently. "Get some rest."

"What about you?"

"Don't you worry about Finn, dear, I've got a few small chores that I would appreciate his help with. It's been a long time since I had a man around the house."

"If you're sure, thanks." Rowan turned to Finn and handed him the car keys. "Could you grab my case from the car? Press the top button to open the boot and the bottom one to lock it."

"Sure. Now go and get that bath running. I owe you, remember?"

"Yes, you do and a back massage, but I'll call on that later," she replied, and blushed.

"Your room is all prepared, second door on the left. The bathroom is just along from there. Take your time, dear, we'll come and wake you when supper is ready."

Rowan left the two of them alone and headed along the small hallway to the foot of the wooden staircase. She took a few moments to admire the beauty of the framework. Weaving its way upwards, the intricate carvings of birds and butterflies were so lifelike it forced her to take a closer look. She almost expected them to fly free or break into song. The craftsmanship was astounding; whoever had created such a staircase was truly gifted.

She climbed the stairs with a strange sort of excitement that bubbled inside. Her hand was almost shaking with anticipation as she turned the handle of the second door and entered the room. A soft gasp escaped. Wildflowers spilling from a crystal vase rested on an ivory dressing table, complemented by the plush purple cushion of the little stool. A matching wardrobe, chest of drawers and two bedside cabinets completed the furnishings. The double bed was covered with a deep purple bedspread that complemented the velour drapes.

Rowan smiled and slipped off her trainers, her toes curled into the softness of the cream carpet. She floated to the window and pressed her head against the pane. The glass was cold and yet comfortable against her forehead. Rowan sighed at the sheer beauty of the landscape outside with its sun-kissed fields and trees that swayed from a gentle breeze. An assortment of colours stretched out for miles ahead.

A soft knock on the door disturbed her daydream.

"Can I come in?" Finn asked.

"Yes," she replied. Rowan's heart skipped a beat as he wrapped his arms tenderly around her waist and drew her close. "It's beautiful here," she whispered.

He nodded. "I've set your bath running."

She brushed her lips against his. "Thank you."

Their mouths met once more, the kiss deepening.

Finn groaned. "Your bath," he reminded.

Rowan mustered what remained of her willpower and pulled herself free from his embrace. "Maybe a cold shower for you," she teased.

Finn's jaw clenched. "Then you'd better go now, as standing there looking at me like that, is killing me."

"I won't be long," she promised and quickly retreated from the room.

CHAPTER THIRTEEN

Middlesbrough, North East England

Kane drummed his fingers on the table and took another sip of his wine. *Where is she and how long do I have to wait?* He scowled at the tavern keeper. *You told me she would be here by now, do you lie?* He finished his wine and stalked to the counter, throwing down some notes. "Are you wasting my time?"

The tavern keeper pocketed the cash and refilled Kane's glass. He shook his head and gestured towards the door. The brunette entering caught Kane's gaze and flashed him a huge smile.

"You really don't want to be doing this, mate," the tavern keeper warned.

"Oh, I do," Kane said and swaggered back to his table. His thoughts shifted to the previous night and the Fallen's conversation he had eavesdropped on.

The Entity had led them to believe the Tracker and girl were hiding in the village and under its protection. *But what if Barrock is right and that it is all indeed a deception? Allowing them to escape unnoticed?*

The time that had passed before Barrock's suspicions were raised could mean they were anywhere in this world and even with the Fallen's heightened sense of smell, the Tracker's scent would be too faint to obtain a location.

Before Kane had passed out he had formulated his plan. *I may not be able to drink from the vial but she said nothing about spilling its blood.* He knew his mother's grimoire, safely tucked beneath his mattress, held inside the spell he needed, having witnessed her perform it once before. Kane patted himself on the back for the foresight that he had to bring this with him.

A map of this world is all that I require to bring my plan to fruition. He glanced across to the brunette walking eagerly towards him. *Yes, and you will be the one to give me exactly what I need and much more.*

"You came back then, sugar," the brunette purred, taking a seat opposite him. "I'd hoped I would see you again." She nibbled at his ear.

Kane smiled and leaned closer, his hand reaching beneath the table to brush against her leg and then slipping beneath the scant material she was wearing.

She shuddered and let out a small gasp. "Not here," she whispered.

Kane sat back in his seat and downed the contents in his glass. "Where would you like to go?"

She glanced at the strange ticking bracelet on her wrist. "We can't go back to mine. Ronan's there."

Kane smirked at the direction of the door and the heavy-set man tearing a path towards them. "Actually, I believe Ronan is here."

The brunette's eyes widened in horror. "Shit." She spun in the direction of the bar. "Jason, you bastard, why?"

Kane eyed the tavern keeper. The little turncoat squirmed. "Sorry, Nicki, I had no choice. I did warn you, mate."

"So, it's alright for him to put it about but not me?" she complained.

"I ain't getting involved. I like my face the way it is," the tavern keeper said.

"Wise choice," Ronan spat out. He seized her by the wrist and dragged her to her feet. "You think you're going to cheat on me?"

"It's what you deserve," she fired back.

Kane rose from the chair, anger bubbling to the surface.

The man turned on him. "You sit down if you know what's good for you, mate. You're lucky I ain't gonna bust your knee cap for screwing with my girl."

The tavern keeper intervened. "Ronan, I don't want any more trouble in my gaff. You've got a problem with him, then take it outside."

Kane glanced towards the tavern keeper and nodded. "Outside it is."

Ronan released his grip on the girl. "You've got some front, mate, I'll give you that." He clicked his fingers into the air, and two other men approached from the back of the room.

Kane had not noticed them before. He laughed as he recognised the one from the previous night. "What is this?"

Ronan smirked. "It's the warm-up act, mate, and after they've finished with that pretty face of yours, I'm going to break your legs."

Kane strolled to the bar and placed a handful of notes down. "Jason, is it? Get the lady a drink, whatever she wants."

The tavern keeper shrugged. "Sure thing, mate, it's your funeral."

Kane turned his attention back to Ronan. "After you, gentleman, lead the way."

He paused as the brunette suddenly reached for his arm. "Sugar, I really like you, but Ronan's right, you won't be walking away from this."

Ronan laughed. "She's a smart girl, my Nicki."

Kane deliberately turned her face to his and brushed his lips briefly across hers. "Enjoy your drink, I shall be back for you in a few minutes."

The laughter fell away from Ronan's face. "Outside now."

One of the men shoved Kane forward, almost tripping him. Kane studied the man's appearance, noting the strange metalwork that buried into his skin.

So, this parasite can tolerate pain, can he? Well, I shall certainly look forward to testing that. Fists clenched to his side, Kane followed Ronan through a back entrance and outside into an alleyway. His mind toyed with different ideas until he finally found the one that would satisfy his anger.

He feigned surprise. "Why gentleman, we are completely alone. I take it no one can hear me scream or come to my aid?"

The one who had shoved Kane positioned himself behind

Ronan and sneered. The other man from last night moved behind him and roughly seized his arms, holding on tightly.

Ronan chuckled and rolled up his sleeves. "That's right, mate, no one to hear you scream or beg for forgiveness. You know, I cannot deny Nicki's an incredible lay, but not one worth losing your legs over. You're either desperate or stupid."

Kane's mouth curled. "I am neither as you will soon come to realise, and I'll be the judge of how good she is at satisfying my needs."

"That will be difficult from your hospital bed. Hold him still," Ronan ordered.

Kane had no intention of moving, intrigued to see what they would do next. The man with the metalwork stepped forward and cracked his knuckles. Kane waited for the contact.

The pain inflicted was insignificant in comparison to what the Master had delivered the previous night. Despite the aching throb of his abdomen, Kane started to laugh.

"How is it he can even breathe?" Ronan shouted. "Hit him again."

Kane absorbed the second blow, although with more difficulty. A third and fourth consecutive strike and he could barely force a smile to his lips. The fifth blow had him sinking to his knees. Kane pulled the air into his lungs. He was dragged to his feet. Kane shook his head at the shadows. The man behind tightened his grip once again. The other had resumed his position behind Ronan.

"Not so cocky, now, are you?" Ronan sniggered.

Kane considered for a moment. *Perhaps I should let them feed, yet I want them to see and know my power.* Closing his eyes, he summoned the incantation. A scream from behind signalled its success, the pressure releasing.

Kane's captor slid to his knees, both arms hanging limply at his side, eyes wide with pain and shock. "My arms, Ronan, they're broken."

"How the hell could he do that? He hasn't even touched you," Ronan shouted.

Kane laughed and reached forward to rip a piece of hair from his scalp. Another incantation filled him with pleasure as the man suddenly threw himself backwards and rolled from side to side. "Get them off, get them off me, they're eating me alive! Ronan, help me."

"Well, don't just stand there, help him," Ronan yelled.

Kane immediately opened his hand and released the cluster of hair into the wind. The scarab beetle dropped un-noticed to the ground and joined the others.

Kane turned his attention to the man now hurtling towards him. Ronan, like a coward, stood back. No matter, Kane mused, he would deal with him later. Raising an arm into the air, Kane called forth the same power the Master had summoned the previous night, only with one slight adjustment to the spell. Before his assailant's fist could make contact, he levitated into the air. Kane laughed as the man thrashed around helplessly.

"Ronan, save me, get me down!" he squealed.

Ronan sprinted forward and wrapped his arms around his companion's legs, pulling him backwards. It was a hilarious sight to behold, and Kane marvelled at the sheer stupidity.

"You won't get away with this," Ronan huffed.

"You said it yourself. There is no one around. No one to hear your screams or hear you beg me for forgiveness," Kane sneered. Turning to the one who dared to lay a finger on him, Kane focused his gaze to the small pieces of metal buried in his nose and lips.

"Ronan, what's he doing to me? It hurts my face, help me, make him stop."

Ronan crossed himself and fell to the floor. Kane laughed insanely as the metal continued to grow in size and multiply. Each slithered like worms and repeatedly pierced through face and scalp until finally fusing around the neck to sever the head. The body fell with a thud to the ground.

Ronan screamed and ran.

How disappointing… I thought this human would have more fight in him.

Kane signalled to the Fallen.

Rivik stepped from the shadows and blocked Ronan's path.

Kane sauntered towards them. "I'd hoped you would present a little more of a challenge. Not so cocky, now are you?"

Whimpering and pleading for his life, Ronan inched his way back towards Kane. "Please, you can have Nicki, just let me live."

"Oh, that was never at all in question. She was always mine to take. As for letting you live, well, your cowardice has earned you no favour. For that I shall let my pets finish you off and what's left of your mate over here." Kane kicked at the headless corpse. "The scarabs have consumed your other friend. He's just bone and rag now."

"Who are you?" Ronan stammered.

"Someone you should never have challenged."

Kane smiled as Barrock and Gallo joined Rivik from the shadows. "Remember, no trace."

'Yes, Commander," Barrock growled.

"Do you need me, Commander?" Rivik asked.

"You can join me in a few hours, Rivik. The girl and I will be finding somewhere a little more comfortable. I have a fancy to take her in his bed."

Ronan sobbed miserably.

"If she is as good as he boasts, then I may let her live. I haven't decided yet."

"Very well, Commander."

Kane sauntered back inside.

The tavern keeper's mouth fell open. "How the hell are you in one piece and not a scratch on you? You're one lucky bastard."

"Luck had nothing to do with it," Kane replied, his gaze travelling to Nicki's.

Silently she rose from her seat, her face a mixture of shock and delight. Kane held out his hand. "Come with me, sugar. We're going back to your place."

CHAPTER FOURTEEN

Achavanich, Scottish Highlands

Finn closed the bedroom door softly and made his way downstairs. A smile touched his lips as he entered the kitchen.

Bessie glanced from the stove and grinned.

He held up his hands in surrender. "You were right. I should never have doubted you."

She gave a soft chuckle. "Excellent, that's the first lesson learned. My lavender bath oil has never failed."

"How long will she sleep for?"

"It depends on what her body needs, but I would say we have at least a couple of hours."

Finn sat and studied her as she busied herself with the various pots on the stove, her back towards him. *How is it you know so much?*

She did not speak, but her words suddenly broke through and disturbed his thoughts. "I shall explain shortly."

The hairs on Finn's arm rose as he tentatively reached out with his mind. *I'd like you to answer my question now if you genuinely can hear me.*

Bessie turned around and waved a wooden spoon in the air at him. His connection accepted. "Patience, young man. Otherwise, it will be burned stew for your supper."

Finn nodded, his mind a torrent of questions.

Placing the spoon on the counter, she reached for a small jar and added a pinch of the contents to a pan. There was a familiar hiss before she covered it with a lid and turned the gas to low. Taking a seat opposite, her eyes flashed with amusement as she met his gaze. "Which of your questions would you like me to answer first?"

Finn considered for a moment. "What was that you added to the stew?"

She laughed. "Indeed, you are perceptive. It was Calla essence. I imagine that confirms your suspicions."

"Of your origin, yes. My mother also used Calla in her cooking."

"I am aware. Did she ever explain its true purpose to you?"

Finn shifted uncomfortably. "That's just a myth."

Bessie arched a brow. "Really? Show me your birthmark." She rose and pulled another chair free from the table. He felt the power radiate from her as she moved closer and gestured towards his leg. "Show me," she repeated, placing the chair to the side of him.

Finn sighed and spun to rest his foot on the cushion. Lifting his right trouser leg, he exposed his ankle and waited as she scrutinised the birthmark. "The pod hasn't been activated." Bessie looked confused.

Finn lowered his leg to the floor, allowing her to take a seat on the chair. "It's just a birthmark."

"Nonsense, how do you explain your gifts?"

"I don't know. Perhaps I'm just one of those fortunate people who have a special affinity with nature," he offered.

Bessie frowned. "What you possess is a little more than just an affinity to nature."

"And how would you know of my gifts or the birthmark? I don't believe we've ever met before."

" I know everything about you. That pod should have activated on your tenth birthday."

"Well, nothing happened because it is just a myth, and that mark is just a simple birthmark. I'm nothing special."

"What happened on your tenth birthday?'

Not a question I am prepared to answer. Finn rose and strode from the kitchen.

Standing outside on the front porch, Finn dragged the air into his lungs. *Who is this woman? How does she know so much about me? About the birthmark?*

A hand touched him gently on his shoulder. "I'm sorry, I shouldn't have pushed for that memory."

Finn spun to face her. "Then, why did you?"

"I need to understand what had interfered with the pod activating."

His jaw clenched, the memory burned and stung his eyes. "Why is it so damn important anyway." He wiped the tears angrily with his sleeve.

"Tell me about your journey here."

"It's been difficult. The Master sent his warlock Kane through the portal."

"I am familiar with him," Bessie said.

"How?"

"That doesn't matter. Tell me."

"I am not sure how it's possible, but he gave the Fallen form, they travel with him. He's been on my tail since I arrived and he's getting close. If it weren't for Mercadia's help, neither Rowan or I would be here now."

Bessie shook her head sadly. "You see as well as I do the predicament we find ourselves. I'm sorry, but there's no time for me to rip this plaster off gently."

"I don't understand?"

She chuckled. "An expression I heard, I thought it quite appropriate. It means that I need to rip the bandage off your wound now. There's no time for me to do it slowly."

"Why would you want to reopen an old wound?"

"Because somewhere is the explanation of why the pod didn't activate, and why you didn't become what you were destined to be. In this war, the Council needs powerful allies, and that means you and Rowan. Protecting her will require you harnessing your full power."

"I haven't done too bad a job so far," Finn muttered.

Bessie patted his arm gently. "I know. Come inside. Rowan will be waking soon. We'll have supper, and then I want to show you both something which I believe will help."

He lifted his gaze to meet hers. "I will as long as you tell me the truth. Is it real?"

She smiled and held out her hand. "I don't lie, and yes, it's time to awaken your power."

Finn's mind whirred with the revelation. *I need a minute.*

Her thoughts connected to his once more, and he noted the plea in the depth of her eyes. "Trust me." Bessie offered her arm.

Finn accepted, and they walked back to the kitchen in silence, both startled to find Rowan stood at the stove stirring the pan. "Sorry, I didn't want it to burn." She handed the spoon back to Bessie.

"Thank you, dear. Did you sleep well?"

"I did, although that wasn't my intention."

She flushed a deep shade of red as she glanced across at Finn who grinned. "Very disappointing," he said, "however thoroughly deserved. You look much better."

"I feel better, who knew a bath could be so beneficial?"

"Do you not bathe at home, dear?"

Rowan giggled. "Of course, but I shower most days. There's never much time to enjoy a bath and Jake hogs the bathroom at every opportunity."

"Jake?" asked Bessie.

She rolled her eyes. "My brother. I love him, but he can be extremely annoying." Rowan planted a kiss on Finn's cheek. "He was fine about us by the way."

"You rang him? What did he say?"

"Well, he wants to meet you."

Finn laughed. "Should I be scared?"

"Of Jake? No. Besides, I'm sure he'll love you."

"I hadn't realised you had a brother. Your parents?" Bessie interrupted.

Some of the laughter fell away from her voice. "Just my mum, my father passed away eighteen months ago."

"I'm sorry to hear that. It must have been hard for you all."

Finn ushered Rowan to the table and pulled her down beside

him. He wrapped an arm around her shoulder, and she snuggled closer. "Are you okay?" he whispered.

She gave a small nod. "It wasn't easy, but we've come through it together."

"Do your family know the truth about Finn?" Bessie asked.

Rowan hesitated. "No. In all honesty, I'm not sure they would understand."

"Why is that important?" Finn asked.

Bessie placed a bowl of stew in front of them both. "It's not, I guess. Although it will have a part to play in the future. Let's not worry about that now. Tuck in."

Rowan leaned forward and inhaled the aroma. "It smells amazing; what's in it?"

Bessie caught his eye and gave him a wink. "It's my secret recipe."

"I'm guessing Finn helped? Does he know your secret ingredients?"

"Perhaps one or two, not all," Bessie replied, setting a bowl in front of herself.

Finn spooned in a mouthful of stew, the Calla essence only just detectable amongst the array of meat, vegetable and aromatic spices.

Rowan groaned beside him. "You have to give me the recipe."

"I'm so glad you like it, dear. Now eat up, you'll need your strength. Training starts tonight."

"Training?" Rowan turned to Finn.

"We need to prepare, Bessie is going to help us."

"Prepare for what?"

"Let's not spoil the meal talking about that just yet, dear."

Rowan nodded an acknowledgement although he could see that she was disappointed. They continued eating in silence for the rest of the meal, Finn rising to clear the table after polishing off two portions of stew.

Bessie shook her head. "The thought is very much appreciated, however, Mortimus will take care of it."

Finn frowned. "Mortimus? As in the stone rabbit?"

"He's not a rabbit. He's a hare, and a very clever one at that," Rowan replied.

"Come now, you of all people understand the unique and special attributes of the animal kingdom. Mortimus will see to the dishes while we are out."

Finn could feel the flush of colour and a sickening churn despite the Calla essence effects. "Where is it we are going?" he asked, changing the subject quickly.

"You'll both need your coats."

"They're still in the car. I'll go get them." Rowan kissed him on the cheek.

As soon as they were alone, Finn turned to Bessie. "Could you not speak of that in front of her?"

"Are you ashamed of your gift?"

"No, but I need to get my head around it first before I share with anyone else, especially Rowan."

"Fair enough but it's part of who you are, and something that cannot be kept hidden. You will have to tell her sooner or later."

"Later then, when I understand and have accepted it."

"As you wish."

Rowan entered the kitchen and passed his jacket, her eyes wary. "Are you alright? You look pretty tense."

Finn relaxed his jaw. "Sorry, and yes, I'm fine. I guess I'm just a little worried about you."

"Don't be. I'm excited, but a little nervous too."

Unable to fight the overwhelming urge to pull her into his arms, Finn hugged her tightly to his chest, inhaling lavender.

"What's that all about?" she whispered.

"Nothing," he said, releasing her from his embrace.

Rowan slipped on her jacket. "You're sure?"

"Yes, I didn't want you to be nervous, that's all."

Bessie cast a glance in his direction but didn't comment. She wrapped a thick woollen shawl around her shoulders. "Follow me, my dears."

Dusk had arrived when they stepped outside. Biscuit appeared from out of nowhere and ran towards them.

"Is everything set?" Bessie asked.

Finn could have sworn he heard the words *'Yes, mistress'*. He studied the little dog in the dimming light as Rowan kneeled to pet him. Large brown eyes turned towards him, Biscuit's head cocked to one side. *Yes, I heard you, and you know it, don't you?*

There was no response. Instead, Biscuit trotted away down the gravel driveway and in the direction of the main road. Finn's gaze shifted to Bessie in time to see the small smile that touched her lips.

"Are we to follow him?" Rowan asked.

"Yes, dear. Biscuit will guide you past the potholes."

"Shouldn't the local authority be sorting those out for you?"

"No, dear. As much of a nuisance as they are, we do not like to be disturbed."

Rowan shrugged and linked her arm through Finn's. They walked in silence, following the little dog along the main road until he turned to the left and slipped under a metal gate into a large field. Finn vaulted over the gate and reached to assist Rowan across. She landed in his arms, gratefully.

He turned to help Bessie, his mouth dropping open when the older woman nimbly leapt over the gate without the slightest of fuss. "I may be old, but I'm as fit as a fiddle," she chuckled, walking away.

Rowan and Finn burst into laughter.

He took hold of her hand. "Well, I guess that told me."

The moon lit their way as they moved silently through the field, Biscuit suddenly diving through the hedging. As they approached, it sprang apart, allowing all three to fit through the hole comfortably. Finn stole a glance behind, noting the entrance had closed as soon as they had passed.

"Just look at all the stars. Finn, have you ever seen a night so clear?" she exclaimed.

Finn had to admit it was quite the show, each one bright and...

Rowan stopped dead in her tracks. Bessie held up her hand, signalling for him to stop. Ribbons of light danced freely from Rowan's fingers.

"You feel the call?" the older woman asked.

Rowan nodded and turned to Finn, her eyes reflecting the night sky, deep dark pools with tiny explosions of silver light. Her mouth formed words, but he couldn't hear them or speak.

His feet felt heavy and rooted to the spot.

Why can't I move?

"Let go," Bessie ordered.

Finn's blood boiled, his skin on fire. *What is this?* The thumping in his head was becoming louder, drowning out her cries. Arms caught him as he sank to his knees, his breath coming in short sharp gasps. *What is happening to me?*

"Bessie?" Rowan's voice sounded far away. "Do something, oh god, Finn, please answer me, what is it?" she begged.

He lifted his face towards Bessie.

"I'm sorry, Finn, the plaster is gone. Now it's time to let it go."

He started to cough. *Let what go? What was he supposed to let go?*

"How?" he gasped and collapsed to the ground.

Rowan sobbed, and rolled him onto his back.

He stared helplessly at the night sky. *Am I dying?*

"Damn it, Finn, do what Bessie says," Rowan shouted.

"You must stop fighting it, let the memory in and force that bloody creature out," Bessie said.

What creature… wait, what is happening? Where am I?

Finn stumbled to his feet and stared around him. *How did I get back here? Why does my jaw hurt so much?* The memory flooded back to him. *That's right, Aaron punched me, but why?*

"Well, do you want me to make the pain stop?"

Who is that? Finn spun to face the owner of the voice but could see no one.

"Must we play this game again?" it asked.

"Who are you?"

"A friend. I can take it all away, the shame you shall bear no more. Just say the word."

The shame? Finn could hear the distant echo of a childish rhyme. It brought a wave of pain and humiliation. The memory of the boy's eyes cold and bitter as Finn had sunk teeth into flesh. His

159

father's embarrassment right before his death. His brother's rage throbbed in his face. Finn rolled his tongue tentatively around his mouth, his cheek swollen from the punch Aaron had landed. There it was that faint taste of copper. *Yes, take it away, now. Wait, no, something is wrong. Rowan? Bessie? I need it, I need my power, stop!*

Finn rolled up his trouser leg and stared in horror at the oozing bulbous mass clinging to his shin. Sweat beaded his forehead, as he bent forward to seize the worm and rip it away. A sharp pain seared through his entire leg and he cried out in agony. He fell to the ground, his head swimming and nausea rising.

"You're making a terrible mistake, the Fae will not make such an offer again," the worm warned.

"It lies, don't listen to it." Bessie's voice echoed through the forest.

Finn groaned and bent forward, his eyes widening as the head of the worm disappeared below the gaping hole in his skin. He could feel it biting its way through flesh, his body temperature rising with each second that passed. Molten lava gushed around the worm's exposed carcass, as it wiggled spasmodically in the air. The dark pink liquid, blood mixed with the worm's viscous white pus, burned and continued to pour from the wound, soaking his boot.

"But the Fae, I cannot refuse," Finn said weakly and fell backwards.

Inside his head, the worm smiled and his own lips lifted in response.

"That thing is not born of the Fae," Bessie yelled. "Act quickly, before it takes control."

"I don't have the strength," he said.

"Yes, you do," Bessie insisted.

"I'll make all that pain go away," the worm crooned.

"Think of Rowan, you cannot protect her with this creature inside you," Bessie urged.

Her words slapped him hard across his face and brought him back to his senses. *Rowan! My power!* Gritting his teeth, Finn lunged forward in time to catch hold of the worm's tail end before it could enter his body. Taking a deep breath, he tightened his grip, and with his thoughts firmly focused on Rowan and his primal instinct to protect her, Finn yanked. The worm, forced free from his flesh, squirmed in his fingers.

"You need me," it shrieked.

"No, I don't," Finn said.

"Destroy it," Bessie ordered.

Finn quickly searched his surroundings, and found a large chunk of stone. He grimaced as he sank to his knees and dropped the worm to the ground. Before it could escape, he smashed the rock repeatedly until nothing remained of the creature except a white sticky residue. With all his strength spent, he collapsed into darkness.

When he awoke seconds later, it was in Rowan's arms. She held him tightly. "Don't move. Bessie?"

"I'm sorry," he whispered.

Her voice was shaking. "You scared the hell out of me."

Bessie knelt and placed a hand over the wound. Finn heaved a loud sigh as the warmth of her healing energy eradicated the damage that the worm had caused.

"Now you are both ready. Well done, Finn."

He met her gaze. "What was it?"

"A parasite. The last of its kind and now extinct."

"I was just a boy. It said it was a friend of the Fae?"

"A lie. It took advantage of your grief and has stayed hidden all this time, feeding on the power denied to you, to sustain its existence."

"Will my power return?"

Bessie lifted Rowan and Finn to their feet. She gave each of them a hug.

Finn could feel the pulse of energy through his skin. The ground vibrated softly beneath his feet.

"In time. Do you feel it now?" Bessie asked.

Finn nodded and grinned.

The older woman smiled and closed her eyes as she stretched her arms upwards and into the night air. "Once the Meridian reveals itself to you, it will always be there when you need it. Be respectful of its home and be open to the lessons it teaches. Trust it and know that its source comes from the highest light and the greatest of power ever to enter this realm."

She clapped her hands together and opened her eyes. A thundering boom caused the air to ripple in waves around them and then stillness.

Finn held his arms in front of him. The same ribbons of silver light he had witnessed earlier now danced playfully through his fingers.

He turned and laughed at Rowan spinning in circles, sparks of silver shooting from her feet as she danced on the ground. "This is amazing."

Bessie chuckled. "Welcome to the Meridian, and now, your training begins."

"What do you need us to do?" Finn asked.

"Each of you possesses different gifts. The Meridian must get to know those gifts and consider what you each require to enhance and build on them further. For you to do this together will only create confusion, and so I shall leave it to you to decide who shall go first."

"I think you should," Rowan said.

"Why?"

"You need to heal first."

Bessie smiled and nodded. "The Meridian does indeed bring healing and much more."

"But it's Rowan that we need to protect. I think she should go first. You said yourself that we don't have much time." Finn argued his point although he could tell from both women's expressions that he was fighting a losing battle.

Rowan folded her arms. "No. Something tells me that tonight is for you, and I need you to protect me by understanding, and using your powers fully."

"She makes a valid point. You came close to death tonight expelling that thing."

"You never said anything about dying when ripping that plaster off," Finn bellowed.

"I didn't know you'd willingly let a Margorian Worm take refuge until the Meridian exposed it," Bessie responded calmly.

He ran a hand through his hair and released a deep exhale. "I have no defence."

Rowan nodded. "That's settled then. So what's next?"

"You and I will be leaving. Finn must remain here alone and spend the night in the Meridian. Biscuit will wait for you on the other side of the hedge and will accompany you home."

"Oh," Rowan said.

Finn sensed her disappointment that they would not be spending the night together.

"And one more thing." Bessie's wicked smile made him suddenly suspicious. "You have to take off all your clothes."

Finn coughed and cleared his throat. "You mean I'm to stand here, completely naked?"

"No, I mean that you will lie on the earth, completely naked." Bessie grinned.

"What if someone sees me?"

"You are shielded within the Meridian, no one can see you. Anyone who does happen this way will see an empty field."

"But why naked?"

"You must be fully exposed to the Meridian, to trust and completely open yourself to its energy. Once you have integrated, then your lessons can begin."

"What about Rowan?"

"Her turn will come."

Finn sighed. "I'd better make myself comfortable then."

Rowan's amusement was evident as she pressed a kiss on his cheek. "A shame I cannot stay. I shall see you tomorrow morning."

The two women turned and left Finn alone. A small bark sounded from the other side of the hedging. "Yes, Biscuit, I'm doing it."

Finn reluctantly removed his jacket and dropped it to the ground. The night air nipped at his skin as he stripped away the rest of his clothing. *This is utter foolishness.* Finn laid himself on the grass and closed his eyes. *Well, I'm ready.*

The anticipation churned in his stomach as he waited, for what, he wasn't quite sure. *At least let it be worth the humiliation of lying naked in the middle of a field in a strange world.*

Time crept by slowly. Still, there was nothing from the Meridian. Disappointment rose, and he shifted uncomfortably, the ground cold and hard beneath him. His patience lost, Finn addressed the silence. "Is this a test? I was ready hours ago. It will be dawn soon, and I feel no different."

The Meridian did not respond. Finn considered whether he should admit defeat and go back to the cottage. *What would Rowan think of me if I did?*

The Meridian's energy had been active when they had first entered. *So why was it silent now? What have I done wrong?*

He reflected on Bessie's words. *What had she said? Trust and give yourself entirely to its energy. Have I not been doing that?* Finn believed he had and yet that inner voice niggled. *Really? Or have you allowed your embarrassment and pride to get in the way?*

Truth acknowledged, Finn stretched both arms and legs outwards and exposed his vulnerability further. *I must release all doubt and yield.* Exhaling deeply, Finn released the last of the tension from his muscles and pushed all other sensations from his mind. He could no longer feel the chill in the air or the ground beneath. "I give myself freely to you."

A current of electricity ignited in his feet and travelled swiftly upwards, passing through his core and into his mind. The pressure in his forehead increased as his third eye awakened and a purple light burst free. Somewhere in his consciousness, he was vaguely aware of the ground trembling. Roots tore through the soil and wrapped gently around him, drawing him slowly beneath the earth. Levitating above where his physical body had once been, Finn stared in wonderment. *I should be shocked and yet it's strange that I am not.*

Many voices instantly gathered around him and whispered his name.

Finn directed his thoughts toward them. "Who are you?"

They replied as one. "We are the Meridian. Are you ready to begin, young Warrior?"

"I am."

Finn's soul catapulted towards the night sky. He lost consciousness.

Suspended in time, he floated amongst the stars while the Meridian set to work.

CHAPTER FIFTEEN

Achavanich, Scottish Highlands

"Will you sit down, dear? You're starting to make me anxious."

"But they should be back by now," Rowan complained.

"The Meridian will release Finn when it's ready."

"I thought you said that would be at dawn? It's nearly midday. I've hardly slept a wink worrying about it all and whether he's alright."

"Of course, he is. Why would you think any different?"

Rowan heaved a sigh and ceased pacing the kitchen floor. Flopping onto the dining chair, she accepted the cup Bessie offered and took a sip of the hot liquid. "That's good, what is it?"

"Lavender tea, drink, it will help you relax."

She slid her gaze to the doorway. "I'm sorry, I can't help it. Finn's been gone for ages, and after what happened last night I need to see for myself that he is alright."

"Don't you worry. The Meridian will heal any damage caused by the removal of the Margorian Worm. Finn has already proven how strong he is by carrying that thing around for as long as he has. You truly have nothing to fear there."

Rowan shuddered. "How could he not know it was there?"

"Like you, Finn has many gifts, some he also has yet to discover. The Margorian Worm invaded one of those gifts and suppressed it from him to enable it to sustain its existence. He was not aware of the worm's existence as he did not accept the fact that he even possessed such a gift. He doubts his abilities too."

Rowan considered Bessie's words. "I don't mean to doubt all of this. Honestly, I don't. It's just that it is difficult to see myself as being this great heroine destined to save another world. I've stepped into something so hard to imagine that I have to keep pinching myself to prove I'm not simply dreaming it all."

"You're not dreaming it all," Finn's voice replied.

Rowan almost spilt the remaining contents of her cup as she lunged from the table and into his arms. He held her tightly and kissed the top of her head. Tears of relief slid down her cheeks. "I've been so worried about you."

"Don't be, I'm fine, better than fine. Look at me."

She lifted her gaze and searched his face, the same and yet different. His eyes held a strength she had never seen there before. *Wait… what is that?* Rowan peered closer. *Have they always been different colours? Why have I never noticed that before?*

Finn cleared his throat. "Something wrong?"

Rowan shook her head. "Sorry, I didn't mean to stare at you quite like that."

Her legs quivered beneath her as he kissed her lips gently. "You do believe me now?" he whispered.

"Yes."

"You're not going to faint on me again, are you?" he teased.

"No, I've got it sorted, see?" Rowan sauntered back to her chair, grateful that her body did not betray her. She sat and beamed at Finn. He laughed and followed her lead, accepting the cup that Bessie offered as he lowered himself into the seat.

"Where is Biscuit?" Bessie asked.

The little dog trotted into the kitchen and barked. Rowan admired his talent for timing.

"I see. Well, that's good. I'm glad you've bonded. Although Finn does look exhausted. Perhaps you should have come back a little sooner," Bessie replied.

Biscuit barked a response and wagged his tail. "Very well, I shall trust your judgement. Perhaps a nap for you both?" He trotted to his basket without further argument and curled himself into a tight ball. Less than a few seconds later, he snored softly.

"What was that all about?" Rowan asked.

"It would seem that following the visit to the Meridian, Finn

167

and Biscuit have been getting better acquainted. That's why they were a little longer than expected, dear."

Finn didn't comment and instead drank his tea. Now and again, Rowan noticed him glance across to Bessie. She frowned. "Have I missed something?"

"Not at all, dear."

Finn released a huge yawn.

Rowan's gaze flicked to Biscuit asleep in his basket. "It seems you've worn each other out."

"Sorry, I haven't rested in hours. All that walking and fresh air must be catching up on me. Bessie, what was in that tea?"

There it is again that same look between them both. Is it the Meridian? Will I be let in on the secret once I have had my turn? Rowan swallowed her jealously. "It's Bessie's blend of lavender tea. Why don't you grab a few hours' sleep?"

Finn cast a look in the older woman's direction. "Will you be taking her to the Meridian?"

"Yes, we shall be spending a few hours there this afternoon, and tonight, she and I will stay the night alone."

"I'm not sure that's such a good idea."

"Rowan is perfectly safe with me. It is a full moon, and she requires a different integration with the Meridian than the one you experienced last night. She and I will be going alone after supper. You will stay here with Biscuit."

"Look at it this way. It's more male bonding time for you and Biscuit," Rowan quipped.

Judging by the look on Finn's face, he wasn't amused. "Will you be staying out all night?"

"Till the early hours of the morning, I imagine," Bessie replied.

"I'm still not sure it's such a good idea. They are looking for her."

Rowan rolled her eyes. "Hello, I am still here, and it is my decision as to what I do."

Bessie gave an apologetic smile. "Of course, I'm sorry, dear."

Finn met Rowan's stare. His lips pressed together, jaw clenched.

"Don't even think of looking at me like that. Besides which I think I have the right to be in on the secret that you two seem to be enjoying."

Another look exchanged between the two, much to Rowan's annoyance. "What secret?" he asked, his voice anything but innocent.

"Don't think I haven't seen the looks between you both. Whatever the big secret is I want to share it too. I'm going to the Meridian with Bessie on my own, and if we are to stay out all night, then you will have to deal with it."

Finn's mouth opened to argue.

Bessie shook her head. "I wouldn't."

Rowan resisted the urge to scream as he clamped his mouth firmly closed.

"Sorry, did you have something to say to me, Finn?" she dared.

"No, I'm going to bed."

"A wise decision," she snapped.

"So much for missing me," Finn muttered under his breath.

Rowan folded her arms.

Bessie cleared her throat. "Perhaps a little air for you, and some sleep for Finn is what you both need right now."

Finn pushed his chair back from the table. "That works for me."

"I'm so glad you approve. Oh, and for your information, I did miss you," Rowan shot back to his retreating form.

"Don't worry. He heard you, dear."

Rowan stood and swallowed her irritation. "I'm not worried. Are we going?" She asked, moving towards the door.

"Could you fetch the wicker basket from the pantry, please?"

Rowan walked in the direction of the older woman's gaze and opened the door to the small cupboard. She lifted the basket from the shelf and handed it across. "What do you need this for?"

Bessie smiled and reached into the fridge, retrieving two silver bundles, some cheese and two bottles of water. Crackers and scones from the bread bin, a small knife and a jar of the strawberry preserve were added to the basket.

"A picnic?" Rowan's mood lifted a little.

"I thought once you've completed your first lesson that we can have a bite to eat for lunch."

"I feel guilty now."

"We shall talk about that when we get to the Meridian. There's no need for guilt, or to doubt that young man upstairs. It's as plain as the nose on your face how he feels about you, dear."

Ignoring the sudden urge to check a mirror, Rowan collected the picnic basket and followed Bessie from the kitchen outside into the sunshine. A comfortable silence fell, as they traced the same route that Biscuit had guided them along the previous night. Rowan's annoyance quickly dissipated and was replaced by a flutter of excitement the closer they drew to the Meridian.

Once more, Bessie leapt over the metal gate with ease and grinned back at Rowan as she offered to take the picnic basket from her.

Rowan climbed gingerly over. "I honestly don't know how you make it look so easy."

The older woman smiled and handed back the basket. "That's because it is, dear," she replied.

Rowan could hear her chuckling to herself as they set off again through the field and towards the hedging. She didn't mind and soon found herself giggling at her awkwardness over crossing the gate.

At Bessie's raised hand, Rowan paused, her ears straining to decipher the words spoken. "Aha, this way."

Rowan was ushered further down the hedging than she recollected from the previous night. A gap opened up in front of them, allowing entry to the Meridian. The energy this time was more intense as it thrummed through her core and bid her welcome.

"It feels different as its attention is solely focused on you," Bessie replied to her unspoken question.

"What do I do now?"

"Sit and close your eyes. Rest your palms on the earth. You must trust the energy, dear. Allow it in."

Rowan nodded and sat, the earth warm underneath her

hands. Straight away her skin itched and tingled with an array of different sensations, an explosion of colour clouding her vision. A giant purple sphere moved from its centre and quickly encased her inside its shell. Her forehead ached with the magnitude of energy channelled from the Meridian's source. A dozen voices spoke at once.

She shook her head, confused by their words. "Slow down. I don't understand, one at a time," she called out.

The voices momentarily fell silent.

Rowan's heart skipped a beat as she waited, both eager and nervous for the reply. Tears burst free and streamed down her face when her father's voice answered above them all. "Welcome, Guardian."

'Dad? Are you there? Answer me, please."

"We are not your father, we are the Meridian, and you are the Guardian. Awaken."

Rowan sprang to her feet. Furiously brushing the tears from her cheek, she turned to Bessie. "Why did I hear my father's voice?"

"I cannot answer that. Only the Meridian knows. Are you sure it was him?"

"I know my father's voice," Rowan shouted.

"I'm sorry, dear. I didn't mean to offend you." The older woman drew her into an embrace and patted her soothingly on the back.

Rowan's anger dissolved. "He spoke to me, Bessie."

"What did he say, dear?"

"He told me I was the Guardian. What does that mean?"

Bessie gave a sharp intake of breath. "It means that you are far from ordinary and possess a rare gift. This world holds secrets that even I had not considered to be possible."

"That still doesn't explain anything."

"Forgive me, dear, but this is unexpected. I had begun to think it would be Finn, given his abilities. You are quite the enigma."

"I'm something alright," Rowan muttered.

"Let's eat. You must be hungry."

Rowan flopped next to Bessie and accepted the foil package. "How can you be so calm about all this?"

Ignoring the question, the older woman took a large bite of her sandwich. Heaving a sigh, Rowan opened the packaging and bit into her own. A soft grumble from her stomach signalled its appreciation. "You're not going to explain anything to me, are you?" she asked in between mouthfuls.

Bessie finished eating. "I will explain as and when the time calls for an explanation."

"Is that not now?"

"No."

"Did anyone ever tell you how frustrating you are? Must it always be a riddle with you?"

Much to her annoyance, Bessie chuckled. "Certain events must fall into place first, and you are only at the beginning of discovering the power that you possess. Too much knowledge at once can be dangerous. The Meridian will assist in preparing you, and the rest will be determined."

"If that's the way it has to be then I guess there isn't anything else I can say. So, what do we do now?"

"Now, we enjoy the rest of our lunch, and then you can go and spend some time with that young man of yours. Tonight, you and I shall return and begin your training."

Rowan nodded and accepted the scone and knife that Bessie offered, the warmth of the sun on her face and gentle thrum of the Meridian soothing her mood. The two women fell into a comfortable silence. Rowan settled against the grass once she had finished eating and gazed at the sky. She studied the cloud formations, memories triggering of her father and the games they used to play. Rowan allowed her imagination to take control and create.

The afternoon drifted by in a peaceful haze. Bessie gently nudged her when it was time for them to leave. Collecting the much lighter picnic basket, Rowan followed the older woman in silence through the opening of the hedge and back through the field. Neither spoke as they crossed the gate, each lost in thought.

She could see Finn sitting on the porch next to the stone hare as they drew close to the cottage. He sprang to his feet, relief written across his face. "You've been gone a while."

Bessie took the picnic basket from Rowan and tutted as she walked past him and into the cottage. "You two need to have more faith," she muttered before closing the door.

He shrugged his shoulders. "I'm sorry. I guess I was a grump."

"Lack of sleep will do that to you. How do you feel?"

"Better now. How was the Meridian?"

"Truthfully? I'm not sure. I guess I'll find out more in a few hours when Bessie and I return."

Rowan accepted his hand, following him around the side of the cottage, and through the little gate into the garden. Her nose inhaled the heavenly scent of wildflowers. Butterflies fluttered in and out of the blooms, and the soft and gentle hum of bees filled her ears. Finn led her to the bench in its centre. She took a moment to admire the intricacy of the owl sculpted within its frame before she sat next to him. His arm encircled, and she snuggled in close. "I like being here with you," she whispered.

"Me too, with you, I mean."

She laughed. "You know, you scared me last night. I thought I was going to lose you."

Finn kissed the top of her head. "I scared myself too. All this time I had no idea."

"Can you explain it to me? I still don't understand."

"I've blocked that memory for such a long time I don't even know where to begin."

Rowan lifted her face and brushed her lips against his. "Try please, for me."

Finn nodded. "In my grandfather's journals, he spoke of a blending that would occur between the kingdoms of man and beast, and that in every tenth bloodline a son would be born, align himself to the animal kingdom and be as one with them. The branding of the Calla would identify the son, and on his tenth birthday, the Calla pod would open and release the power of convergence. Although I bore the mark, we always believed it to be myth as the journals spoke of there being no such power given in my family's history. My grandfather wasn't even sure where the legend originated." He scratched his head.

"Don't worry about that," she said softly, encouraging him to continue.

Finn dropped his hand and frowned. "On my tenth birthday, I remember I quarrelled with someone who I used to consider my friend. He had so proudly flaunted the hide of a young deer he had tracked and killed that morning. I don't know what came over me, but I was so consumed with anger that he had taken an innocent life I grabbed hold of him and sank my teeth deep into his arm. There was so much blood. He ran from our home, promising that my family would pay for my actions. My father refused to speak to me. But his eyes said all I needed to know. He left around noon. I guess he couldn't stand to be near me. He died that same day. Aaron found me in the forest and of course, blamed me for killing him. We got into a fight, he landed a punch on my face, and I took off. That must have been when the Margorian Worm found me. I thought it had been one of the Fae that had come to ease my pain. I didn't know what it was."

"The Fae? As in Fairies?"

He looked confused.

"Tiny magical people with wings?" she explained.

"Close enough," he replied.

"Sorry, I didn't mean to interrupt. Please carry on."

Finn ran a hand through his hair. "My mother enlisted the help of the Council to look into the cause of my father's death. She never truly believed Quinn or his family were capable of killing him, and she wanted the argument between Aaron and me to cease. Mercadia confirmed my father was murdered, but she would not tell my mother any more. Aaron forgave me eventually, and I buried the memory."

"Why would Mercadia not say who murdered your father if she knew?"

"I don't know. When I challenged my mother, she told me that she had made a vow not to go looking for the answers. A part of me wonders if that was the reason why Aaron deliberately sought Mercadia out and joined them."

Rowan gently traced her fingers down his cheek. "Thank you for opening up to me. I can see how much this still hurts."

"Do you mind if we don't talk about this anymore?"

"Sure, what do you want to talk about instead?"

"I'd rather not talk at all," he whispered and pressed his mouth to hers. The kiss continued and deepened. When they finally broke apart, neither could speak. Finn's eyes, full of need, matched her own desire. With what little resolve she had left, Rowan prised herself from his embrace. "Perhaps it's best that we just sit?" she suggested.

"I think I need to go and occupy my hands. I'll check if Bessie needs anything doing. Are you coming back inside?" Finn asked.

"Do you mind if I stay out here a little longer and enjoy the peace?"

Finn was silent for a moment.

"Finn?"

"Sorry, I just wanted to make sure it was safe."

"It is and I'll be fine, go on and occupy those hands of yours."

He gave her a brief kiss before heading inside the cottage. "Don't make it too late," he called.

Rowan settled against the seat, and took a deep breath in and exhaled. She repeated four more times and with each exhale willed any tension that lingered to be released. Pushing all thoughts aside, she allowed herself for once to enjoy simply being in the moment.

A sound broke her reverie and she smiled. "Hello again, Albion," she whispered, instantly recognising him from her dream.

Albion hovered in greeting and rested on her knee. He seemed contented to stay there at first but then suddenly lifted and flew away. Rowan's instincts confirmed he had not gone far.

"He watches from the tree. I believe our arrival disturbed him," Charles commented.

She sensed him take a seat beside her. "Do you think it odd for a dragonfly to behave in such a way?"

"Nothing is what it seems here, Rowan," he replied.

"I'm not sure if you mean that in a good or bad way."

"I sense no threat to you, and you seem to have benefitted by being here. Your energy is stronger, and your senses are sharpening."

Rowan paused. "Wait a minute, you said our?"

Aliyah stepped forward. "Apologies, Rowan. Charles had mentioned there had been a change in you. I wanted to observe your aura for myself for a few moments."

"It's fine, I understand. Is he right? Am I much changed?"

"There are differences. You are coming into new power," Aliyah said.

Rowan sighed, "I feel it. Bessie is taking me back to the Meridian tonight."

"Is this the energy source that you cannot enter?" Aliyah asked, turning to Charles.

"Yes, I've not discussed this with the Lightkeepers, as I need to understand and study its effects first. But I have to be assured that in doing so Rowan is safe," Charles said.

The fact that her guide couldn't gain entry slightly concerned her. "I'm sorry, I didn't know this." She felt the strength of his love as he wrapped his energy around her shoulders.

"As long as you don't think I have abandoned you," Charles replied.

"I admit I had wondered about your silence. We haven't spoken since yesterday morning, but I'd never think that you've abandoned me."

"Don't worry, brother," Aliyah said, "there is no suggestion of any harmful energy. In fact, quite the opposite, the transformation she is going through is amazing."

Rowan smiled. "Thank you, both of you for looking out for me, and my family."

"You're welcome. Is there anything else you need from me?" Aliyah asked.

"Only news of home, if you would? With everything that's happened, I haven't been in touch with mum since Saturday. I am surprised that she hasn't sent any messages by now."

"Truthfully? She's taken your lack of contact as a positive sign that things are progressing well and Finn is keeping you extremely busy. She's really happy for you."

Rowan blushed. "And what about Jake?"

"Not that he would openly admit it but he's missing you, although Harry did say that Jake is somewhat pleased he has swerved Saturday's movie night. He's hoping by the time you come home, you will have forgotten."

"Not a chance, I owe him a good musical."

Aliyah laughed. "I would give them a call soon. Secretly Jake is missing you and I am sure Christine will want to know how you and Finn are getting along."

"I will. Do you know if Jake is working tonight?"

"Harry didn't mention anything about watching the entertainment so I am guessing not."

"Entertainment?"

Aliyah sniggered. "A certain acquaintance of yours decided to pay Stan a visit with a couple of his not so intelligent friends. They've been providing an endless source of amusement to all, until Stan finally put them out of their misery and sent them home with a giant footprint on their backsides."

"When will Philip learn?"

"He doesn't catch on very quick for one who claims to have an IQ of 162. You would think he would stay away especially with his luck around bar stools."

"No? He did it again?"

"Harry said Philip's on his way to scoring a hat trick, whatever that means."

"It means three times in a row. How did he manage that?" Rowan asked.

"It wasn't me," said Charles.

Aliyah snorted. "I have my suspicions, but Harry is keeping quiet on the matter."

"I bet Tarwin is as well!" Charles roared with laughter.

"Now brother, as much of an ejit as Philip is, the fact that he has suffered a misfortune is no laughing matter," Aliyah admonished.

"Of course, my apologies," Charles replied sheepishly.

Rowan bit down on her trembling lip. "So, when does Adeybo take over?"

"Tarwin believes it will be tomorrow. I am quite sure he will be the one to put an end to Philip's antics. Teach him how to use that IQ of his to improve his manners and have more respect for furniture." Aliyah's voice quivered with amusement.

"For Philip's sake let's hope so."

Aliyah hugged her. "I've really enjoyed our conversation, Rowan, but my apologies, I must leave now. Christine is attending her first yoga class, and I've so wanted to try it."

"Mum is doing yoga?"

"Yes, your dad suggested it to her. She's really excited, as am I."

Rowan felt a pang of jealousy. "I'm glad he still visits her and she isn't alone. When you get chance will you tell him that I miss him and I love him?"

"Yes, and don't worry about Christine, she's doing fine." Aliyah brushed her lips against Rowan's cheek. "Goodbye for now, Rowan." She left the two of them alone.

"I must go too," Charles said. "I shall check in on you once you have returned from the Meridian."

Rowan sighed as he disconnected his energy. She glanced towards the tree, disappointed to note that Albion had also abandoned her.

A cold nip at the back of her neck signalled that perhaps it was time for her to leave too. Rising, she rubbed the ache in her back and buttocks, her stiffness easing as she headed back inside the cottage.

Bessie nodded an approval as she entered the kitchen. "Good timing, supper is ready."

Rowan surveyed the contents of the plate offered, and her mouth watered.

"I hope you like salmon, dear."

"I do."

"Finn, I'm sure you'll enjoy this too."

Already seated at the table and armed with cutlery, he nodded. "Thanks, it smells good."

The fish was cooked to perfection, and Rowan demolished it with ease. She was almost disappointed when the empty plate stared back at her. "I could just eat that all over again, if of course, I wasn't so full."

Finn groaned his appreciation and leaned back in his chair. "You sure can cook."

"I'm glad you enjoyed it. Would you do me a kind service, Finn, and wash the dishes for me? Mortimus is studying tonight. It's almost time for Rowan and me to leave for the Meridian."

"Are you sure I can't come with you both? I promise I won't interfere."

"I'm afraid not. Tonight, it must be Rowan. Do you want to get yourself ready, dear, while I help clear the table?"

"Will you be alright, Finn?"

"I'm not completely comfortable, but I know you're in good hands, and I cannot deny you if it means keeping you safe."

"Give me a couple of minutes, dear, and I will meet you on the porch."

Rowan nodded and left the two of them alone. She headed to the bedroom to quickly pass a brush through her hair and collect her jacket before making her way outside.

Bessie arrived a few moments later, clutching a satin bag. Although curious as to its contents, Rowan resisted asking the question, knowing it was doubtful that the older woman would answer in any event.

They walked in a comfortable silence, Bessie slightly ahead to guide Rowan around the potholes. When they arrived at the Meridian, Bessie paused at the opening in the hedging. "Are you alright, dear, you've barely said a word?"

"I'm fine."

"Are you nervous? There's no need to be as I will be with you the whole time."

Rowan shook her head. "It's not that, it's just, never mind, let's do this."

"If you're sure, dear?"

"I am."

Rowan could barely hear herself think over the constant whirr of energy as they approached its centre. It was as though the Meridian had been building itself up for this night.

"Now it's your turn," Bessie said.

"For what?"

"To remove your clothes."

"Seriously?"

"The moon is full. Our time is now. While you undress, I shall prepare the crystal grid."

Rowan reluctantly did as she was told. "Where do you want me?"

"At the centre."

The crystals pulsed with energy, lighting the shape of a pentagram. Strange patterns formed with smaller tumbled stones cast at each point.

"What do those mean?" Rowan asked. She stared at the runes that glowed from the ground and within the pentagram.

"They represent the elements from both yours and Finn's world. Now lie down, dear, and place your hands either side of you. Are you ready?"

Rowan nodded. Excitement and fear somersaulted inside her.

Bessie smiled and placed three tiny crystals across Rowan's forehead. "See you soon." There was a sudden whoosh of energy and Bessie was gone.

The humming grew louder and louder. Rowan's soul, free from its constraints, plunged into the dark void. A silence was followed by a burst of brilliant silver light. Shielding her vision, she studied the many constellations that gathered and moved around her until her gaze fixed onto one. Spellbound, she willed herself closer, eager to reach out and touch it. The other constellations blinked into darkness. Her father's voice spoke softly. "Welcome home, Guardian."

"Why is it you sound so much like my dad?"

"We took the voice of the one your heart yearns for the most."

"I don't understand."

"We believe it is easier for you this way, to listen and accept our teaching. To trust in what we ask of you."

"And what is it I am here to learn?"

"The Guardian must awaken."

"Guardian of what?"

"That is for you to discover."

"Why me?"

"You waste time asking irrelevant questions."

"Perhaps I would have fewer questions and more relevant ones if someone would care to explain this all to me. You're asking me to trust and yet I have no idea in what and who."

Bessie's voice broke through. "It's a fair point."

"You are not to interfere, Bessantia. We have allowed you only to observe."

"My apologies but our time is short."

"We are aware. Valoria's Veil is thinning, and neither world will survive if the Guardian does not awaken."

"Are you saying that my world is also at risk of harm?" Rowan asked.

"Yes, Guardian, and others like it."

"What must I do?"

"Are you ready to trust?"

"Yes."

"Then, we shall begin."

CHAPTER SIXTEEN

North York Moors, North East England

"Commander," Rivik growled, "we were not expecting you back so soon."

Kane completed a quick surveillance of the camp, instantly suspicious. "Am I interrupting something?"

"No. You seemed to be enjoying your time with the girl so much, we thought you may wish to spend another night."

Kane reached into his pocket and retrieved a book. "The girl has acquired what I need, I have no further use for her."

"Then what are your orders?"

"If you mean, do I want the girl killed, not now."

"Very well, but my brethren and I need to feed."

"Then go, Rivik. I am tired after last night's exertions and need to rest. When you return we shall make our preparations to leave. The Master will not allow any further delays."

The Fallen nodded. "Understood, Commander."

"When you return, do not wake me. When I am sufficiently rested, I will summon you."

"Yes, Commander."

"And make sure that Barrock knows under no circumstances is he or any of the others to disturb me."

Kane didn't wait for Rivik's response and strode to his tent. Dropping the book to the floor, he collapsed onto his bed, closed his eyes and drifted into sleep. He groaned as he was suddenly jolted free from his physical body and catapulted into the void. Kane sensed the creature following close behind him. Ignoring Morbae's call, he lingered purposefully in the darkness. "I know you're there."

It drew closer. "Yet, you are not afraid. Why is that?"

"I fear nothing."

"Bold words, but we both know it's a lie. You know what dwells here, Warlock. A fool you are not."

Kane smiled and traced his fingers across the scar. "Perhaps. Tell me, did you intend to mark or kill me?"

"I meant to kill you."

"And now?"

"Now, I cannot."

"Why? What is it that you have done, to me?"

Its laughter rang through the darkness. "Too late, Warlock, too late."

Kane lurched forward and landed with a sudden thud on the stone flags of the Great Hall. He stood quickly and slammed the dust from his clothing. "You had no right."

Morbae cast him a cold glare. "You will immediately obey us, apprentice, and come as soon as you are summoned."

"I am here now."

Morbae tutted. "Not good enough. She knows that you lingered in the void and why."

Kane faltered. "You're lying."

"I am many things but a liar is not one of them."

The chamber doors crashed open, Kane's retort dying on his tongue. Her voice ordered them both to silence. Morbae nodded and skulked quietly back to his chair, his eyes simmering with annoyance. Kane shifted uncomfortably underneath her intense scrutiny.

"When?" she demanded.

He feigned innocence. "When what? I don't know what you're asking?"

She stormed across the hall, her face a mask of fury as she seized Kane's head in her hands. Pushing her lips against his, she forced his mouth apart with her tongue, the kiss bruising as it deepened. Without any care for his sanity, she delved further into his mind and searched through his memories. Kane fought against the unwelcome desire that stirred in his groin. His fingers sought her arms and dug deep into her skin. She flinched with the pain he inflicted.

Kane wrenched himself free of her embrace. "That's enough," he spat out.

Morbae rose abruptly from his chair.

"No, leave this to me," she snapped.

Kane made no attempt to hide his smirk as the guardian slumped back.

"Don't think yourself clever. She can kill you where you stand," Morbae muttered.

He laughed. "She won't kill me."

"What makes you so sure?" she asked, her hand stroking his face. "You have no idea of what is to come."

"I know that I do not fear it."

"You should," she warned and turned her attention to Morbae. "My suspicions are confirmed, although I don't understand how this has been allowed to happen again."

Kane glanced to the guardian noting a flicker of recognition cross Morbae's face.

"You're sure, Mistress? There's no chance you could be mistaken. To happen once is rare, to happen twice... well..." Morbae shrugged.

"You said yourself, he lingered in the void and the creatures did not attack."

His irritation grew. "Perhaps you both would care to indulge me?"

Morbae ignored him. "If this is true, Mistress, you cannot know it will end the same."

She frowned and turned to Kane. "When did you come into contact with it?"

"The night you seared your sigil into my skin. It attacked after I left you."

Morbae laughed. "You know what this means, Mistress?"

Wrapping her arms around Kane, she pulled him close and brushed her lips briefly against his. "It means that this time is different; he belongs to me. The Nyrvallia will evolve."

He seethed inside. *I belong to no one, and you will tell me what you know.*

Oblivious to his rising anger, she turned to Morbae. "We must prepare."

"Yes, Mistress." The guardian clapped his hands gleefully. "I forgive your previous insolence, apprentice. You are quite the marvel."

"I have not said I forgive yours," Kane muttered, impervious to the compliment paid.

Morbae hopped from his seat. "Mistress, you are permitted one visit. Should I arrange this now?"

"Yes, but it must be at the time of my choosing. I shall need to study the charts."

"Of course, I will leave them in your chamber."

Kane swallowed his anger. "You still have told me nothing. Why did you summon me?"

She reached into her robe and passed him a potion. "Drink it."

"What is it?"

"It will ensure you survive the transformation of the Nyrvallia."

So, it is something I am to become? I must know more. He released the gold cap from the vial and sniffed the mixture. "There's blood in here."

She raised her brows. "Your sense of smell has developed. Indeed, there is. A few drops of my blood to ensure your obedience."

He glared. "Why is that you both insist on inflicting your poisons to ensure my allegiance. Is my oath not enough?"

"I have not inflicted but openly given you the potion. As for your oath as you stand here, yes, but when you become the Nyrvallia, a different matter."

Kane scowled. "What if I refuse to drink?"

"You claim to be loyal to me. Why would you refuse? Unless you have something to hide?"

Kane shook his head and tipped the contents into his mouth.

She moved towards the chamber doors. "Wonderful, well done, my apprentice. We shall speak again in a couple of days. Now I must consult the charts."

"Mistress, wait," Morbae croaked.

She spun, her eyes widening in horror at the sight before her. Kane's arms wrapped tightly around his stomach as he doubled over and continued heaving. The vomit was a black sticky pool that hissed as it spewed onto the cold tile floor.

"What is this?" she shrieked.

Kane rose slowly and shook his head. "I don't know."

"Morbae?"

The guardian moved to examine the vomit. "I've never seen the like of it before, Mistress. But I do not believe he has knowingly rejected your potion."

"The creature?" she asked, her voice shrill.

"Does not possess such ability."

"What do you feel?" she asked, her eyes narrowed as she appraised Kane.

"Nothing, the pain has gone."

She glanced down. "Lift your shirt, I must see."

Kane immediately obeyed, small bumps appearing over his skin as she traced her fingers across. "I only see my mark. The Lyboria wound has healed. It couldn't have possibly caused this. I do not understand."

"Neither do I," he replied.

"Leave me, I must think. Morbae, the charts." She stormed to the chamber doors and slammed them closed behind her.

Kane opened his mouth to address the guardian, but the words didn't come out. His consciousness catapulted back through the void.

Kane sprang to his feet, cursing the one who had disturbed him.

"My apologies, Commander, but the fire is prepared. The Master draws close."

"You are?" he spat out.

"Dorgu," the Fallen replied hesitantly.

Kane hissed an incantation and lifted the creature into the air. Dorgu wailed loudly. "Please, Commander, forgive me, I was only asked to deliver the message."

"More fool you," Kane snapped, and with a click of his fingers tore Dorgu apart.

Storming into the clearing, he glared at the others gathered around. "I said that I was not to be disturbed."

"The Master is here, Commander, and as you are aware, he waits for no one," Barrock hissed.

Kane stared into the flames.

The Master leaned back in his seat, hands clasped and face contorted in anger. "You have something more important than me?"

Fighting to regain his composure, Kane shook his head.

Rivik stepped forward and addressed the fire. "Our apologies, Master, the Commander was studying an important text that may lead to the girl's whereabouts."

Much to Kane's relief, the Master's interest had piqued, his anger forgotten. "What is this text?"

"A book that contains maps of this world. I was in the middle of preparing it for a location spell," Kane said.

"I had not known you were so well versed."

"My mother's powers may have been taken from her, but her knowledge of the craft wasn't. I discovered some of her spells before she died."

The Master studied Kane for a few moments. "And how did you come by this book?"

"I had a human girl acquire it for me. She serves me well."

"Be careful, consorting with these creatures."

"I have no intention of impregnating any of them."

The Master rose from his chair and stepped free from the flames. The Fallen retreated as he strode purposefully towards Kane. "Your shirt," he ordered.

Kane obeyed for the second time that night.

"You heal quickly. There will be no further delay."

"The skin has healed, but it still causes me some discomfort. I have not been well," Kane said.

The Master nodded. "Your lesson learned. Do not disappoint me again."

"I will not fail you," Kane said.

"Good. However, I shall require proof of your loyalty."

"What is it you ask of me?"

"Bleed for me."

Kane immediately withdrew his dagger and slit his arm. Ignoring the blood gushing from the wound, he raised his eyes to the Master. "My blood."

The Master seized hold of his arm and drew a rune; the gash healed immediately. "I'm glad we have an understanding."

Kane gestured towards a log. "May I?"

The Master nodded and laughing, walked back into the fire.

Kane glared a warning across to the Fallen. They took note of his silent threat and remained quiet, none daring to move except for Rivik, who edged closer to the fire and watched the flames intently.

"What news have you on the scorpion's tail?" Kane asked.

"Your mother was indeed gifted."

"She was right? He possesses the ability of the Shade?"

"Yes, most pleasing."

Kane could barely contain his excitement at the prospect. His mother, vindicated at last! *You scoffed at such 'a ridiculous notion', Mercadia. You refused to accept my mother into your tutelage and instead stole her power and cast her out of Astyllis. The Council of Elders swallowed your lies and it ruined my mother. She died with everyone including her son believing her to be crazy. But you are the fool! These tiny red scorpions my mother discovered hold magic, absorbed from deep beneath Elyssia's sands. The ritual she created to transfer the magic from the scorpion's stinger and rebirth a Shade worked! No longer the crazy ramblings of my mother's fever as you will soon come to discover.*

Kane's hands gripped tightly to the wood to steady his trembling limbs. He searched the Master's face. "The Council do not suspect? They've sensed nothing?"

"Far too busy protecting the Selensia and saving their precious villages."

A momentous day, for I have succeeded where my mother failed! The Chosen One arisen from the grave and sooner than my mother predicted.

Could that be due to the additional magic that flowed through his veins? Did he carry it forward after his death? I must study him!

Rivik growled and rose to his feet as something moved quickly from behind the Master. Kane shifted closer. Had it been there all this time? Can it hear my call?

The Master's attention turned towards the dark shape as it leant forward to whisper something in his ear. Kane strained to hear its words above the crackling wood.

The Master nodded and threw a final glance towards him. With a sharp clap of his hands, he extinguished the flames and disappeared.

Kane stared at the glowing embers, his previous elation smothered by the churn of resentment at how the Master had so easily dismissed him.

"What was that?" Rivik growled.

"I believe that was the Chosen One," Kane said.

"You need to be careful of it, Commander."

"Of him, and yes, I will consider your warning. I did not hear its words, did you?"

"No, Commander. It whispered in a foreign tongue," Rivik replied.

They fell silent as Barrock walked towards them. "We are fortunate that the Master accepted your lie. I have completed a count, and our numbers remain intact, apart from Dorgu."

Kane sighed. "Dorgu was a necessary sacrifice, Barrock. Had I not, the Master would have seen the fullness of my anger. That would not have ended well for the rest of your brethren."

"Forgive me for saying this, Commander, but you cannot blame us for his early arrival," Barrock said.

"Then who lit the fire?"

Rivik released a growl. Barrock glared but noted the warning and swiftly retreated, the other Fallen following him into the trees.

"Explain, Rivik," Kane demanded.

"You witnessed how easily the Master extinguished the flames, much in the same way that he created them. We were as surprised as you. Barrock sent Dorgu to find you as soon as he appeared."

Kane considered for a moment. "You're sure?"

"My brethren do not willingly choose to summon or be alone in the Master's presence. Not even Barrock, he values his existence too much."

Kane nodded. "Indeed, his powers are growing. We cannot afford to be caught off guard again, Rivik."

"The Chosen one crawled from the ground. It is he who has something to do with the sudden change of power, I'm sure. You need to be wary, of both of them."

"Do not concern yourself, Rivik," Kane said.

"Very well. What are your orders?"

"I will study the text and complete the location spell. Do not allow any other interruptions. When I am ready, I will summon you and Barrock."

"Yes, Commander."

Rivik turned and sprinted into the trees. Alone, Kane released a deep breath and gathered his thoughts. He could not deny that the Master's parting look had unnerved him, almost as though he had detected the undercurrent of deceit that flowed through Kane's veins.

How long had the Chosen one been there, and what message did he whisper in the Master's ears? Will he betray me to the Master? Was sabotaging the blood of the scorpion, not enough? He trusted that when the time came, his mother was right.

Stifling a yawn, Kane strode to his tent, eager for a glass of wine to take away the unpleasant taste in his mouth. There had been no conscious thought or plan to expel the potion he had consumed and nothing to explain his violent reaction to it. *Perhaps the creature? Does it even possess such magic? And why? What was in it? Does she lie to me?* Glancing down to the scar on his hand, he considered the night of the attack. *Can it be the creature is warning me? Are we linked?*

Kane's head ached as he entered the tent. Ignoring the book that was laid next to his bed, he headed for the table, and whispered a quick intonation. A bottle uncorked accompanied by a large glass appeared. He studied the label, not a vintage that he was familiar with but still it would do. Kane filled the glass to its brim and downed the contents in seconds.

Collecting the book the girl had given him and the grimoire hidden beneath the bottom of this mattress, Kane sat on the floor and retrieved the vial from his pocket. He carefully measured a few drops onto the book's cover. Placing the book in front of him, Kane lifted the grimoire and flicked through the pages until he found the spell required. With the Tracker firmly fixed in his thoughts, Kane spoke the words aloud and waited. The blood seeped slowly into the cover and disappeared. A sudden gust of wind blew through the tent. The breeze turning through the pages of the book until it found the one it sought. The air fell silent.

He smiled, as the vibrant red liquid trickled from the top of the page and stained a path. It slowly travelled across the paper until it had reached its destination. Satisfied, Kane closed the cover and placed the vial into his jacket pocket, the grimoire hidden safely in his trunk.

Returning to the table, Kane poured himself another glass of wine, and studied the location to which the blood had travelled. When the village and road names had been successfully imprinted to his mind, he closed the book and placed it with the vial. Moving to the doorway, Kane pulled the fabric back and called for Rivik to join him.

Rivik did not keep him waiting long, Barrock as he had requested was also in tow.

"May we enter, Commander?" Rivik asked.

"Yes."

The two Fallen moved quickly inside, Barrock sniffing the air. "I smell blood."

"Magic performed to locate the Tracker and the girl," Kane said.

"What are your orders, Commander?" Barrock asked.

"We leave camp tomorrow as soon as the light fades. I want you to ensure the others are prepared. It would be prudent for you to regenerate early ahead of the journey. We shall be travelling quite some distance, North, I believe."

Barrock nodded and retreated from the tent.

Rivik's cold amber eyes studied him closely. "And what is it you need from me?"

Kane sighed and seated himself on the mattress. "The truth, Rivik."

"I do not understand, Commander."

"What do you know of the Nyrvallia?"

"I know very little."

"Don't lie to me, your body has already betrayed you. I know that you sensed something."

Rivik growled. "You asked for me to say nothing, Commander. I would suggest that we both continue to follow that advice."

"Why? What is it that you fear?"

"It is not for my benefit, Commander but for yours. I fear nothing."

"Neither do I," Kane snapped.

"Then your transition will be so much easier. Now, if there is nothing further you need of me, I shall join the others and regenerate."

Kane glared. "You will tell me what I want to know."

"Soon," Rivik promised and he strode out of the tent.

Simmering, Kane considered whether to follow Rivik and punish him in front of the others for such insolence. Yet there was something in the Fallen's words that made him uneasy. What that was he could not put his finger on.

Instead Kane downed the last of the wine and undressed. It had been a long and arduous day. He climbed beneath the covers and recited a grounding spell, having no desire to be summoned again to her chamber.

Firmly pushing all thoughts of her, the creature, his reaction to the potion and Rivik's avoidance to divulge what he knew of the Nyrvallia from his mind, Kane closed his eyes. The turbulence that raged slowly began to calm. Only when Kane sensed a heavy weight anchor itself to his limbs did he give in to sleep.

CHAPTER SEVENTEEN

Achavanich, Scottish Highlands

Finn raised his head groggily from the pillow and groaned loudly. The mantra that had hummed persistently in his ears subsided as he finally succumbed to her will. With a grunt, he pushed back the covers and swung his legs out of bed.

"You know, I could have summoned the dead much quicker," Mercadia complained.

Ignoring her sarcasm, Finn reached for his clothing and dressed. He sensed her irritation rising the longer he held his silence and hid a smile. Perhaps it was childish of him but better that than to engage in a futile exchange of insults.

"Do you know what the hour is?" she demanded.

Finn heaved a sigh; in all truth, he didn't care what the hour was. Shifting his eyes to the window, he estimated it, by the sun's position, to be late afternoon. Perhaps it was a little longer than he had initially intended to sleep, but not too surprising given that he had been restless and awake all night waiting for Rowan and Bessie to return.

"When I ask you a question, I do expect a response. The matter is serious."

"I am fully aware of that fact, Mercadia." Finn ran a hand through his hair. "It may have slightly escaped your attention that sleep is a necessity, especially if I am to complete the quest that you sent me on." He could have kicked himself for biting back at her.

"Watch your tone, Finn. I am an Elder, which I'm sure hasn't escaped your attention either. As for your quest, it is well past midday, and I see nothing other than you laid in your bed."

Before he could respond, a less intrusive connection gently pressed for his attention. With a shrug of his shoulders, Finn allowed the entry and waited for Bessie to speak.

"Good afternoon, Mercadia. I trust you are well?"

"This discussion was private, Bessantia."

"Acknowledged, but you have invaded my home and woken my guest."

"With good reason. I see nothing of his or your progress."

Bessie's voice remained steady. "Not entirely true, and we did agree that you would leave this to me."

"We agreed that you would prepare the girl and send her to our world without delay."

"Which is what I am doing. However, it would be remiss of me not to prepare Finn too, especially given his abilities. You shared nothing of his background."

"In truth, I was not aware of how deep his power ran, nor of its source. Admittedly I had sensed there was something. It briefly revealed itself within the Lemure."

"Yet you kept this information to yourself," Bessie said.

Mercadia sighed. "My power was drained. I could not be sure at the time, that what I had glimpsed truly existed."

Finn rubbed the ache in his forehead. "Would either of you care to enlighten me?"

Mercadia changed the subject. "Has there been any progress made on the location of the amulet?"

"Not as yet. There have been other matters to attend to."

"We do not have the luxury of time, Bessantia. Why has this not begun?"

"You know very well that certain events must be done in the correct order, and according to the prophecy. There is little chance of Rowan finding the amulet unless she is fully prepared."

Mercadia was unable to hide the desperation in her voice. "You do understand that our situation is dire? The Master's forces are relentless. Elios is exhausted. I must take over the protection of the Selensia to allow him to regenerate, or we risk losing him. I need to ensure that all is in hand. The girl cannot travel to our world unless she possesses the amulet."

"I do understand, but Rowan must be prepared for what is to come. You cannot throw her straight into a war, or you will repeat the mistakes of the past."

"We may not have a choice." The pressure suddenly eased as Mercadia abandoned her connection.

Bessie sighed. "I'm sorry to have to admit this, but she is right. We don't have much time."

Finn nodded and glanced to the window. Although there was no sense of Kane and the Fallen close by, he knew it would not take long.

Bessie acknowledged his thoughts. "By my calculations, we may have a day or two before you must leave. I suggest what time remains we spend it within the Meridian. I'll go wake Rowan and meet you downstairs."

"Are you going to explain what it is that you and Mercadia know?"

"In time." She released her connection before he could respond.

Finn cursed under his breath and strode to the bathroom. His thoughts steered to the recent exchange between the two women, and the calm but firm way Bessie had dealt with Mercadia. It was clear they knew each other well. *But from when? And what of this power I have inherited? What did Mercadia see within the Lemure?*

Determined to find out, Finn narrowly avoided colliding into Rowan, standing on the other side of the door.

"You really should lock it behind you. I almost walked in," she said.

Although there was humour in her eyes, her face was pale and strained. Pushing all thoughts of Bessie and Mercadia's conversation to the back of his mind, Finn stroked a thumb lightly across her cheek. "Sorry, I wasn't thinking." He studied her face. "You look exhausted. Did you not sleep at all?"

Rowan shook her head. "It was just a bad dream. Nothing for you to worry about."

Finn wasn't convinced, her tone and expression enough to cause him concern. "Do you want to talk about it?"

"I'd rather just forget about it." She hopped from side to side and signalled towards the bathroom door. "Do you mind if I go? I'm desperate."

He hid his hurt and stepped aside. "Of course, sorry."

Rowan gave him a brief smile and sprang past him. The door closed firmly behind her, the lock sliding into place. Reluctantly Finn made his way downstairs and to the kitchen, unable to ignore the unsteady swirl of his gut.

Bessie caught sight of his expression and ushered him swiftly to the table. "What is it?"

"It's Rowan. She didn't sleep well. She told me it was a bad dream and nothing for me to worry about."

"But your instincts tell you otherwise?" Bessie asked.

"The pain on her face tells me otherwise." Finn's hands repeatedly clenched at his side. "I don't know, there's something about it that feels wrong."

Bessie pressed a finger briefly to her lips. "We'll discuss this later. Eat something, you'll need your energy."

Finn nodded and reached for the platter of sandwiches she had made, stacking his plate high. Rowan entered the room, looking suspiciously brighter than he had seen her moments earlier. He sensed she was hiding her emotions as she took a seat next to him and helped herself to the large jug of fruit juice.

She poured them two glasses and set one down in front of him. "So, what's the plan?"

Finn caught the flicker of concern in the older woman's eyes. "We'll be spending the rest of the day together at the Meridian."

Rowan reached for a sandwich. "Are we allowed? I thought the Meridian required us to be integrated separately?"

"Yes, that's true, but unfortunately we are running out of time, and there is the small matter of your amulet."

"The amulet…? Is this the one you mentioned before? The one I need to travel?"

"Yes, my dear. It is important that… what on earth is going on?"

All three stared as Biscuit ran into the kitchen, barking repeatedly.

Finn sensed the older woman bristle. "She's done what? And where is she now?"

The little dog sat back on his haunches and growled.

"Well, that course of action won't be necessary, although I do understand your sentiments. You leave this to me."

Bessie hurried from the kitchen.

Rowan shook her head. "I wonder what that was all about? Are you okay, Biscuit?"

He wagged his tail in response.

"Are you hungry?" Rowan tossed him a sandwich.

Finn studied the little dog. "I'm not quite sure he eats that."

The sandwich was obliterated in seconds. Biscuit licked his lips noisily.

"Or perhaps he does," Finn corrected.

Rowan smiled and dropped another to the floor. Biscuit nuzzled her hand. "I hope she's okay."

"Who? Bessie?"

"Yes, whatever it was she didn't look happy."

"I'm sure she'll sort it. She doesn't strike me as the sort of woman to be messed with," Finn said.

"She's amazing, and…" Rowan hesitated for a moment.

"Go on?"

"Well… it's just that I know she's from your world. She doesn't belong here."

"Did she tell you that?"

"No, Charles did."

Finn felt a stir of jealousy. "Oh? And what else did Charles say?"

Rowan bit her lip and fidgeted in her seat. "Actually, it was very little. He came to make sure I was alright, after the dream."

"And did you tell Charles about the dream?"

She looked confused. "Yes, why wouldn't I?"

"I thought it would be me that you would talk to."

Rowan met his gaze. "Are you mad at me?"

"No," he said a little too quickly.

"Why don't you just admit it?"

"Admit what? I'm not mad with you," and he wasn't really although he could not say the same for Charles.

"Why don't I believe you?" she asked.

Finn tilted her face to his. "I'm disappointed that you didn't come to me first, not angry."

Rowan shook her head. "I'm sorry, Finn. I don't want to hurt you but you have to know that Charles is my guide. He has always helped me to make sense of things since I was a child and so you cannot just expect me not to automatically reach out to him first."

Finn released a sigh. "All I need for you to understand is that I am here now to protect you. I have to know when something is wrong."

She pressed a kiss against his cheek. "I do understand that. Please don't feel that I am deliberately shutting you out."

Finn nodded, although in truth that was exactly how he felt.

Bessie returned to the kitchen and paused in the doorway, her thoughts immediately connected to his own. "Is something wrong?" she asked silently.

"No," he responded.

"Well, do you want to tell your face that? It doesn't seem to agree with you." Bessie released the connection and approached the table.

"Is everything alright?" Rowan asked.

"Yes, dear, it's just old Lady McGinty being a nuisance as usual." She turned towards Biscuit. "It's all taken care of. There will be no more of her nonsense, at least not for today."

"Whose old Lady McGinty?" Rowan asked.

"My own personal stalker from the village," Bessie replied.

Finn stood abruptly. "Can we go now? I'm ready."

Bessie arched a brow. "I see, and you, my dear?"

Rowan pushed her chair back and gave him a pointed look. "We both are."

"Excellent, then let's go. Biscuit, you remain here, please. Let Mortimus know we'll be back for supper."

"Before we go, you mentioned the amulet?"

"Your talisman, dear."

"What does it do?" Rowan asked.

"I do not know the full extent of its power for it has never belonged to me," Bessie said.

"Then how is it you know of the amulet?" Finn asked.

"The Council of Elders studied the ancient texts relating to the prophecy. There is an image of the amulet. They believe it to be a conduit that will enable Rowan to travel to our world."

"Do you know where it is?" Rowan asked.

"No, dear. The amulet has always belonged to you therefore it is only you that can find it."

"I've no idea where to begin."

"Let's talk about this tonight. Are you both ready?" Bessie said.

Finn offered no resistance as Rowan dragged him outside into the sunshine. Releasing her hand from his grip, she fell in step beside him, neither of them speaking as they followed Bessie towards the Meridian. Occasionally Finn would catch her eye and note the amused smile that tugged at her lips.

Finally he broke the silence. "I'm sorry. I'm an idiot."

She gave him a gentle nudge in the ribs. "Yes, you are, but if it helps any, you're my idiot."

He shot her a wounded look. "Gee thanks."

"What? You were hoping I would disagree with you?"

"Yes, although I admit I did deserve it."

Bessie chuckled ahead of them. "Now that's sorted, could you move a little quicker, we don't have much time."

The Meridian's energy pulsed in the distance, as they turned off the main road and into the field. Although Finn had witnessed it before, he could not help but gape at how easily the older woman leapt over the gate.

Bessie tossed her long silver hair over her shoulder. "I still got it." Laughing, she continued towards the hedging.

Finn wiped the beads of perspiration from his face. "I wish I knew how she did that so effortlessly."

"I only hope to have half her energy when I am her age," Rowan said.

Climbing onto the top bar, Finn jumped over and offered his arms out to her. Rowan brushed her lips against his before he lowered her gently to the ground. "Thank you."

He winked. "Glad to be of service."

"Feeling better?" she teased.

Finn kissed her softly. "What do you think?" he asked.

Rowan's voice trembled. "I think we should go before we lose Bessie."

"I suppose we should."

Neither moved. The energy shifted and weaved around them. "You feel that?"

"Yes," she whispered.

Their mouths met again, arms locked tightly around each other. The kiss deepened and suddenly spiralled out of control. Somewhere at the back of Finn's mind a warning signalled. With great difficulty, he mustered the strength to pull away from her.

"What is it about this place?" he panted.

Rowan's eyes were dazed and heavy with desire. 'I don't know what came over me. I can't believe I almost wanted to... and here."

Finn took hold of her hand. "We need to go."

She nodded and followed him in silence to the Meridian's entrance.

Bessie raised a brow as the two of them approached.

Finn cleared his throat. "I have no explanation."

The heat in Rowan's cheeks flushed deeper. "Neither have I," she managed.

Before the older woman could respond, Rowan dived between the parted branches. Bessie immediately followed. Stealing a few moments for himself, Finn took a steadying breath in and out, willing his heart to resume its regular rhythm.

"Enter Warrior. We must begin."

The Meridian's energy greeted him warmly as he complied, the entrance sealing quietly behind him. A sudden sense of panic swept through him as he joined Bessie. She was stood alone.

"Where's Rowan?" he demanded.

Her finger pointed towards the centre of the Meridian. Finn's eyes widened at the vision in front of him. Stood in a whirlpool of silver and purple rays was Rowan, her arms outstretched and head tilted towards the sky.

"What is that?" he murmured.

"All you need to know is that she is perfectly safe," Bessie whispered.

Finn's stomach clenched. Rowan had levitated into the air, light flying free from her hands and feet.

"Are you sure? She's at least ten feet in the air."

The older woman grinned. "Quite sure. Now it's your turn."

Finn cleared his throat. "Why don't I like the sound of that?"

Bessie didn't reply, instead she signalled for him to follow her. They strode towards the far edge of the Meridian and away from where Rowan was floating, oblivious and in a trance-like state.

"Now what?" he asked, glancing around nervously.

The ground trembled beneath Finn's feet, branches breaking through the surface, spiralling together and spinning upwards. They formed into the shape of a tree.

Bessie stepped forward and caressed the trunk with her hand. "Hello, old friend."

Finn's eyes widened, the tree bursting into a lavish bloom of white and silver. His nostrils filled with the divine scent of its blossoms. Their fragrance soothed his inner turbulence and left him with a profound sense of peace and calm.

"Enwen only reveals herself to those who are deserving," Bessie explained.

Finn reached his hand upward and gently touched a petal. A soft chime sounded from its centre as the bloom tipped towards him and revealed a pearlescent orb.

"You mustn't remove the orb without Enwen's consent."

He gently released the petal and stepped away from the tree. "Of course. But why is she here?"

"The Meridian summoned her," Bessie said.

"For what purpose?"

She gestured towards the tree. "I cannot answer that question. Only Enwen can."

An opening had appeared in the centre of the trunk. The older woman nodded encouragingly, and he stepped forward. Tentatively he placed an arm inside.

"You must go in."

Finn glanced towards Rowan.

Bessie placed a hand on his shoulder. "I'll keep an eye on her. Now go and find the answer you seek."

Taking a deep breath, Finn stepped into the darkness.

"I have waited a long time for you." Enwen's voice spoke in soft lyrical tones.

"Forgive me for asking, but I'm not sure why?"

There was a gentle pressure at the centre of his forehead.

"Now, you shall see," she whispered.

A blinding white light and everything changed instantly around him. When Finn's vision returned, he found himself standing in the chamber of a great hall. There were seven men gathered around a large oak table.

"Can they see me?"

"No, this is but a memory of the past," Enwen replied.

Finn moved closer. His heart thumped wildly, as he caught sight of the giant golden rune carved in the centre. The very same rune that Rowan had shown him a few days ago. Fascinated, he observed as each man stood, retrieved a sword from their belt and swore an oath.

"By the grace of Enwen, I do hereby swear my allegiance to Morvantia. Guardian of the Light and Protector of the Realm. Blade to Blade I stand by my brothers."

The swords were lowered in silence, a pearlescent orb gleaming from each hilt. When the last man had taken their seat, all seven turned in the direction of Finn. A chill ran down Finn's spine and passed through his core, the coldness releasing when another man appeared, his back kept toward Finn as he passed him and quickly joined the others. The oath was repeated, his blade placed to the direction of the rune. Finn's legs almost crumpled beneath him as his father raised his head and clasped his hands.

"It is done, my brothers."

"Regretful that this must fall on your shoulders, Kyle."

His father's eyes filled with sorrow. "We knew this day would come."

The one who had spoken hung his head low.

Finn sensed the depth of his pain and his heart ached in response.

"You cannot blame yourself, Frieyll. The child died in Hannah's womb."

Frieyll turned to the man seated to his left. "But I failed to protect them, Calyd."

His father shook his head. "The failure was mine. I had not anticipated such magic existed. It is only just that I give my life for the one taken."

"Morvantia's lack of blessing suggests a failure by us all. It is not right for you to carry this alone, Kyle," Calyd insisted.

"Have faith, brothers. All is not lost. Morvantia has granted Enwen's protection of my unborn child and agreed to the exchange. What is mine shall soon be his."

"When, Kyle?" another spoke.

His father sighed. "I have forty seasons to prepare him, Saadu."

"But he is so young?" Saadu argued.

Tears slowly slid down Finn's cheeks as he waited for his father to respond.

"I have no choice, Saadu, nor do any of us in this."

"I sense there is something else. What is it, brother?" Frieyll asked.

The burden was evident in his father's face. "You should know that when I fall, I will be the last."

"Then, we must prepare. Do all we can to prevent this evil

from taking grip. Ensure that this doesn't come to pass," Calyd shouted.

The other men nodded.

His father's voice was solemn. "I will fight by my brothers' side until my very last breath. But I fear this will come to pass. Let us hope that we have done enough to secure the new order." He turned to Frieyll. "How is Hannah?"

"The night terrors grow each day. I fear that she is losing her mind."

"Myrialle may have a salve to ease the pain. She'll prepare it tonight after Aaron is asleep. Come by in the morning."

"I am grateful to you both, Kyle."

Finn did not hear his father's reply. All eight men had disappeared. The great hall dissolved into particles of silver dust.

"You understand?" Enwen asked.

"That I let him down? I spent so much time in the forest with my friends and not with him," Finn replied angrily.

"No, you were where you were meant to be and under my protection."

"But he said he needed to prepare me. I never gave him the chance to do that."

"Search your memories, find the truth," Enwen replied.

Finn closed his eyes and scoured the furthest recesses of his mind. The images swirled in and out of focus until one remained.

Kyle crouched beside Finn as a boy and pointed towards the stag that observed them from the trees ahead. He whispered encouragement in his ear and the boy nodded.

Finn smiled as the younger version of himself placed his hands firmly onto the ground and reached forward with his senses. Even now, Finn could feel the strength of the stag's heartbeat that day as it thumped a wild rhythm in his chest, his thoughts connecting and power pulsating through his core. The stag bowed its head, before it turned and sprinted off into the undergrowth.

Kyle rose and reached for the young Finn's hand. "Follow him."

Finn recalled the sudden pull of energy as he released his

awareness, allowing his senses to take him further and deeper into the forest. It was as though he were watching the world through the stag's eyes. Their hearts beating together as one. Speed and strength coursed through Finn as they ran in and out amongst the trees. The stag reaching the summit of the forest looking down at his kingdom with pride.

Kyle's voice broke the vision. "How do you feel, son?"

"Free," Finn had replied.

The memory faded, and with it, the weight of guilt. "I had forgotten," Finn said.

"Your father had many gifts that he wished to share with his children. But you were destined for another path, the moment Morvantia bestowed her blessing. You are her child now. You are ours."

"I am not sure I am deserving of my father's sacrifice."

"The fact that you question this speaks otherwise. Morvantia does not share her life force with those who are not pure of heart," Enwen confirmed.

"But I have done things I am not proud of."

"You have done what is necessary."

Finn sank to the ground. "He stopped coming into the forest with me and spent most of his time training Aaron. Although he offered for me to stay, I refused."

"Your father accepted that you were ours. He set you on your path and when you were ready, released you to us. Kyle knew you would be safe but he needed to ensure the protection of your brother for what was to come."

"And what of my mother, and her protection?"

Finn sensed Enwen smile. "What do you know about your mother's childhood?"

"Very little." He considered for a moment. "But I guess I never really asked."

"Do you know of her friendship with the Fae?"

"Not really, I know that she holds a connection. She taught me how to communicate with them when I was a boy."

"Their friendship had begun long before your father

met her. Myrialle had leapt into the waters of Tahlia to save a young Fae trapped amongst the Gylliac reeds. In doing so she almost drowned herself. Touched by the strength of her heart, I gave her a helping hand, and your mother and Lilly survived."

Finn's eyes widened. "Lilly? As in the Queen Lilly?"

"Yes."

"What was she doing in the Tahlia?"

"Lured into the waters by one who claimed to love her. But Bryndell never loved anyone, other than himself of course," Enwen said.

"What happened to Bryndell? His name is not spoken of in the Fae realm."

"His brother Tymoria banished him as soon as he'd discovered what he had done."

"Tymoria? The Queen's Guard."

"And lover, at least he was up until a few nights ago. Tymoria has disappeared."

"Could Bryndell be behind this?"

"A possibility. He was banished to the Winter Marshes. No one knows if he survived."

"Does my mother know about Tymoria?"

"Myrialle and Lilly have not spoken for some time." Enwen sighed. "Such a shame, theirs was a beautiful friendship. I had so looked forward to their visits to the forest."

"It all explains where my mother's knowledge of healing comes from. My father always joked that the Fae had secretly birthed her."

"Some, but not all. Morvantia had blessed you while you grew in your mother's womb. It was inevitable that her life force would pass onto Myrialle, enhancing her knowledge and gifts beyond anything that the Fae could teach."

Finn shook his head. "I knew none of this."

"Which is why the Meridian summoned me. I am to undo the damage caused by the Margorian Worm and heal the wounds of the past. For me to achieve this, you must understand what took place and why it had to be so. You must understand who you are and why the Elders chose you."

"Thank you, Enwen."

"You are welcome. Now go, give my blessings to Bessantia."

"I will."

Stepping free, Finn was surprised to find moonlight bathing the Meridian. The ground vibrated beneath him, Enwen's branches unfolding and spiralling back beneath the earth once more. Finn hurried towards the centre of the Meridian.

Rowan jumped up from where she sat. She ran towards him and wrapped her arms around his neck, hugging him tightly. "I was starting to worry."

Finn released himself from her hold. "What about you? Levitating at least ten feet in the air. I think I had more cause to worry than you."

Her smile quickly turned into a yawn. She tried to smother it but failed. "Sorry, I'm exhausted."

"It won't have helped you not getting much sleep last night."

"After today, I'm hoping I sleep much better. It's been such an incredible afternoon."

Bessie approached them. "Are you alright?"

"I'm fine. Enwen sends her blessings to you."

"She never forgets," Bessie murmured and lowered her gaze.

"Never forgets what?" Rowan asked.

The older woman shook her head. "Perhaps another time, dear. Shall we go? Mortimus will have supper ready. Then it is straight to bed. Finn is right. You do look exhausted."

"I could do with a long sleep," Rowan admitted.

Finn took hold of her hand and squeezed it gently. "Let's eat and then get you into bed."

Silence fell as they crossed the Meridian, and made their way back towards the small cottage. Finn couldn't recall much of the journey, a vague awareness of lifting Rowan down from the gate, but that was all. His thoughts were consumed by Enwen's visions. *What had happened to the other men in the order? Was my father murdered, or did he sacrifice himself for me? And what of the news shared. Who had captured Tymoria? Had it been Bryndell's revenge or another of the Master's attempts to weaken the Council's position? Why do Queen Lilly and my mother no longer spend time together?*

The past continued to haunt him through supper, his questions circling. Finn sought another distraction. "Can you tell us about the amulet now?"

Bessie nodded and dabbed at her mouth with her napkin. "Yes, but there isn't much I can say."

"You said that the Council of Elders had seen an image of my amulet?" Rowan asked.

"The drawing is faded and there is only a brief reference in the ancient texts to the amulet. From what Mercadia tells me it is an oval shaped pendant hanging from a silver chain, given the nature of its abilities. The jewel is an emerald discovered in the dwarf mines during the war of the ancients. It was last known to be in the possession of a mage named Aurora. There are no references in the texts after that."

"I don't understand how the amulet could be mine," Rowan said.

Bessie smiled. "I am sure your friend can help you there."

"My friend?"

The older woman nodded. "To find the amulet, you need to take a step backwards. Your friend will know how."

"What do you mean, Bessie?" Finn asked.

"She means that she knows about Charles and that I am to regress," Rowan said.

Bessie stood from the table. "I shall leave you and Charles to explain this to Finn. I'm off to bed now. Mortimus will straighten the kitchen, so leave your dishes. I suggest you get your rest too. Tomorrow is another big day for you both."

Rowan's face flushed. "Good night, Bessie."

As soon as they were alone, Finn turned to her. "I didn't tell her about Charles, I promise. It wasn't my secret to tell."

"Don't worry, I believe you. I have never discussed Charles with Bessie either, and he only ever visited me when I was alone. Although it doesn't surprise me that she would sense his energy."

Finn sighed. "What does she mean about showing you how to regress. What is that?"

"She's referring to past life regression. It's a form of hypnosis which takes a person back through time to a previous incarnation and allows them to access memories or experiences," Rowan explained.

"Have you ever done it before?"

"No, although I have always been curious about it."

"I take it from Bessie's parting comment that Charles is here with us too," Finn said.

Rowan smiled. "No, he's just left. Aliyah needs to speak with him. But he will be back as he wants to do the regression tonight once I am asleep. It will be easier to guide me through then."

"Whose Aliyah?"

"She's my mum's spirit guide."

"Right, do all humans have spirit guides?"

"Yes, they do, Harry is Jake's guide. But I don't really talk to him, and it is only recently that Aliyah has connected with me."

"I see, and is this regression thing safe?"

"There could be a risk I unlock a memory that isn't good. It depends how far back in time we have to go and what previous incarnations I have held. Don't worry, Charles has promised he will keep me safe, and at the first sign of trouble he will waken me."

Finn frowned. "He'd better. Is there anything I can do at all?"

"No, it's something I must do alone. But thank you for offering."

Finn rose. "It would seem today is one for revelations."

Rowan released a loud yawn. "Sorry, I hadn't realised how late it was. Perhaps today is what the Meridian intended."

Finn reached for her hand and lifted her to her feet. "Come on, let's get you into bed."

She giggled as he scooped her into his arms and gently carried her upstairs and into her room. The covers were already turned down as he placed her on the bed and removed her shoes.

"I could get used to this," she whispered.

He pressed a brief kiss against her forehead and pulled the duvet around her shoulders.

"If you need me?"

She smiled. "I'll shout for you. Goodnight, Finn."

He closed the door softly behind him and headed downstairs to the kitchen. Bessie glanced up from an armchair that had appeared next to the fire. "I thought you were going to bed too. Is something wrong?"

Finn sighed and ran a hand through his hair. "I don't think I can sleep just yet. I've too many questions spinning around in my head."

She was silent for a moment, her thoughts connecting to his. "Your mind does appear to be somewhat overwhelmed."

"Do you have anything that can help? Something that doesn't involve me taking a bath? Not that I am against bathing," he added quickly. "I wouldn't normally ask but it's been a difficult day."

"I imagine seeing your father again has been quite painful for you." Bessie rose from her chair and patted his hand gently. "I'll prepare something."

Finn nodded and shifted his gaze to the fire whilst waiting for her to return. Mesmerised by the flicker of the flames, and the sound of crackling wood, his thoughts drifted to the memories of his youth, and the nights he had spent camping in the Spring Stones with Indigo and the soothing melody of his pan pipes. *What had become of his elven friend since leaving Valoria?* Mercadia had made no mention of his arrival into Astyllis, and up until this moment, Finn had never really given Indigo much thought. Strange that he should suddenly pop into his head now.

"Perhaps you are meant to reconnect," Bessie said, reappearing with a small bottle in her hand.

Finn frowned. "We were best friends once. I don't understand how so much time has passed, and why I had forgotten him?"

She tipped the liquid into a glass, and filled the remainder with water. "I am sure the answer will come. In the meantime, drink this."

Finn sniffed at the contents suspiciously. "What is it?"

"That which you have asked me for," Bessie replied.

He stared dubiously at the violet substance. "Should I drink it now?"

"I would wait until you are in your bed. The potion will take effect almost immediately."

"Thank you. I really appreciate you doing this for me, and for everything that you have done for Rowan."

Bessie's eyes flickered with sadness. "You're welcome. I do understand why you have asked for this, and know that it is my choice to give it to you. It is imperative that you have strength of mind for what is to come."

Finn studied her face. "What is it that you are not saying?"

Bessie shook her head and lowered herself into the armchair. Biscuit moved from his basket and jumped onto her lap. He gave a small yawn and curled into a tight ball.

"No more words are required. Off to bed with you," she said, stroking the little dog.

Reluctantly, Finn did as she requested and carried the glass with its strange violet contents carefully upstairs and to his room. Placing it down on the bedside unit, he undressed and slipped beneath the covers. The sheets were soft but cool against his skin and he gave an involuntary shiver.

Reaching for the drink, he downed the liquid and returned it to the unit as the potion took its effect. Heat rose instantly through the soles of his feet and spread out through his core. His limbs were weighted by an invisible force, eyes heavy. All thoughts of his father and the events of the Meridian were now a fuzzy fog as he fell back against the pillow. The name, Indigo, whispered somewhere from the depths of his subconscious as he slipped into slumber. Finn entered the realm of dreams and with his burdens released ran through the forest once more, wild and free.

CHAPTER EIGHTEEN

Achavanich, Scottish Highlands

Aliyah crossed the room and took his hand in hers. "Thank you for coming, brother. I am sorry to have called you."

"What is it? You look upset."

"The Lightkeepers have allowed David's visitations to continue. It seems to be working, and Christine's energy is restoring. I haven't invaded the time that they have shared at David's request, but something she has said concerns me."

"About Rowan?"

She shook her head. "About Jake. Should I tell Harry?"

"To do so may upset the balance, particularly if Harry were to intervene."

"Even if Jake were at risk? I know our role is to guide our wards along their path and assist when it is their time to return. But these events are influencing a path that to my knowledge was never agreed. It could cause significant harm to their soul if we are not careful and do nothing."

"What is it Christine has said?"

"She is repeating a mantra, 'I will not release Jake's light'. I just have a feeling she means Jake's spirit."

"What does his life map say?"

"That's the problem. The Lightkeepers have refused me entry to the hall of records."

Charles shook his head. "Strange that they would do this. Since when? Did you explain?"

"Yes, I've just left Raphael but he would not comment. I am not sure what he knows and thought perhaps you might find out when you next speak with the Lightkeepers."

"I'll talk to Nicolai, but I cannot promise he will share their reasons."

"What about the Sages? Will they know?"

"Eleanor, possibly as she is the closest to Raphael."

Aliya hugged him. "Thank you, brother. Should I say anything to Harry?"

"For now, the safest option would be to let Harry know that he's to keep a close watch on his ward. All the guides have been instructed to do the same. The threat has not passed; the creatures remain in our world. We all need to remain vigilant."

"Understood. I'll speak to him," Aliyah replied.

Charles nodded. "Now I must ask a favour in return."

"What is it, brother?"

"As you are aware, the Meridian has changed Rowan. She is coming into a different power. Her aura radiates energy that has never been known to exist in our world. It is a highly attractive beacon. Last night, one of the lost ones tried to attach itself whilst she was in the dreamscape."

"Rowan knows not to allow them entry. She has rescued many spirits and knows the dangers that her gift can bring," Aliyah said.

"Yes, but the lost ones grow bold. In the guise of a child grieving to be reunited with its parent, they can all too easily manipulate her compassion and use it against her. Had I not arrived to her when I did, it would have attached itself, subdued her spirit and attempted to seek possession."

Aliyah frowned. "It should never have been in the dreamscape. How did it cross the boundary?"

"A matter for the Lightkeepers. I have spoken with them and they do not want Rowan to enter the dreamscape, at least for the present time. That is where I need your assistance. Is there a temporary spell that you can do that prohibits her entering?"

"Yes, I can prepare one for you. When do you want me to cast it?"

"Not tonight. Rowan has asked me to regress her in the hopes of finding the amulet that Bessie spoke of. I will send for you when we are ready. I must speak with Rowan first, and ensure that she understands this action is necessary."

"I shall prepare it as soon as I have spoken to Harry."

"Thank you, Aliyah. I am grateful to you. I must go, I sense Rowan drawing close."

She nodded.

Charles gave her a brief peck on the cheek and took his leave.

He returned to Rowan's bedside and immediately connected his energy to hers, pulling her back to the edge of the dreamscape, and away from the images that were taking shape. Her confused eyes met his own.

"You wanted me to regress you, Rowan."

A flicker of recognition crossed her gaze, and she nodded.

Charles reached for her hand. "I must ask first. Are you sure you want me to do this?"

"Yes," she replied.

"Very well, but you should know that when this is done, the Lightkeepers do not wish for you to astral project or travel to the dreamscape."

"I don't understand why?"

"You are evolving. The lost ones are drawn to the source of power that is emanating from your aura," Charles said.

"But they should never have been in the dreamscape in the first place."

"I know. While the Lightkeepers deal with the breach, I must protect you. Bessie and Finn seek to arm you with power to aid their world, however neither of them know of the threat that exists in ours. I have therefore asked Aliyah to prepare a spell to prevent you from entering. It is temporary."

"As long as it is, then I agree. When will she do this spell?"

"It will be soon. She is preparing it tonight. That will give us time to complete the regression. Are you ready?"

"Yes," Rowan said.

Charles recalled the words he had been taught by his Sage Eleanor and spoke them softly into her ear. Rowan's eyes closed briefly, and the dreamscape faded away.

Darkness surrounded them.

Rowan trembled at his side. "Nothing's happening," she whispered.

"Patience. It may take a little time."

They lingered in silence until an explosion of light and the first incarnation revealed its memory. Charles felt the stir of a breeze and shuddered beside her.

Rowan gave a small gasp as her gaze fell to the youth laid on the blanket. His arms locked around a young woman with auburn hair. She cradled the slight swell of her belly and sighed.

"Who am I?" asked Rowan as tears trailed down her face.

Charles stared at the mirror image of himself. "Anna, my beloved wife."

"We look happy together."

For the first time, Charles lifted her hands to his lips and kissed them softly. "We were, Rowan."

"You never told me of our connection. I felt the love from you, but I had no idea that you were my husband."

The light around them dimmed and the image faded. Another appeared in its place. Anna stood alone, her gaze locked onto the paddock and the young Charles riding a magnificent black stallion. He turned to beam at Anna.

Charles groaned. "Please not this."

"What is it?" Rowan asked.

He squeezed his eyes shut and gripped her hand tightly, knowing of the anguish to come. The horse's squeal, closely followed by her cry of horror, ripped through him. When Charles opened his eyes, his dear Anna knelt to cradle the man he once was in her arms and repeatedly begged him to come back to her. Rowan cried beside him.

Charles pulled her into his embrace. He swallowed the lump in his throat. "I never meant to leave you so soon."

"The horse… it just…." Her words trailed off as she stared across to the sobbing Anna.

"It wasn't Goliath's fault. He was startled by a prairie snake. My foolhardy decision to ride him before he was ready."

Rowan wiped her tears and cradled her stomach. Her voice was strained. "I lost our baby too that day. The grief was too much for me to carry."

Charles choked back the tears. "I am so sorry. The Sages wouldn't let me see you, my spirit too traumatised following my transition. But I swore as soon as I was able, that I would be there for you. I will always be there for you."

Rowan smiled. "And I'm so glad you were. I can feel how much Anna loved you. How much I love you. Do you know what became of our child, Charles?"

"I am told we would have had a son. He reincarnated before I healed. I do not know any more than that," he replied sadly.

"I hope he was born into a happy family," she sniffed.

The image vanished, returning the two of them into darkness. Charles released her from his embrace and together they waited for the next incarnation to arrive. He prayed it would be less traumatic, for both of them.

The second brought with it the scent of desert. Charles appraised the landscape around him, a flow of blue rippled against golden banks occasionally splashed with greenery. Behind him palm trees stood unaffected by the gruelling heat, a welcome contrast to the stark sand dunes that spread out for miles. In the distance, the monolithic splendour of the ancient pyramids stood proud. He turned his attention to the woman alone on the riverbank. She was clothed in a simple sheath dress, her hair plaited and adorned with gold ribbon, her emerald eyes pleading to the sky. "Isis, I beg of you to return him to me." She fell to her knees and cradled her stomach.

"What do you remember?" Charles asked.

Rowan's face lit with anger. "My husband committing adultery with my sister." She shuddered, her expression one of disgust. "When I discovered her betrayal, we fought. I lost. I remember praying to Isis to save me. She took pity and healed my wounds but she failed to return the child growing in my womb."

"These are painful memories, Rowan."

"I know. I cannot help but think in my lifetimes there has been a pattern emerging. Maybe I was never meant to bear a child." Her voice hitched.

He waved his hand and released the memory, returning them both into darkness. "It's time we stopped. This is too much for you."

"But I haven't found the amulet yet. We have to try again, please."

"One last time," he conceded. "I need you to focus your desire to be reconnected to the amulet. Imagine how it would feel against your skin once more. Let its energy combine with yours. Only when you are certain, release the memory." He waited.

"I feel it," she finally murmured and reached for his hand.

They were pulled so fast into the next incarnation, Rowan lost her balance and tumbled head first into a pile of straw. Charles chuckled and lifted her free. Rowan picked the pieces from her hair, her expression confused as she stared around the empty barn. "I don't understand. What is this place?"

Charles had no opportunity to respond as the doors to the entrance suddenly flew open, and a woman with thick raven hair garbed in a long red gown, ran inside. Her companion, much younger, wore a dull grey linen dress, and clutched a small baby to her chest. "What are we to do, Mistress Aurora?"

Rowan gasped as the dark-haired woman unclasped a silver chain from around her neck. She held it out in front of her, the green pendant swaying momentarily before she thrust it towards her companion. "You must use this. Take Abigail through the gateway. Start a new life with her. On her thirteenth birthday give her the amulet. Its power belongs to her now."

"But I cannot raise a child," the younger woman wailed.

"Deliverance Hobbs, you can and you will. Now go before he discovers us both and realises what I have done."

"Please come with me, Mistress Aurora. I don't know how to use the amulet and I cannot travel to another time alone."

"Impossible, Damon has marked my soul. Wherever in time, I travelled he would find me. I'm afraid it has to be you, there is no one else in this world that I trust. The amulet will work for you,

Deliverance. Abigail is with you and will activate its power. The portal I have already prepared." Aurora grimaced and clutched her face. They both glanced towards the doors. "He's near. Deliverance, you must leave now. The gateway will close as soon as you are through." Holding her cheek, she lowered to kiss the top of the baby's head. "Goodbye, my sweet Abigail, know that I will always love you."

With a frantic wave of her hand, Aurora signalled for Deliverance to leave. The younger woman obeyed and hurried to the other side of the barn. She pressed along its wall until the concealed panel clicked open. Deliverance stepped through and sealed the gap behind her.

"That baby was me," Rowan said softly.

Charles didn't reply, his attention fixed firmly on the woman that now stood alone. Something about her expression, and the thick mass of jet hair that fell around her shoulders all too familiar to him. When Aurora released her hand from her cheek, he felt a surge of anger at the spiral welt that glowed so fiercely from her skin.

Rowan nudged his arm gently. "Why hasn't the memory ended when Deliverance left with the baby?"

Charles was interrupted by the sound of wood splintering. A man with silver hair burst into the barn, his face full of fury. Charles presumed this was Damon.

"Thought you could hide from me, Aurora?"

She shook her head. "You are too late. The last egg has turned to dust."

"You lie," he spat out and seized her arm. "Where is she?"

"Gone where you can never find her. Use your power, dear husband, if you do not believe me."

"You whore." Damon flung her to the ground.

Aurora laughed hysterically. "There will be no more of its kind. You've lost."

"We shall see about that." His hands grasped her waist, and he tossed her onto her front, pushing up her skirts. "I shall make another child, and with it return the creature's fertility," he snarled.

"Do what you like. You could put a thousand babies in my belly, and none would give you what you want. She will age and die by the time the season changes."

"You're wrong, and I shall prove it."

The vision ended abruptly.

Rowan turned to Charles and smiled. "I know where the amulet is."

His response was cut off as Rowan was shaken violently awake.

CHAPTER NINETEEN

Achavanich, Scottish Highlands

"What is it?" she asked, her eyes squinting against the sudden onset of light.

"Get dressed, we need to leave now." Finn thrust a rucksack into her hand.

"Where did you get that from?"

"Courtesy of Bessie, there's no chance of taking that case with us now."

Heart pounding, Rowan scrambled out of bed and reached for her clothes. Finn turned his back as she changed out of her pyjamas.

"I'm done," she said and hurried to the chest of drawers. Grabbing a handful of clothes, she rammed them quickly into the bag.

"I don't understand," she muttered.

"Neither do I," Finn replied angrily. "Why did she do it? It makes no sense."

"She? You mean, Bessie? What did she do?"

"I asked her for something to…"

A crash from downstairs interrupted him and he cursed loudly.

"What was that?" Rowan's voice trembled.

Finn met her gaze. "Two of the Fallen are inside. The others and Kane are almost here."

"Where is Bessie?" she asked, hoping for the best but fearing the worst.

He shook his head and looked away, his hands balled tightly into a fist.

Rowan forced back her tears. "Please don't say it. She's not…"

"No, but she doesn't want us to go downstairs, until she gives the order," Finn said sullenly.

"You are kidding me, right?"

Finn didn't reply.

"So we are to just sit up here and do what? Leave her to those creatures?" Rowan cried.

His jaw clenched. "I don't like it any more than you do but she is very clear on this."

"But…"

Finn cut her argument off. "Bessie is a powerful mage, she knows what she is doing."

Rowan stalked to the bedroom door. "We'll see." She turned the handle. It was locked. "Where's the key?" she demanded.

"I don't have it."

"I don't believe you," she said and strode towards him.

He shook his head sadly as she rifled through his pockets. They were all empty. Heaving a sigh, Rowan lifted her face to his, suddenly feeling incredibly stupid. "I'm sorry, I thought that…" Her voice trailed away.

Finn took her hand in his. "I know how you're feeling, but honestly it is no use. She won't be reasoned with, believe me, I've been trying."

"Are you communicating with her now? In the same way as Mercadia?"

He nodded. "I've been able to since we arrived. She didn't want you to know of her origin, until we had completed our training in the Meridian."

"It's alright, I should have made the connection myself the moment I realised she came from your world."

The sound of glass shattering below had them both spinning in the direction of the door.

"Finn, we have to get out of here now, we need to help her."

"How? She's locked us in with magic."

"Then we'll have to use magic to break ourselves free," Rowan said, freeing her hand.

"Great idea, now why didn't I think of that," he muttered.

She ignored his sarcasm and rolled her eyes heavenwards, calling for Charles.

There was another loud crash from below, this time accompanied by a chorus of snarls and howling.

"Do you know of any spells?" Finn asked, his voice full of desperation.

Rowan raised her finger gently to her lips and nodded.

She turned to address Charles and gestured across the room. "Can you get it open?"

His energy instantly released. Seconds later he returned, only this time he was accompanied by a female presence.

"It's sealed with a spell, a pretty impressive one at that, but nothing that I cannot undo," Aliyah said.

Rowan beamed her relief when the door flew open minutes later.

"How did you do that?" Finn asked incredulously.

She slung the rucksack over her shoulder and grabbed his hand. "Never mind, let's go."

"We'll be with you," Charles said.

Finn held tightly to her hand as he led them silently downstairs and towards the kitchen. Bessie stopped them in the doorway. She dusted what appeared to be black ash from her skirt. "I thought I ordered you to stay upstairs until I was ready?"

"We couldn't leave you," Rowan said peering past her. There were no other signs of movement. She grimaced at the overturned furniture and glass littering the floor.

"Then you jeopardise all of our futures, dear. You must stay alive. I assume it is your two friends who assisted?" Bessie scolded.

"You sensed Charles and Aliyah here now?"

"My home is well warded, I know when others are here."

"A very gifted witch," Aliyah murmured.

Bessie turned her attention to Finn, their eyes locked. "It is time."

He shook his head. "I'm not ready to show her that yet."

"Show me what?"

Her question was ignored.

"I'm afraid you have no choice. The cottage is surrounded. I have enough power remaining to give you the time you need to escape from the Fallen, but it is impossible to do it on foot. Rowan will not be able to take her car, Kane is approaching from the front entrance. You'll escape at the back. Biscuit will be going with you."

"What about the Guardian?" Finn asked.

Bessie raised her brow. "Attuned but neither will awaken without the amulet."

"The Guardian? What are you talking about?" Rowan demanded.

They continued their conversation. "I don't want to frighten her," Finn said.

"You were meant to protect her, it is a gift."

Hello, I'm still standing here. Rowan resisted the urge to scream. She turned her thoughts to Charles. "Why aren't they listening to me?"

He placed a hand gently on her shoulder. "Wait a moment."

Bessie slid her gaze to Rowan and gave an apologetic smile. "I'm sorry, dear. We did not mean to exclude you, I…" She spun to face the front door. "Kane has reached the driveway. I'm sorry, there's no time for goodbyes. Go."

Finn nodded and seized Rowan's hand. Her protests falling on deaf ears, he pulled her along the narrow hallway and through a door situated at the back of the cottage. Biscuit was standing outside, his fur bristling and his gaze locked in the direction of the trees. Rowan pulled her hand free and turned to stare into the darkness. Ice travelled the length of her spine and her heart beat a wild rhythm in her chest. The creatures were watching.

"What do we do now?" she hissed.

"We wait for Bessie's signal, but first I must choose."

"Choose?"

"A form," he replied simply.

Rowan's eyes widened. "Are you saying what I think you're saying?"

He nodded. "Can you ride?"

"You mean as in a horse?"

"Yes, can you?"

"I don't know, I've never…"

Charles squeezed her shoulder and whispered, "You're still my Anna. The knowledge is inside you. Trust me."

"Rowan?"

"I'll try," she said and gave Finn a weak smile.

He released a sigh and nodded. "I'm still me, please remember that."

"Wait, have you done this before?"

"Yes, when Biscuit and I had our male bonding time as you put it."

A realisation occurred. "That explains it."

"Explains what?"

"Your eyes that day."

"My eyes?"

"When you arrived back from the Meridian, your eyes appeared a different colour."

"You noticed?"

They both flinched as Biscuit barked furiously. Rowan could hear a high-pitched whistle and covered her ears as it grew in strength. Seconds later a brilliant white beam burst past them and rippled outwards. Dozens of reptilian-like amber eyes suddenly glared back at her, now exposed by the light that hurtled towards them. The creatures turned and ran for the darkness, their wails of agony and rage ricocheting through the trees.

Rowan spun to Finn and released a loud cry as she found herself staring into the eyes of a stallion. It snorted and nodded its head repeatedly up and down.

"You haven't much time, Rowan," Charles warned.

She took a calming breath. "How do I even mount him?"

"We'll help you," Aliyah said.

"Wait a minute," Rowan requested and unzipped the rucksack. Tipping it upside down, she emptied her clothes onto the ground. Kneeling, she called to Biscuit and opened the bag.

As though attuned to her thoughts, the little dog ran towards her and jumped into the bag. Rowan lifted the rucksack, Biscuit's head poking free from the top. She slipped her arms through both handles and slung it onto her back.

"I'm ready," she said to Charles.

"Hold onto Finn's mane and raise your leg," he instructed.

She followed his directions and was immediately thrust upwards, her right leg automatically swinging across Finn's back.

"Move forward slightly… that's it," Charles said.

"This would be a lot easier if I had a saddle," Rowan muttered.

"You've ridden before without a saddle or bridle, it will come back to you, I promise."

"Better get out of here before those things come back," Aliyah advised.

With the little dog nestled against her back, Rowan gripped tightly to Finn's mane and leaned forward. "I love you."

The stallion gave a soft whinny and set off in the direction of the trees.

A cold clammy sweat crept across her skin as they continued forward in silence. She flinched with every snap of branch underneath Finn's hooves.

"The Fallen… can you sense them, Charles?" she whispered.

"I sense a darkness ahead. But don't worry, I have a feeling I know where Finn is going," he reassured.

"I hope so or they'll be eating him first," she hissed.

After a few minutes Finn turned right and picked up his pace. They emerged from the wood and entered a field. Rowan's relief to be in the open air, however short lived as several howls could be heard from behind them.

Finn broke into a gallop.

Rowan held onto his mane tightly and closed her eyes momentarily. She searched for Anna's memory, her mind moving beyond the pain of Charles's death and to the memory of the ride in the valley. Allowing the knowledge to return to her body and her instincts to take over, Rowan adjusted her posture and moved confidently in sync with Finn.

The snarl and sudden snapping of teeth from behind had her head spinning. Three of the creatures were in pursuit of them. Their fangs gleamed in the moonlight and eyes focused on their prey. Rowan sensed their thirst for blood.

The little dog growled and wriggled in the rucksack. "Stay, Biscuit," Rowan ordered and facing forward, she nudged Finn with her feet.

Acknowledging her urgency, he increased his pace, tearing towards the furthest edge of the field. Rowan gripped his mane and steeled herself for the jump that was coming. Finn leapt into the air and cleanly over the fencing. He didn't stop. There was a familiar thrum of energy in the distance and she smiled briefly.

Biscuit barked furiously from behind.

One of the Fallen had gained speed and had closed the distance between them.

Rowan turned her head at the moment of its attack.

"No," she screamed, the anger rising. Her hand swiped through the air. The creature released an agonised wail as it flew backwards and sailed straight into the other two. Swallowing her shock, she faced forward and continued urging Finn on. They leapt across another fence and crossed into the field. The hedging at the far end leading into the Meridian parted swiftly and eased their entry. It sealed behind them.

Finn stopped running.

CHAPTER TWENTY

Achavanich, Scottish Highlands

A wind gathered and shifted the air around them. Kane lifted his gaze to the sky. The clouds were forced apart, exposing the moon. *Did the woman summon it?*

Kane could clearly make out her features. There was something oddly familiar to him. *Where have I seen her face before?*

"You're too late. They've gone," she called out.

"Not possible. I have the cottage surrounded," he replied.

"Yes, and I took care of those miserable creatures."

He gestured for Barrock to leave. "Find the others," he snapped. Turning his attention back to the woman, he muttered, "If you have that is quite an accomplishment."

"You almost sound impressed," she replied.

"Unexpected, that's all, given the limitations of you humans." Kane would give her no more than that.

"Well then, since you've wasted your time here, I suggest you return. The Master will need his pet."

Kane's brow arched. "Who exactly are you?"

"No one to concern yourself with," she replied.

"We shall see."

Rivik sprang towards her and released a howl as she held out her hands and released a blast of purple energy. Rivik was sent crashing to Kane's feet. He rose quickly and snarled. Kane shook his head in warning.

"It is as I suspected. You are not from this world."

"I am not," she confirmed.

"Then you must realise you are no match for me, old woman."

"Do your worst," she said, having the audacity to mock him.

Furious, Kane raised his hand into the air and closed his fist. The woman sank to her knees, holding her throat. Her power invaded his mind. "Release me now, Warlock, or he will make you pay. We both know who it is that I speak of."

Surprised and confused he acquiesced to her request. "What is your name?" he demanded.

"Bessantia," she croaked.

"That's a lie. She died a long time ago."

The woman rose to her feet slowly and smiled. "Don't be so sure." Raising her hand into the air, she used the very same power he had summoned, against him.

Kane's throat constricted and he fell to the ground gasping for air. His hand fumbled frantically in his pocket for the dagger. Still holding his throat in a feeble attempt to release her grip, the other hand hurriedly carved a rune in the ground in front of him. The pressure instantly released and he rose to his feet, still gripping the dagger.

"We can do this till dawn," she said, her gaze sliding to the blade.

Kane sensed a slight quiver in her voice. "You continue to lie to me, old woman."

"Do I? How can you be so sure?" she replied boldly.

Kane sneered and strode towards her. A fork of lightning struck the ground in front of him. He sprang back, dropping the dagger. The old woman smiled and gave a nonchalant shrug of her shoulders.

"Be careful, Commander," Rivik warned.

Kane appraised her for a few moments. "It truly is a convincing act but I'm no fool. I'm sure the Tracker has told you that."

"Not really, you were not that important enough for us to discuss," she replied.

Fury channelled into power, and energy exploded from Kane's core. The woman was knocked off her feet and sent hurtling backwards through the open doorway of the cottage. There was a loud crash from inside. Kane spat his disgust and retrieved the blade from the ground. "She will soon see how important I am."

"Commander," Barrock called, approaching them.

"Well?" Kane snapped.

"All but three of my brethren have suffered injuries, but they live. Gallo is unharmed, he has taken Grynn and Minious with him. They are in pursuit of the Tracker and the girl."

"Good. He may yet redeem favour with me," Kane sneered. He glanced upwards at the sky and cursed loudly. "Dawn will soon be approaching."

"What are your orders, Commander?"

"Go with your brethren and have them set up camp. They can begin their regeneration. Return with the coordinates once you are done, Barrock."

"Yes, Commander."

"Rivik with me. I shall deal with her."

The Fallen nodded and followed Kane inside the building. There was a loud scraping from a room to their right.

"I scent no other presence," Rivik confirmed.

Kane entered into what appeared to be the remains of a scullery. The woman was seated in a large chair, her arms folded in her lap and posture relaxed.

"You do not fear me?" Kane said, surprised by her nerve.

"No, I do not." She raised the sleeve of her clothing to expose her arm.

Kane strode towards her and glared down at the mark on her skin. A knot tightened in his gut and his head swam with shock and rage.

"Tell me, how is it possible?" he demanded, leaning in for a closer inspection.

She didn't falter, her eyes meeting his with an equal intensity.

"You are not privileged enough to hold such knowledge," she answered, suddenly rising from the chair and out of close proximity to him.

Kane's temper exploded once more, the windows shaking in

their frames and shattering. Somehow the woman made a quick calculation and moved effortlessly out of the path of the rain of glass shards. He picked up the chair she had been sitting in and threw it against the wall.

She didn't flinch. "It doesn't matter what you do, you still won't get the answers that you are seeking," she said, calmly rolling down her sleeve.

"I can still hurt you, Bessantia," he spat out, his blood boiled.

"So, you've accepted who I am, have you?"

"Yes, and you will tell me how it is that you have managed to live all this time, undetected?"

"You couldn't possibly understand the how. You neither possess the power or the ability. As for hurting me, you know that I can easily heal," she replied, her voice unfazed by his threat.

"Foolish woman, my bloodline is more powerful than you think."

"Really? Is that why your mother was stripped of all her powers, whilst you did little to stop it?"

"I should have guessed, Mercadia! Was she the one to have extended your life, when he abandoned you?"

She tutted loudly. "There you go again, you give me very little credit for one who claims to know who I am... who I really am."

Kane's eyes narrowed. "What do you mean?"

"The Master hasn't told you everything, has he?"

"The lies come tripping off your tongue so easily," Kane hissed.

"And yet you're uncertain. I sense the doubt picking away at your insides and what remains of the wrinkled black prune you call a heart."

Kane slapped her hard across her cheek. A red welt instantly appeared and her eyes watered. Infuriatingly she stood her ground.

"You don't scare me. Both you and I know the truth. You cannot kill me, he forbids it."

"How will he know? I doubt he knows you are alive?"

"Come now, even you cannot be so foolish. You know what the mark means."

Kane grabbed her arm, his fingers digging cruelly into her skin. She offered no resistance as he dragged her outside into the night air and flung her to the ground. Rivik followed them in silence.

Pacing back and forth, Kane's mind sifted through time, searching through the deepest crevices for the information he needed, his anger building at her sheer arrogance and audacity to ridicule his power.

"Commander," Rivik growled out in warning.

By the time Kane's attention had snapped back to the old woman it was too late.

Bessantia had gone.

EPILOGUE

Lake Samsara, The Moren

Alone on the shoreline of Samsara, Aaron lowered to retrieve a pebble and send it skimming across the once crystal-clear waters. Watching the dark pools ripple outwards, memories of Lake Tahlia and the game he and his brother had played as children, stirred a powerful emotion. He quickly whispered an intonation, hoping that the infusion of words and love would one day prove to be enough.

With a heavy heart, he walked back to the western side of the water's edge and glanced down at the body lying on its embankment. Reaching into his robe, he retrieved the worn black leather journal and released the gilt catch. Quickly he thumbed through the pages to the spell that the Master had marked with his seal. He quietly read the words and imprinted the verses to his memory.

Slipping the book back underneath his robe, Aaron bent to scoop the lifeless form of the Fae warrior into his arms and raise him into the air. Once the incantation had been spoken aloud, he threw the corpse into the crimson water, the warrior's death the last sacrifice required to seal the rite, and ensure the Council of Elders remained powerless to repeal the gateway.

The Master knew all too well the Fae would not forgive the slaying of their own, and by the blood of one whom they considered to be their own. Aaron's betrayal ensured the destruction of the sacred covenant, and denied the Council their only weapon against the Gydgen.

Tymoria's body descended into Samsara's depths and joined the other twelve, murdered by his hand. He shook his head and walked to the east of the lake, attempting to escape the scent of death and wrongdoing that haunted him. Each task the Master allocated, worse than the one before, and piece by piece poisoning his spirit. Aaron mourned for the man lost.

A hefty price paid for the knowledge of his father's untimely death. He cursed his ability for getting him into this position and yet at the same time was grateful to it for allowing him the opportunity to keep his secrets. The Master remained unaware that Aaron was the mole hiding within their ranks.

His thoughts shifted to the family he had left behind, and his cheeks burned with the shame. He imagined his mother standing there, her face stained with tears and her eyes full of disgust for the monster he had become.

Pulling the black onyx shard free from his pocket, he drew the rune into the sand and sat cross-legged. The Master would not keep him waiting for long.

A cold mist drifted across the waters, heralding the arrival of another. Aaron sprang to his feet at the intrusion. "I did not request your presence."

It sneered at him from below the dark grey cowl. "I had my doubts about you, but it seems I am mistaken. You have served him well."

"Where is the Master?" Aaron demanded.

"He had other matters to attend to."

"My orders were to contact him when the task was complete. I report directly to the Master, not to you."

It laughed. "There is no need. The Gydgen sensed the gateway shatter as soon as the thirteenth sacrifice was made. The Master already knows of your accomplishment." It moved closer to study him. "I must admit I never believed you to be capable of betraying your mother. The Master is most impressed by your loyalty, as am I."

"I have no feelings for my mother," Aaron declared.

"That is most reassuring, Warlock, particularly as I have your next orders."

"Oh?" He didn't care for the glee detected in its voice.

The Chosen one clasped a bony hand to Aaron's shoulder and hissed, "You will kill your mother."

Printed in Great Britain
by Amazon